The Running Kind

a Hector Lassiter novel

CRAIG McDONALD

BETIMES BOOKS

First published in the English language worldwide in 2014 by Betimes
Books

www.betimesbooks.com

ISBN: 978-0-9929674-3-7

The Running Kind is a work of fiction. Names, characters, places, and
incidents are either the product of the author's imagination or are used
fictitiously. Any resemblance to actual persons, living or dead, events, or
locales is entirely coincidental.

Cover design by JT Lindroos

Also by Craig McDonald

PRAISE

"With each of his Hector Lassiter novels, Craig McDonald has stretched his canvas wider and unfurled tales of increasingly greater resonance." —Megan Abbott

"Reading a Hector Lassiter novel is like having a great uncle pull you aside, pour you a tumbler of rye, and tell you a story about how the 20th century 'really' went down." —Duane Swierczynski

"What critics might call eclectic, and Eastern folks quirky, we Southerners call cussedness – and it's the cornerstone of the American genius. As in: "There's a right way, a wrong way, and my way." You want to see how that looks on the page, pick up any of Craig McDonald's novels. He's built him a nice little shack out there way off all the reg'lar roads, and he's brewing some fine, heady stuff. Leave your money under the rock and come back in an hour." —James Sallis

This novel is dedicated to Charlie Stella

FOREWARD
By Craig McDonald

The year is 1950: Author and screenwriter Hector Mason Lassiter stands at his own half-century mark as this book unfolds in a snowbound, Youngstown, Ohio, hotel.

Hector's sidekick in this book is the Irish cop prominently featured in the previous novel, *Roll the Credits*, James Butler Hanrahan.

As fictional characters in Hector's universe go, Jimmy has his own secret history. Jim was originally a key player in what was my long-ago first completed novel, *Parts Unknown*, a fictionalization about the Cleveland Torso Slayer that I penned as the 1980s wound down. The Torso Slayer, or so-called "Mad Butcher of Kingsbury Run," was a puckish fiend who killed upwards of a dozen people in and around Cleveland—always by beheading—and was never officially caught.

Eliot Ness of Untouchable's fame—then Cleveland Safety Director—doggedly pursued the serial killer through the dark Depression-era years to no successful legal end. The post-cards mailed to Ness mentioned in this book (as well as *Parts Unknown*, now available as an eBook original as part of my ongoing Lassiter-companion Chris Lyon series) are based on historical fact. So is the hinted-at, identity of the murderer portrayed here and in *Parts Unknown* (that latter book functions as Jimmy Hanrahan's elegiac swansong in the larger Lassiter-Lyon universe).

As is always the case, the historic figures cropping up along the way in *The Running Kind* are portrayed in as close to their actual historical settings and contemporary locations as possible.

Rod Serling of *Twilight Zone* fame came and went through Yellow Springs many times in the course of his woefully foreshortened life and as dictated by the ebbs and flows of his career.

Many years back, I sat writing in the same booth as Hector in the particular stagecoach stop-cum-bar faithfully described in this book, writing and also listening to some academic old-timers reminisce about Serling's informal writing lectures delivered in that place over countless beers.

The Kefauver hearings were every bit the TV sensation described in the pages that follow, and an abject embarrassment to FBI Director J. Edgar Hoover who spent decades denying the existence of the mob until the televised hearings forced Hoover to a hated capitulation that, *Yes, Virginia, there is a Mafia.*

This novel also marks a kind of cresting of a last hill, in a sense.

Although I reserve the right to compose future, stand-alone Lassiter novels, the series was originally conceived as a nine-book, unified arc, as I've said many times since the series launched in 2007.

Just three more novels in the original arc remain to be published by Betimes Books, but only one more will be entirely new.

The Running Kind, then, is in every real sense, the *penultimate* Lassiter adventure. Call it the beginning of the end.

—Craig McDonald
October, 2014

PART I

— YOUNGSTOWN, OHIO —

December 1950

"You often meet your fate on the road you take to avoid it."
— French proverb

"It is a long road that has no turning."
— Irish proverb

1

No happy ending ever started in a bar.

The old friends had chosen to murder the afternoon drinking in the shadowy hotel pub mostly to evade December's bitter chill.

"All I'm sayin' is that any son of a bitch who sets off in a plane for California—and who *then* ends up landing in feckin' *Ireland*—that son of a bitch is deserving of something far better than simple scorn," Jimmy Hanrahan said, tapping a blunt finger against the other man's chest. "Besides, he's from *your* neck of the woods, Hec. He's another Galveston boy."

Jimmy looked out the hotel pub's window at the fresh flurries accumulating atop old, too-high drifts. He shook his head and sighed.

Hector Lassiter rose and fished change from his pocket. He said, "Jimmy, only a romantic Irish expatriate like you would still think of defending Corrigan. Mention your motherland and you get positively dewy. As calamitous decisions go, you leaving Ireland was some flavor of tragic, I think."

Jimmy was big and beefy and about Hector's height—topping out over six feet, but also coming in a good bit over Hector's weight. Jimmy went at least two hundred fifty pounds. He had graying-brown hair, blue eyes, and a nose broken so many times it looked like something no anatomist had invented a word for yet. Jimmy snorted and sipped his Irish whiskey. "Not already calling it a day, Hector? Eager to get back to the writing table? Or maybe you're just off to siphon the python?"

"Huh-uh," Hector said, flipping a nickel and then catching it in his hand. "Just going to improve the music." He didn't call it loud but checked: the coin came up tails.

Nat King Cole was singing *Mona Lisa*, a song Hector regarded as syrupy, yet it had been played nearly to death the past few months. Increasingly, Hector felt out of touch with the sorry drift of popular culture. The crime novelist sauntered over to the jukebox, scanned his options and plugged in a Percy Mayfield tune as well as Vaughn Monroe's cover of *Riders in the Sky*.

Returning to his stool, Hector held up a finger for another shot of Jameson. Jimmy said, "What'd you opt for, Hec? Not more of that hillbilly crap you favor these days, I hope?"

The rangy Irishman had been Hector's good friend since their late teens, going all the way back to Europe, and, later, to the bloody bootleg wars waged along the Great Lakes.

Back then, Jimmy was a relatively new cop. In '36, the year Hector last reconnected with Jimmy *in* the Buckeye State for any real time alone, "Untouchable" Eliot Ness had been fresh from Chicago and chasing Al Capone. Ness had recently been appointed director of public safety for the Mistake on the Lake. Jimmy was swiftly tabbed as one of the force's rising stars and promptly promoted to detective by Ness.

Because of the most recent European war and some lingering, bloody business spinning out of all that, it had been a long time since Jimmy and Hector had last crossed paths.

Jimmy was taking a rare vacation in Youngstown, of all places. Because Hector was also roaming the east on the way back south from a meeting with his New York-based publisher, they'd agreed to risk hooking up close by the Ohio-Pennsylvania border.

Mostly, their first couple hours together had been spent in grisly, *Police Gazette*-style shoptalk. Seemed Jimmy was in Youngstown chasing clues to a long unsolved series of mutilation murders—still doggedly pursuing his *bête noire*, the so-called "Cleveland Headhunter," a.k.a. the "Mad Butcher of Kingsbury Run."

The Butcher was credited with disarticulation and decapitation murders across the upper Midwest, crimes spanning decades and thousands of miles, but mostly grisly slayings committed around Cleveland, Youngstown and Pittsburgh.

Hector had relatively recently gotten caught up around the edges of a similar crime in Los Angeles, the harrowing case of the "Black Dahlia" as the breathless newspaper boys dubbed the tragically murdered and mutilated would-be actress Elizabeth Short. Some in police and conspiracy-theory circles thought the "Black Dahlia Avenger" and "Headhunter" killings linked. A letter sent the press a few years before the Dahlia's mutilation murder claimed the Cleveland killer was fleeing the chilly Buckeye State for the City of Angels. The letter writer even referred to a severed head buried in almost exactly the location where Beth's bisected body was later found.

For reasons of his own, Hector didn't buy the theory of the Dahlia-Butcher link, not even a little, but he wanted to see Jimmy, so he'd made the icy run down from New York.

Percy Mayfield began crooning *Please Send Me Someone to Love*. Hanrahan listened to a few bars, grunted and said, "This isn't so bad a tune. It'll do."

"It's a great song," Hector said. He stared into his glass, then said, "Jimbo, you've really gotta commence letting go of this Kingsbury Run business. You've been decades on this mess. The guy who murdered all those folks around these parts, that hombre's gotta be long gone south of the sod by now. Please don't let yourself be run crazy by it anymore, buddy."

Jimmy rolled his eyes. "If only that seemed so, Hec. It bein' over, I mean. But another lassie was cut up this past July. Just like the others. *Exactly* like the others. It's the same fiend. I'll stake my life and reputation, such as it remains, on all that."

Hector narrowed his pale blue eyes. "You really believe that?"

The cop shook his head. "Not a scrap of doubt. And something else happened at an industrial site in Cleveland recently. A fairly large fellow was seen sunning himself on some steel girders that had been sitting there for almost two years. The man showed up every day for nearly six weeks. He spent about twenty minutes in the sun there each day." Jimmy sipped his whiskey and shook out a Lucky Strike. He shrugged off a little chill.

Hector picked up his old Zippo and tossed it to the Irish detective. Jimmy caught it and said, "Now, this place is not the kind of place you lay out to catch some rays, Hector. Really not that kind of garden spot." Jimmy said that last through a haze of smoke. He closed the lid and glanced at the engraving on Hector's lighter that read, "One True Sentence." Jimmy ran his fingers over the surface of the Zippo then handed it back to its owner.

Hector slipped the lighter into his sports jacket's pocket. He said, "What'd this fella look like?"

"Fiftyish, like us," Jimmy said. "That'd make him a young man when the Butcher was in his natural prime. This man, he had thinning gray hair and he was heavyset."

Hector bit his lip. "How exactly does this tie back to the Kingsbury Butcher?"

"The boyo stopped sunning himself, stopped right in the middle of summer. About the time he ceased cosseting his tan, the workers around the area started to notice this stench. Then, on July 22, a couple out for a walk found a severed leg in a field. Limb was still fairly fleshy. That set minds working about the stink under that steel pile, and we started poking around there. Under the steel, right where that sunbather had sunned for six weeks, we found a torso. Also some severed parts. One leg and both arms. The head turned up a few days later, close-by. Under the body was a May 1949 copy of the *Cleveland News'* sports pages and a couple of pages torn from a phone book. Listings under the letter K."

Hector blew smoke out both nostrils. "K for Kingsbury, you're thinking?"

"Who's to say with certainty?" Jimmy said. "But even our crazy coroner back in Cleveland, Mariposa, he admits it looks like the Kingsbury Butcher all over again. What do you think?"

"I think it's just this side of chilling," Hector said. "More than a tad skin-crawling, even. I think maybe—"

Hector was cut short by an urgent tug at his sports coat's sleeve. He glanced to his side; saw nothing. Another tug. He looked down.

A blue-eyed, blond girl, maybe five, perhaps six, looked up at him, scared and imploring. "Please, mister, my mommy needs help!"

Hector exchanged a glance with Jimmy and they rose together. They drained their drinks and ground out their cigarettes. Hector called to the keep, "Room 301. Put it on my room's bill, won't you, sport?" Then he took the little girl's tiny hand and looked around for a parent.

The little girl was dressed well and had festive ribbons in her hair. She was wearing a Black Watch plaid wool coat with attached cape and a furry muff dangling around her neck. High-gloss, black patent-leather shoes on her tiny feet. The girl clutched tightly to a lookalike doll dressed in a miniature version of her own outfit.

Jimmy lifted the little girl up and wrapped an arm under her to support her. Getting her face up even with his own and smiling, he asked, "And where's your mother, angel?"

"Down there," the little girl said. She pointed across the lobby to a descending flight of stairs under a sign that read "Restrooms & Shoeshines."

The little girl said, "Mommy really needs your help, right now!"

Hector jerked his head for Jimmy to follow. He said over his shoulder, "What's your name, honey?"

"I'm Shannon," she said.

"Let's hurry then, Shannon," Hector said, patting his left side and then remembering he'd left his big old Colt '73 hidden in his luggage upstairs. He cursed under his breath.

Hector took the steps three at a time. A sign at the bottom pointed left for the women's restroom, and right for the men's. He drifted leftward but the little girl in Jimmy's arms said urgently, "No mister, the *other* way!" Hector obeyed.

An old black man was sitting in his own shoeshine chair near the door of the men's room, fiddling with a brush and looking scared and ashamed for his own fear.

A woman yelled, "No!" There was the sound of a slap, then she snarled, "I said *no*, damn you!"

A man yelled back, "Bitch! You are coming back! Now do it quiet-like or we'll hurt that kid. Boss man gave the all clear to rough her up good. Joe is up there right now looking for her. If he finds that girl first, it will not be a good thing for anybody. Do you get me?"

Jimmy deposited the little girl in a vacant stall. Closing the door on her, he pressed a big finger to his lips and said, "Sit tight, angel eyes. And do please *hush!*" A reassuring smile as he closed the door on her.

Hector could see the woman now—two women, really.

A pair of men were waving guns at the ladies. The thugs were dressed in down-market hats and overcoats but expensive-looking shoes. They turned at the sound of Jimmy's instructions to the scared little girl.

Both men pointed their guns toward Hector and Jimmy. Hector turned to make himself a narrower target, then kicked the one standing closest in the crotch. The man doubled over and Hector grabbed the man's overcoat lapels and tossed him behind for Jimmy to finish with.

The second man was shifting his aim, preparing to point his gun at Hector's chest. Hector kicked that man's hand and the gun went off, blasting a hole in the restroom ceiling. Hector grabbed the brim of the man's fedora and jerked it down over the stranger's eyes. The gunman was pointing wild now, as likely to hit the old shoe-shiner or the little girl cowering in the stall as to put a slug in his attacker.

Hector got hold of the man's elbow while he was still blinded by his own hat. Hector put the man's arm against the jamb of a vacant toilet stall and then slammed the stall door against the man's wrist several times until bone crunched.

The man's hand went limp and the gun smacked the tile floor, chipping marble. Hector scooped up the rod, a taped, skeleton-grip .38, and tossed it to Jimmy. The Irish cop's man was out cold on the floor.

Hector's man groaned again, tugging at his hat with his one good hand. *Tsking*, the author hauled the man up and then flung him headfirst into the toilet bowl. The man was still moving, so Hector did that a second time and then pulled the flush chain on the overhead basin.

Jimmy opened the stall door and picked up the little girl. "Everything's fine now, puddin'," he said. "You're safe and so is your mother, darlin' Shannon."

One of the women, blond and blue-eyed like the little girl, fell to her knees and hugged the child close. "Oh, thank God," she said. The woman wore an expensively tailored skirt with matching jacket and a long fur coat that looked real enough to Hector. The blonde's hat sported a dangling fringe of black mesh that nearly reached her bottom lip. She was quite the looker, that was evident even through that mesh veil.

The other woman was prettier still and platinum blond. She was expensively appointed, too, but not in quite so business-like a fashion as her companion. There was more *va-va-voom* in the second woman's slinky dress and half-stoll. The sexier one stroked the little girl's hair and then squeezed her friend's arm and said, "Katy, we have to go, *right now*. We have to do that before Joe gets back!"

Joe? Hector said, "Now what's up with these toughs? What are they to you two, ladies?"

"There's no time for that," the slinky blonde said. She hauled her friend up from her knees. "Katy, come on! We have to fly!"

This loud *click*. No mistaking that sound, and particularly not amplified as it was off all that tile and porcelain in the men's john: the sound of a gun cocking.

Hector cursed and said softly, "Howdy-do Joe!" Raising his hands, Hector turned slowly to face the gun.

Joe shook his automatic once at Jimmy, directing the cop to drop the revolver they'd taken off the other thug.

Jimmy lowered the hammer on the gun. He slung it in a sink basin, scowling. The Irishman evidently seemed to think it good strategy to rile the man. Jimmy said, "So, ya sorry pup, ya, you're clearly a Dago thug. Which family do you work for? No denials now, 'cause you're clearly of that oily ilk if ya get my drift. And you're no *Joe*, you're a *Giuseppe* at best."

Joe sneered. "Who the hell are you two? I only ask so we'll know whose funerals to send flowers to."

Laying his accent on thicker, Jimmy said, "We're just passers-by. Ya know the old Celtic saying, don'tcha boyo? Is this a private fight, or can anyone join in? In that spirit, we helped ourselves to a dab o' bedlam, going in assured of the happy outcome on our end."

"Ain't *you* the tough, Joey," Hector said, smiling. "But you better rethink this bad business, old pal. Jimmy here is plain-clothes heat. Shooting Jimbo would be sowing the wind in wicked ways you don't want to contemplate too hard. You know how cops are about police-killers. Hell, even the Feds would pile up on you for a bloody stupidity like that."

Joe pointed his gun at Hector. "Okay, mouth, and who are *you*?"

"Smith's my name," Hector said. "John Smith."

Joe sneered. "Yeah. So you're another *cop*?"

Hector just shrugged.

Joe sneered and jerked his head a little to one side, cracking his neck. "What are doing with these two? Kefauver send you to protect them? If so, that woodchuck's sure going on the cheap, 'cause you two mugs ain't all that much."

Hearing Jimmy was police put some spine into the old shoe-shiner. The elderly bootblack lashed out with his hand towel, striking Joe's gun hand and resulting in a second bullet hole, this one in the men's room's floor. Hector grabbed hold of Joe's lowered gun hand, forcing a finger behind the trigger before Joe could get off another wild shot.

In the mirror, Hector saw the slinky woman put a gloved hand over the child's eyes. He thought, *Good for her, gal must sense what's coming.*

Jimmy snarled and grabbed Joe by both ears and wrenched him back toward the sink.

There was an array of bottled colognes between the sink basins. Jimmy sprayed mist in Joe's eyes and then turned on the hot water tap. He shoved Joe's face under the scalding spray, then got him back up on his feet and rammed his head into the wall twice.

Hector nodded at the shoeshine man. "Thanks, brother. You carried the day. That said, if I was you, I'd surely be missing when these three come back around."

Jimmy scooped up discarded guns, then took "Katy" by the arm. She was carrying the little girl now. Hector grabbed the sexy, still-unnamed blonde by her arm and they legged it up the stairs.

"Best we get distance on this joint," Hector said, taking point across the lavish lobby. "These rats rarely travel in trios, more like battalions. And Jimmy's right: they're all mobbed up. They stink of Mafia." Narrowing his eyes he asked the women, "So what are you two to them?"

Silence. Hardly any expression at all there on their pretty faces.

Jimmy said, "One of the boyos mentioned *Kefauver*. That'd be Estes Kefauver, I guess. You know, the toothsome Tennessee senator who's conducting all these inquiries into organized crime. Am I right? Yes?"

More silence as they hustled the women across the lobby and out into the December cold. The icy wind lashed their faces and made their eyes tear up.

The sidewalks and gutters were still mounded high with the snow and slush of the freak Thanksgiving blizzard that had swept over the Appalachians, spawning out-of-season tornadoes, knocking out power to an estimated million and killing more than three hundred people.

The thaw was just setting in south of Cleveland. Consequently, flooding from the melting snowdrifts, some more than twenty feet deep, posed a new threat throughout the Ohio River Valley.

"Car's just around the corner," Hector told Jimmy.

The Irishman nodded. "Always the Chevy man, you. Is this sled fast, Hector?"

"It's a Chevy, dark blue. And yes, it's very fast." Hector's wheels were *brand* new, a 1950 DeLuxe Styleline Sport Sedan with rear fender guards and chrome stone guards. Hector had also sprung for the optional sun visor because he lived in the desert—not that he got home to New Mexico so terribly much in recent days.

Jimmy nodded and squeezed Katy's arm. "I asked a question back there, missy. Well, several questions were posed, but as I'm the one with a badge, I get priority on answers. That man said something about Kefauver and a protection detail. Are you a witness for the senate committee? Are you two tied in some way to one of the crime families who've been targeted by Kefauver's hearings?"

Katy looked at her friend; the other woman shrugged.

"Honey, after what we did back there, you owe us. What are you called, doll face?"

"Megan Dalton."

"Hokey-doke, Meg," Hector said, brushing some strands of yellow-white hair back from her eyes. Her hair was soft and maybe even her real shade. Surely didn't look or feel like a peroxide job. She moved her head away from his hand. Hector smiled at that. Some spirit behind that tarted up face.

The women exchanged a last long look. Jimmy frowned and flashed his badge, just enough to show it was real, but he kept a big thumb over the name of the city emblazoned on the tin.

Katy nodded and hugged her daughter closer. "My name is Katharine Scartelli. My husband is—"

"Vito Scartelli," Jimmy said, raw-voiced. "Hec, this woman is married to a monster."

"I read the newspapers, too," Hector said, cold all over now. "The boss of all bosses in the Great Lakes region." He tossed Jimmy they car keys. "We're dealt in, like it or not, Jimbo." Hector added, "Or don't you think?"

"Oh, I figure we're already in deeper than we can conceive," Jimmy said. "Always the way, it seems, when our paths cross for any time at all." Jimmy stroked the little girl's hair. Hector figured his friend was remembering another city, one a continent away, many years ago. Remembering another little girl in desperate danger. Lyon, France, and the last big war: all of that was certainly on Hector's mind presently.

"Then pull around back of the hotel and wait for me, Jim," Hector said. "I'll exit through the service doors."

It was starting to snow as Hector turned to head back into the hotel. A tiny voice, "Thanks, mister. Thank-you for saving my mommy and Megan."

Hector almost said, "We're nowhere near having done that yet." Instead he smiled over his shoulder at the little girl and said, "You sure are cute, darlin'."

Meg called to Hector, "Joe asked you what you do. Are you police? Perhaps a private detective?"

"Don't insult me." Pausing, Hector said, "I'm just a writer, sugar. But a careful one."

Meg frowned. "Your name does seem familiar. Are you a journalist?"

"Not so much that either," Hector said. He trotted across the parking lot in the snow.

Hector ducked back into the cozy hotel, straight into the barrel of a gun.

2

It was Joe, unsteady on his feet, but still dangerous enough. Joe's face was livid and blistered from his scalding. His nose looked more than a little like Jimmy's pushed-around beak now.

Hector had to give the thug points for durability. Joe had stayed smart through all that pain, too: he was standing several feet away from Hector, safely away from reach of fists or being kicked at with feet.

"Back through that door, you son of a bitch," Joe said.

There was some motion behind Joe. It was the shoe-shiner. The old man raised his wooden box and slammed it against the back of Joe's head. Hector dove right, just in case the gunman got off a shot on his way to the tiled floor. But Joe just groaned, dropped his gun and collapsed. The old man smiled at Hector. "Tough one, ain't he?"

"Very much so," Hector said. He stooped down for Joe's forty-five and slipped it into his pocket. He looked down the hallway to the lobby. Nobody could see them, presently. He said, "Thanks again, Pops. Can you do me one last favor and get the door?"

The old man looked uncertain but complied. Hector grabbed Joe by the ankles and hauled him out into the snow. He propped Joe up against the wall of the hotel and angled his hat to obscure the man's blistered face.

A Styrofoam cup lay on the ground near Joe's feet. Hector picked that up. He put it in Joe's hand, and then reached into his jacket's breast pocket and pulled out a couple of the number-two pencils he favored for writing; he dropped them in the cup. Joe would either freeze to death or eventually be busted for panhandling for pencils, he reckoned.

Hector fished out his roll and skidded off two fives. He passed them to the shoe-shiner. "For your trouble, pal. I think you'd best look for another hotel to work out of, at least for a few days. Best expect he's gonna be vengeful."

"My thought, too," the old man said. He looked at Hector's feet and said, "Wish you'd kill him now. Nice snakeskin boots you got there, sir. That accent of yours, is it Texan?"

"That's right," Hector said.

The shoeshine man smiled and nodded. He said, "Civil War sides aside, I've always liked that state. Thanks, cowpoke." The old bootblack then walked briskly away.

Jimmy was waiting out back with the trunk of the Chevy open. It was snowing harder and the flakes were stoking fresh accumulation. Hector slung his suitcase and portable typewriter in the trunk. Jimmy tossed Hector the car keys. The writer dropped his fedora on top of his suitcase, slipped off his overcoat, folded it, and placed it in the trunk, too. The Chevy had a good heater, so he figured he'd soon be plenty warm.

"You could drive," Hector said to Jimmy.

"No way," Jimmy said. "I know how you are about your cars. Honest to God, I think you care more about your wheels than your women. Certainly, the cars tend to linger longer."

"Not true," Hector said. "It just that they can't drive themselves away." He nodded at the backseat. "What about the ladies? Do I need to make another run upstairs for their luggage? I hope not, because I had to take another shot at one of those bastards. The guy you scalded was up and about. He's one tough hombre."

Jimmy smiled. "Yet you didn't even muss your hair." He jerked his head at the back seat. "No, no luggage with them, presently. The sleek cooze, the one I suspect you have your eye on, this Meg, she's a resident in there. Hotel's a mix, that way, she says. The woman and the child were hiding with Meg overnight."

"How does Megan tie into this?"

"Seems Miss Meg is Vito Scartelli's mistress," Jimmy said. "Every cheating man's nightmare, wouldn't you concede? I mean, the missus and the mistress throwing in together? No conceivable good can come of that."

"Not an ideal scenario under these, or hell, under any conditions," Hector agreed.

"Particularly not if hubby knows you're chummy and you're the wife who is legging it," Jimmy said. "Meg's was the first place he looked, I'd wager. I know it's the first place I would search if it was me."

"Where are they headed?"

Jimmy closed the trunk. "Damned if I know. You didn't give me that much time alone with them. But reluctant as I am to admit it, the better angels of my nature say we need to step in here, Hector. We need to get 'em someplace closer to safe. They'll not last the night on their own. That's obvious."

Hector felt something whiz close by his cheek; an instant later he heard the shot.

A man was running at them, firing at them through the snow flurries.

It was the thug Hector had dropped face-first in the toilet.

Jesus, Hector thought, *I really must be losing my touch*. Both of his men had come back around. Only Jimmy's man seemed to stay down for the long-count. But then Hector decided he had used bad logic on that last one dropping him in the toilet bowl. Hector had aimed to drown his man, but instead likely just brought the man back around with the gush of all that cold toilet water.

All that went through Hector's head in a flash. The thug was getting ready to shoot again.

Hector drew; Jimmy too. The other man fired again.

Hector couldn't say for certain how many shots were fired by the three of them, though he knew he'd cocked and pulled the trigger on his Colt twice.

A red spray obscured the thug's chest and face.

Hector winced, remembering little Shannon was in his Chevy's backseat. God willing, she hadn't seen those bullet strikes. He hoped one of those dishy molls found the presence of mind to cover the child's face again or, better still, to push the kid to the floorboards when the shooting started. Hector had seen more than once what a stray bullet could do; he knew far too well what a single errant shot could cost a man.

Jimmy hefted his own gun. "Not my service weapon, so I'm not too worried about anything being traced back to me."

Holstering his Colt, Hector nodded at the dead man and said, "You figure that was you or me who put that son of a bitch down?"

Jimmy waved a hand. "Figure it was me. At least with the first one. There's only one hole I see. Straight through the pump."

"See, I figured you for a between-the-eyes man," Hector said. He could hear the nervousness in his own voice under all the callous, macho bluster. Hector could hear it in Jimmy's usually smooth brogue, too. Adrenaline and cordite so easily made men blood simple, even men of their years. Hector clapped his friend's beefy arm, said, "We rolling now, or are you flashing your badge again, Jimbo?"

Jimmy opened the passenger side door. "We flee with all dispatch, Hector. For all I know, the entire Youngstown police department is on this godless Scartelli's damned dole."

As they rolled by the hotel, Hector pointed at Joe, still propped up against the wall in the falling snow. But someone had stolen Joe's hi-tone shoes.

Hector figured with the bitter cold his shoes' theft would probably cost Joe his toes.

Two blocks later, they spotted the shoeshine man wearing Joe's shoes. Jimmy elbowed Hector's arm, gesturing at the shoe-shiner leaning into a garbage pail to root around.

Jimmy said, "Boyo wears 'em much better'n Joe, don'tca think?"

Hector never got to answer. He was stopped by the burn of cold metal at the back of his neck.

Hector turned just enough to see another gun was pressed to the base of Jimmy's skull. "Okay, you lugs," Meg said. "We really do appreciate all you've done. We do. So now you just let us off up here and we'll let you two handsome bruisers go about your business as reward."

Hector balked. Sexy Meg pulled back the hammer on the gun against his neck. She said, "I mean business, Mr. Lassiter."

3

Hector sighed; it sounded like it came up from his heels. "I am not pullin' over, Meg," he drawled. "Abandon that thought now, sweetheart. You haven't thought this through. If you shoot me, you'll find yourself in the worst kind of car wreck. So let's stop fritterin' away time and instead figure out what our best and shared next move might be."

The gun was still at his neck. "Put the damned iron the hell down, Meg." Hector hesitated, then said, "And drop the hammer with the gun pointed *out* the window, okay?"

The way his luck was lately running, Hector could too vividly envision himself slain by an accidental discharge.

"First red light, we're getting out of here, mister," Meg said.

"Sorry, but *no*." Jimmy slowly held up his left hand. Two slender pieces of chrome rolled back and forth between his big thumb and forefinger. "These are the stems from the backdoor locks," Jimmy said. "I unscrewed them when you two were fussing with loading young Shannon." Jimmy opened his hand and the stems fell to the floorboards. "And now, in my clumsiness, I've lost them." He turned around more in his seat as Meg tried her door. "Am I not the devious Irishman?"

Meg threw herself against the door a last time.

"Locked the doors before I unscrewed the stems," Jimmy said. He held out his hand, palm up. "Give me the guns, lassies. As has been recently pointed out, you don't hold a firearm on a cop, regardless of your trouble. I can run you in now for that and something close enough to kidnapping to ensure you'll both miss Shannon's college graduation and her first child's christening. Give me the rods right now, or Hector here is headed to the station house where we'll turn you in to just any old probably bought-off cop we see. For all any of us know, I'm the only badge-carrier in this town who isn't living fat off Vito's roll."

The guns were still at their necks.

Jimmy said, "Left at the next crossroads, Hector. At least if they shoot us in the precinct parking lot they won't get any distance at all before they're caught. Whatever happens to us, this only ends one way for you skirts."

That did it—the two guns were passed into Jimmy's hands. He emptied each of bullets. The ammo he put in his overcoat pocket; the guns went in the glove compartment with the thugs' guns they'd taken.

"Wise choice," Hector said, stealing glances at Meg in the rearview mirror. "We're truly your best bet." He said that to her reflection. He studied Meg's face; savored that flush in her cheeks and neck. Spirited, that was the word for that one, he thought.

"You don't even know what's going on," Katy said.

"Oh, I think Jimmy called it correctly enough," Hector said. He nudged the car heater up a notch as he saw Shannon shiver. "For whatever reasons, you two are turning witnesses for Senator Kefauver. The whole breathless world is awaiting those hearings like they're a poor man's *Gone With the Wind*. Any bar or pub with one of those television sets is packed to bustin' with elbow-benders fixing to gawk at the big crazy show unfolding. So I figure for two pretty women who could hand up Vito Scartelli and his crew, old bucktoothed Estes would pull out all the stops. New identities, maybe a little house in a quaint and remote corner of Canada or down in coastal Mexico. Maybe even one-way tickets to Europe and some seed money to put down roots in some forgotten corner of the Old World. Close enough to actual facts?" Hector smiled in the rearview mirror. "Will it stand?"

Hector searched Meg's blue eyes with his. As he watched her in the rearview mirror, he saw Meg and Katy exchange nods. "Close enough," Meg said. "But we have to get to Kefauver, first. That's looking to be even harder than we expected, based on what just happened."

Jimmy lit a cigarette and shrugged. "That hoodlum, Joe, he wondered whether Hec and I might be Kefauver-sent sentries. Begs the question, why don't you two have some official escort? Why didn't Estes detail a crew to bring you ladies safely in?"

"He was supposed to," Katy said. "They were to pick us up at noon. They didn't. Instead, Joe and his crew turned up in the lobby."

Jimmy said, "You in touch with Kefauver directly?"

"Never," Katy said. "We were working through an FBI man in Cleveland," Meg said. "He was in charge of bringing us in. We should call him."

"Or maybe you shouldn't," Hector said. "I mean, he hasn't exactly distinguished himself today, and this was only step number one. You're both still relatively low-profile. Messing this earliest phase up doesn't bode well for the tougher future. So I think we write that FBI fella off. At best he's incompetent. At worst he's in Vito's hip pocket. Hell, he may well have set you up back there by tipping your husband's muscle."

Meg said, "So now you're making all our decisions, is that it? A writer and a plainclothes cop against the northern Ohio Mafia and crooked G-men? I fear we're doomed."

"Haven't said yet we're taking on your problem as our own," Jimmy said. "But if we do, you'll be lucky to have us."

Hector glanced over at Jimmy. "Thought you had unfinished business here in Youngstown."

"Looks to be another dead-end already," Jimmy said. "It's kept this many decades, Hec. And Cleveland? Well, you know…"

Cleveland was Jimmy's home, his inevitable next destination. Cleveland was Jimmy's city.

He said, "What about you, Hec? You know, the two of us together might stand something like a dim chance." This silly grin on his face. Hector owed Jim this one. Similar circumstances in Europe during World War II had found Hector pleading to Jimmy for help with the plight of a young Jewish orphan.

Jimmy had stepped up under circumstances more circumspect men would have bolted from. Hector had asked Jimmy in nearly the same words to ride shotgun across occupied France, pursued by the might of the Nazi army.

Hector smiled and shook his head. "I am sorely at ends, Jimmy. Signed another two-book contract in New York and handed over two complete manuscripts on the spot. Got a backlog of works, presently. So I've certainly got some time to spare."

Jimmy put a hand on Hector's shoulder and patted. "Badge doesn't leave me much choice, Hec. But you've got options. You do know what you'd be throwing in against? You do this with open eyes?"

What was the Mob compared to the goddamned Nazis? Hector's waved a dismissive hand. "It's no great thing. So, we go to Cleveland?"

Jimmy squeezed Hector's shoulder. "Yes, boyo, we go to Cleveland. By the time we get there through all this snow and probable detours for closed roads along the way, I figure we'll have had the time to formulate some plan as to what to do next."

Rubbing his jaw, Hector checked the rearview mirror again. Meg and Katy were taking it all in. Katy said, "We were supposed to be taken to Cleveland and questioned there. Then we were to be sent on by train to Washington and Mr. Hoover and his men, prior to seeing the senator."

Hector whistled. "J. Edgar himself, eh? No joking?"

"So they promised," Meg said.

"Funny thought—I mean old John Edgar now racing to get out in front of this mob stuff," Jimmy said. "For years, for decades, really, Hoover has denied the existence of a Mafia. But now with the Kefauver hearings, he's got himself in a public relations bind, one supposes."

The little girl said, "I'm hungry."

Katy said, "She can wait." In the mirror, Hector saw Meg give Katy another look. Anger there. Irritation, sure, but something else he couldn't yet define. He asked, "When was the last time the child had food?"

Meg searched Hector's eyes in the mirror; hard to read her expression. "Yesterday afternoon. These past several hours, well, there's never been a chance."

Christ. "She must really be starving then," Hector said. "We need to remedy that, pronto. We'll hit a drive-in. Stay warm in the car."

"And keep us prisoners in the bargain," Katy said, an edge in her voice.

"There is that," Hector said. "But we have to deal with a tail, too. Need to shake him."

Meg said, "She desperately needs to eat." Then Hector's last statement sunk in. Her eyes widened. She said, "Wait, there's someone following us?"

"Pretty sure, and right from the hotel parking lot," Hector said.

Jimmy grunted and said, "The gray Olds, three cars back?"

"I do think so," Hector said.

"Had my eye on him, too," Jimmy said. "There's little doubt it's so if we both seized on him."

"More of Vito's men," Katy said, sounding defeated.

"Doubtful," Hector said.

Katy said, "Why not? Why doubtful?"

Jimmy turned around in his seat. He pushed his hat back on his head with two thick fingers. "Because no guinea hoodlum would be caught dead in such a drab car. Not the Ohio flavor of hoodlum, anyway. They get a little gelt and in a jiffy they get notions of grandeur. Get above their raisings. They pour it all into their wheels and threads. At least their shoes…"

Katy said, "Who is following us, then?"

"Time will tell," Hector said. He thought, *And all of us will surely not like the answer.* Hector chewed his lip. *Hell, probably certainly that'll be so,* he concluded.

4

They found a Don Juan's drive-in between Youngstown and Boardman. The comely carhops wore puffy coats with fur-lined hoods and big boots. Their usual roller-skates and saucy short shorts had been swept away with the November blizzard. Once again, Hector rued the wicked weather.

He ordered up several hamburgers, baskets of wavy fries and Coca Colas. While they waited, Jimmy and Hector parked their backsides on the warm hood of the idling Chevy and lit up a couple of cigarettes. The gray Olds was parked in a service station across the street.

"Sitting here like this," Jimmy said, "we could just be giving them time to gather resources or forces, Hec."

"If they're official, we might be doing that," Hector said. "If they've got a radio in that car. But like you, I *already* figure they are official. But they've got no antenna on that car that would support any kind of radio to worry us, right?"

"Those are also rental tags," Jimmy said, spewing smoke. "So I suppose I concur."

Hector nodded. "So you also figure we sit and eat?"

"Figure one of us does that," Jimmy said. "Figure the other one of us sneaks up on them. But then what?"

"Figure I'll figure that out when I do it," Hector said. "Try and keep my burger warm. I'll wolf it down on the lam. But first, a distraction of some kind would serve the cause."

"Done," Jimmy said. He began to whistle "The Parting Glass" as Hector drifted away.

First Hector walked toward the drive-in's interior, like he was maybe headed to the can. He slipped around back and then jogged a block through snow flurries. Hector crossed the street and made his way around to the back of the service station.

Hiding behind an air pump, Hector looked over the Olds and its occupants. The two men inside looked husky and Federal enough. Hector surely wouldn't want to tangle with them individually, let alone in tandem.

A tow truck was parked about ten feet off the Olds' rear fender. Hector cast a look around the scene. Jimmy was out in front of the Chevy with the hood up, pretending to futz around while chewing his lip. The Feds seemed to focus their attention on Jimmy.

The service station attendant was busy with an elderly female customer. That exchange looked heated, fingers in faces and spittle spraying.

Hector bit his lip and took another look at that tow truck, then made up his mind. He released the brake on the towline and tugged loose about fifteen feet of metal cord.

Ducking down, he made his way to the back of the Olds and rolled onto his back, sliding under the car on the icy pavement. Quietly as he could, Hector wrapped a couple turns of towline around the Olds' rear axle and secured it with the big rusty hook. He wriggled back out from under the Olds and crouched his way back to the truck.

Hector re-engaged the towline brake and crept back around behind the station, brushing snow off his back and ass. He shoved his hands into his pants pockets and trotted back around the block to the drive-in. As he crossed the street, Hector stole a look back at the gray Olds. He hoped for taxpayers' sake the Feds had forked over for rental insurance.

"*Ho-ho*, probably bent their axle," Jimmy said, looking back over his shoulder in delight at the disabled Oldsmobile. "Particularly with you fleeing the scene with such gratuitous speed and forcing those hapless lads to do likewise. So puckish, you can be. Were they Feds, Hector?"

"Quite probably," he said.

Jimmy winced. "Then fond as you are of this fine car, Hec, I suggest we change wheels."

"No," Hector said. "I don't think they could do much with that information that they haven't already done by now. Not standing back as they've been. Suspect by now they have my identity off the hotel desk clerk. They saw what almost happened with that thug back in the hotel lot and didn't raise a finger to help us or to arrest us for putting down that torpedo. As Federals go, these fellas seem rather passive to me, even when bullets are flying with terminal intent."

"Righty, then," Jimmy said. "I suppose I concur again. At least so far as your logic goes."

Hector checked the rearview mirror. The women were silent. Shannon suddenly said, "*Mister!*"

"*Hector*," Hector said.

Shannon said, "*Mister Hector!* I need to go to the bathroom *real bad!*"

"Ah, that's grand, isn't it?" Jimmy shook his head, grinning crookedly. More *déjà vu*.

"Just let me find a filling station," Hector said. Two-tenths of a mile later, he palmed into the lot of a Sinclair station. A big green Brontosaurus statue loomed on the station's rooftop. Hector unlocked the passenger-side rear door from the outside. He said to Meg, "You take her. We'll wait."

Katy leaned down where she could see Hector's face. Her eyes were blazing. "I'm her mother."

"Precisely why you're staying here," Hector said. He was distracted a bit by the expression on Meg's face. Anger? Confusion?

Either way, Hector couldn't yet read it. So he pressed on with Katy: "You and Shannon together? I figure that pairing for more of a real flight risk. Meg and Shannon together? Not nearly so much. Sorry, Kate, but it's the way things are going to be, at least presently. Once we feel you've all lost the impulse to rabbit, things could change." Hector let his voice trail off on what he intended to sound like a hopeful note.

He held out a hand and Meg took it. He drew her up out of the backseat. "Good to stretch, huh, Meg?"

She shrugged and put out her other hand to the little girl. "Come on, Shannon," she said.

"Please, try to be fast," Hector said softly to Meg. "There's only one real road out of this town on the way to Cleveland and those boys in the Olds are going to rightly figure we're on it. Afraid that seconds count, now."

Meg nodded. Standing next to her he saw how tall she was. How tall she stood with the heels on, anyway. Her sexy shoes raised her up to about five-ten, maybe five-eleven.

She said, "Thank you, Hector, really. Clearly we're in over our heads." Meg hesitated, then said, "Even with you two helping us, frankly, I'm not very hopeful."

"That's okay," Hector said. He admired her hard-eyed honesty. He said rather dopily, and very falsely, "I've got hope to spare, darlin'."

She smiled—one filled with doubt. Maybe even a bit rueful. Meg said, "I don't know about that, but you've certainly got confidence to burn. You're a cocky, fool-hearty man."

"That's me all over," Hector said. "Get a move on now. Hustle, won't you two? It's a hundred miles to Cleveland, give or take, and we're in the snow-belt. Hell, roads out this way may never have been cleared after that wind-driven pile that fell around these parts on Turkey Day. Given all that, I'd rather make Cleveland before nightfall."

He watched the dishy moll, swaying on her stiletto heels, carefully crossing the slick lot to ask the attendant for the restroom key. Shannon kept looking up and pointing at the big dinosaur model atop the station. Watching them from behind, Hector was stuck by how pale the little girl's hair was, nearly as yellow-white as that of the gangster's mistress.

Sliding back behind the wheel, Hector rubbed his hands together and blew into them to warm fingers.

"We have some time alone now, Katy," Jimmy said. "Now would be the time for frank talk, away from the child's innocent ears. For starters, what did you tell this FBI man that you were prepared to give the Kefauver committee?"

Katy stared at her gloved hands. No hesitation: "Everything. Names of his lieutenants, phony fronts for my husband's various so-called enterprises." A long pause ensued while she considered her hands. Then, "And a ledger."

Jimmy sighed. "Any of that would be more than plenty for your husband to sign your death warrants. And what's in that ledger, Katy dear?"

"Names. Account numbers. All the kinds of things you'd probably expect. My husband's memory has never been particularly good, and now it's only getting worse. Dementia runs in his family, and it seems he's reaching that age. He repeats himself constantly. He gets furious when he's called on it, but in more lucid moments he grudgingly registers it's a problem. So he writes things down these days. He writes down everything. He does that all the time."

A low whistle. "That would make him an exceptionally rare and dangerous duck in his sordid line of work," Jimmy said. "It makes him a real risk to this heathen brethren. How'd you wrest such a dangerous document from hubby's blood-stained hands?"

"I hired a man," Katy said. "We made it look like a robbery, like a break-in at our house. I sacrificed some money and some of my jewelry to further the illusion. My hired man got me the ledger, and, essentially, all the contents of the safe in our bedroom."

Hector said, "But your ruse didn't fool Vito?"

"Not for long, it seems," Katy said, bitterly. "What are we going to do in Cleveland?"

"Try to lose ourselves in the damned city," Hector said. "It's no New York or Chicago, but it's a hell of a lot easier to hide there than in these tinier Buckeye environs. And I have some contacts of my own in the Bureau, trusty folk. Honest ones, and time-tested. Least ways, they don't always lockstep behind old J. Edgar's nefarious marching orders."

Katy just shook her head. "These FBI friends of yours, are these men in Cleveland, or in D.C.?"

"The latter," Hector said.

"Then it might as well be China," she said, sour-voiced.

"They have their own friends," Hector said. "They may know some honest agents in Cleveland. And more importantly, Jimmy has friends in Cleveland, too."

Jimmy held up his badge. This time he held it so she could read the locale emblazoned on his tin. "So you see, Cleveland is Jimmy's town," Hector said. "Now, are you two going to try and bolt on us? I hope not, because standing guard on you three is getting tedious and cramping our damn style. It's a drain on our energies that could best be spent helping you gals. You really don't want us distracted."

"We're with you two lugs for better or worse now," she said. "Who else do we have? I don't think you can truly help us in the end, but our chances without you are hopeless. Today has made that clear."

"This damned ledger," Jimmy said, "you've got it on you? It might be better if we sent it ahead of us, via mail, or something. Surely wouldn't do to be caught with it. That'd be a colossal mistake. Endgame, stuff, really."

"The ledger is just pages of stray paper now," she said. "I tore them lose from the binding, the better to hide them, you know? They're safe enough and I'm not letting those pages out of my sight. They're my bargaining chip. They're our life insurance. For my baby and I."

Sighing, Hector stretched his fingers in front of the car's heater vent, still trying to warm them. "Meg and you should be blood enemies, Kate. How'd you end up in cahoots, particularly with such life-and-death stakes in the mix? Have to confess, the dynamic between you two women has me plum foxed."

Katy shrugged. "How terrible for you, then. I'm afraid you'll simply have to stay foxed, Mr. Lassiter." She nodded. "Here they come back." Edge in her voice as she said that last.

Hector turned, watching the two cross the icy lot together. The little girl had one hand wrapped around the pretty moll's hand. Shannon's other arm was wrapped tightly around her dolly.

Something there, a thing Hector still couldn't put his finger on.

He looked at Jimmy. The Irish cop nodded and said softly, "Yes, me too. And yes, me *neither*. Not yet, at any rate." Jimmy wet his lips. "But I will figure it out of course. It'll come in due course, as it always does."

5

Passing through Warren, Ohio, Jimmy and Hector decided it was best to get off the most obvious trail to Cleveland. Consequently, they cut across a wide spot in the road called "Delightful" where an old filling station attendant assured them rural roads were open all the way through to Twinsburg. That path would take the quintet into Cleveland, via Maple Heights.

But it was a white-knuckle drive all the way northwest.

The drifts and plowed piles of snow stood two- or three-feet higher than the roof of the Chevy. To Hector's mind, it was like driving through the launch chute of a pinball machine—the monotony of those high, white walls began messing with Hector's eyes. A glossy veneer of ice also covered the pavement. Hector was soon regretting having turned down the car dealer's offer to equip his new car's tires with a set of snow chains.

Jimmy said softly, "We've both been profligately to and fro in this mad, bad world, Hec, and plenty at that. Yet I have to say, I've not seen snow like this, not ever."

Hector nodded his agreement, keeping his eyes on the road and his hands firmly on the wheel.

Shannon yawned loudly. Jimmy smiled and began to sing "Carrickfergus," lullaby smooth:

> *So I'll spend my days in this endless roving*
> *Soft is the grass and my bed is free*
> *Ah, to be home now in Carrickfergus*
> *On the long road down to the salty sea.*

Eventually Jimmy veered into Gaelic: "*Do bhí bean uasal.*"

Somewhere around Aurora, Katy said softly, "Shannon's asleep."

"Poor child has had the Devil's own hard and trying day, and that's for certain," Jimmy said. "I could sleep myself, I think."

"Do that if you want," Hector said. "God knows there's no scenery with this goddamn snow." Hector smiled. "But don't expect me to serenade you to sleep."

"Shall sleep later," Jimmy said. "Wouldn't want the ladies ganging up on you." He shook his head and said, "Any objections to me turning up the heat a few notches?"

"Not at all," Meg said. Hector saw her rubbing her arms with her hands. She'd spread her fur wrap over the sleeping child. Katy was still wearing her coat.

Jimmy said, "I'm parched. Could use a fiery drink." He fished around in his overcoat pocket and produced a silver flask. "Sweetest Jameson," he said. "Any takers?"

Meg smiled and shook her head. She opened her purse and pulled out her own flask. "Bourbon," she said.

Katy produced a third flask. "Gin."

Jimmy waved his flask at me. "You surely won't disappoint me, will you, Hector?"

Steering with his left hand, Hector reached down into the cuff of his right boot and retrieved his own flask. "Whisky without the 'e'," I said. "Single malt, in other words."

Jimmy snorted. "Ah, you *Sasanach* heathen! God love ya at least for your taste in booze."

They hoisted their four flasks. Hector toasted, "*Pro rege et patria*," then he added, "Ain't we the sorry juicer quartet?"

They found themselves a motel on the outskirts of Shaker Heights. Still at least naggingly uncertain in their minds whether the women might try and dash on them at any instant, Jimmy and Hector got adjacent rooms with a connecting door they agreed would be left open all night.

Hector sat with the women while Jimmy made some calls back to Cleveland and his cop confreres.

Hector said, "You ladies hungry for supper? There's a diner across the lot. We should eat while we have the chance."

Shannon, looking up at him with big shiny eyes, made it clear she was starving.

Meg said, "But your friend, Mr. Hanrahan?"

"He'll find us," Hector said. "Hell, he's a detective after all, and one of the rare good ones."

It was dusk and the heavy snow flurries flitted, glittering in the parking lot lights. Hector watched Jimmy making his way toward them, snow swirling around him. Hector stood and slipped on his overcoat and put on his hat. "You ladies eat up. Be back in a jiffy."

He left them there with their diner food, the joint only had one way in or out and Hector figured to park his ass outside that single door. He met Jimmy under the diner's metal awning. Jimmy fished out a Lucky Strike and leaned into Hector's old Zippo. "You don't look so right, Jimmy."

"Christ, Hector, I almost wish I hadn't placed that damned phone call."

"Who did you talk to, Jim?"

"Josh Gordon, my partner. He's the one cop in Cleveland I trust, and I mean all the way up."

Something strange in Jim's voice; Hector felt this void yawning close. Their breath was frosty on the night air. Their cigarette smoke trailed from their mouths and nostrils in sinister tendrils. Hector figured they must look like fidgety dragons through the frosted-over display window. He said, "And what did your partner have to say?" Hector didn't like the sound of his own voice, suddenly. Jimmy's palpable unease was maybe contagious, Hector thought.

"My badge isn't going to do a lick of good for us, I fear," Jimmy said. "If that woman's monster husband all but owns the Youngstown police force, his fingers reach deep into Cleveland, too. Word is out on both of us. By that I mean about who we've got and what Kate means to do to Vito given less than half a chance."

Jimmy rubbed his neck and sighed. "I'm trying to figure out how they made me. Enough guys from the old days know you and me to be friends. I guess maybe me being in Youngstown too might have been enough for some to figure I'd throw in with you to protect the gals."

Jimmy blew smoke out both nostrils. "Hell, either way, we're up against it hard, Hec. Anyway, it seems I'm going to have my own people keeping an eye peeled for me. Some of them are ready to sell me out." He spat into the snow and said, "Crooked sons of bitches."

"There is one good thing," Hector said. "If they run a DMV check on me they're going to be looking for a blue

Chevrolet Fleetmaster Convertible. That was my previous car. I've still got temporary tags on the new one. Only bought it two days ago, and it being the start of the weekend, well, we get a few days' leg up."

"At best, that buys us a few more days before the county offices open up and that auto registration gets updated," Jimmy said. "After, we're squarely behind the eight ball on that front, as well."

Hector looked across the street at a five-and-dime. Scads of gaudy toys littered the front window. Sleds and air rifles were arrayed amidst puffy piles of artificial snow. A placard in the window told how many shopping days remained until Christmas. Hector did some math and realized that there were not many left at all. He thought that countdown might have meant more if he had anyone to buy gifts for this year.

So far, it was another of *those kinds* of Christmases. There had been too many of *those kinds* of Christmases in his life.

"I'm freezing my ass off out here," Hector said. "Let's get back in there and warm with those gals. Put on brave faces. Get some grub for you and then I think we divide up. You take Katy and the little girl back to the rooms and see what more you can get from her. I'll focus on Meg."

"That's about all you've done since you laid eyes on that pretty, long-stemmed piece of trouble." Jimmy held up his big hands as Hector started to object. "Just saying what I see, Hec. It's no big deal. As always, I expect you to be you, and so far, Hector, you haven't disappointed, and thank God for that—I mean given the promised mayhem."

Jimmy shook his head and stared at the end of his cigarette. He said, "That gal in there is no Duff Sexton. Based on tales you've told me of her in your cups, Meg's certainly no Brinke Devlin, either. You step careful around this one, yeah?"

6

Meg watched the trio walk back across the lot to the hotel, Shannon holding hands with Katy and Jimmy gripping Katy's other arm at the elbow, steadying the woman on the icy pavement as she tottered on her heels.

Meg said, "So is this some divide-and-conquer strategy you boys have in mind?"

Hector sipped his cream-laced coffee. "Afraid you're gonna have to define conquer for me, Meg."

"Sure. I mean cop tricks, though you insist you're not a cop. But you easily could be, you know. You have that kind of mind and the right kind of wrong-headed attitude. I suspect you and Hanrahan angle to split us up and see if our stories mesh. I suspect that you aim to undermine Katy's and my bond to one another. I suspect you two men mean to run some good-cop bad-cop act on us. Is that your strategy?"

Hector brushed a comma of hair back off his forehead. "Bond, you said. Singular. Not bonds, but bond. So there is just one solitary thing holding you two together." Hector sipped more of his coffee. "What is it exactly that has bound you to that woman, darlin'?"

Meg just looked at him. She at last said, "Damned author. You would seize on the nuances of a single word, wouldn't you?" That snide observation struck Hector as a diversion.

"Writer or no, I can maybe make some good guesses as to what's happening," he said, pointedly ignoring Meg's crack about his craft.

She shrugged and sipped her coffee. "So do it, Hector Lassiter. Take your best shot, you writer."

Hector put it out there with one true word: "Shannon."

Meg flinched. Hector of a sudden felt like a heel. She said, "I like that little girl plenty. I don't want to see her hurt." Her eyes didn't meet Hector's when she said all that.

"It's much more than that, honey. Don't insult my intelligence."

"What do you mean?"

"The hair color is a tipper, Meg. I'd like to say it's in the eyes and the bone structure, too. The smile. And I suppose it is, though I didn't see it at first. Mostly it's just the way you look at that child that clued me in."

"What are you saying, Hector?" Her tone made him squirm just a little.

He offered her a cigarette and she held up a hand. "I don't smoke."

"Then neither will I presently," he said.

"You were saying?"

"I was about to say Shannon is your blood, Meg. Shannon is your daughter. Isn't she?"

Meg just looked at him, her eyes smoldering.

He pushed ahead. "I don't pretend to fathom how that can be, Meg. But I know to my bones I'm right. That little girl is your blood."

Meg sat back in the booth and crossed her arms over her chest. Her eyes were focused on something very far away now, those blue eyes verging on violet, just like Shannon's. Violet eyes, pulling the rug from under a ruse, again. Hector shook his head to escape the déjà vu. Sometimes it struck Hector if God maybe did exist, the old bearded fella was a sorry-ass, one-trick pony.

"There's a bar around the corner," she said. "I could use a real drink."

"Me too," Hector said, voice going to gravel. "Maybe even several drinks. Let's go get some of those right now."

It was bitterly cold and windy. "Damn lake effect weather," Hector said aloud as the wind whipped the tails of his coat and made his eyes tear up again. He slipped a bit on the sidewalk, despite his newish Catspaw heels. He took one look at Meg's high heels and offered her an arm. She considered the overhead lights' glare on the treacherous concrete, then slipped her arm around Hector's.

She nodded across the lot at the fuzzy lights of their lodgings, winking through the flurries. "Some dump you two checked us into."

"Hell, it's merely rustic," Hector said. "Americana. Sorry if my pockets don't run so deep as your former beau's." Hector smiled and shook his head. "Jimmy has a saying: 'If you want to know what God thinks of money, just look at who he gives it to.' And anyway, that dump is just for one night. Jimmy tells me the Hollenden Hotel, on Superior Avenue, is quite nice."

"Very nice indeed," Meg said. "Also very conspicuous."

"You've been there?"

Her voice went a shade flat. "A time or two."

"Vito do a lot of business here in town?" That was a knife-twist of a transition, Hector knew.

"In this town, yes," Meg said, her breath trailing frost. "Hell, in every town. Ohio, West Virginia and western Pennsylvania. Even a bit of Canada, up around Windsor." She gripped Hector's arm a bit harder as her feet betrayed her. "Do you have even the remotest sense of what you're up against, helping us?"

"Yeah, I do," he said. "Don't you entertain any fears on that front. Have no qualms about Jimmy and I not grasping the scale of the danger."

"Then you're just more the puzzlement if that's so, Hector. I can't decide if you're crazy, a thrill-seeker, or just some kind of suicide case."

"And here we are." Hector held the door for Meg. A couple of wolves gave her the eye as they slipped in from the cold. Hector figured he would have stared at her too—she had those kinds of looks. Patti Page on the jukebox: "Tennessee Waltz."

He helped Meg off with her coat. As he held her hand while she slid into the Naugehyde booth, a waiter drifted their way. Meg jacked a thumb at the cardboard advertisement balanced on a chrome napkin holder, a promotional piece for White Rook sparkling water. "Some of that, please, with some white wine," she said.

Her order didn't seem much of a drink to Hector. He ordered them both rum St. James, thinking of winters many years past and toying with trying to recapture some memory or two tied to all that. Twenties Paris was very much on his mind lately, for some reason.

Meg said, "Shannon and I? It's a closed subject, Hector. At least for now."

He narrowed his eyes. "But why exactly is that?"

Meg bowed her head, tugging at her gloves. "Because I can't afford for you to hate Katy. Not while you're committed to seeing us through this thing."

Just like that, Hector of a sudden loathed the other woman. But he said, "Then I'll respect your wishes on just that point. I won't push. But only for a time. I can't promise more than that."

She let a little smoke into her voice. "I appreciate it."

Their drinks came. They toasted, Hector resorting to one of Jimmy's hoary Celtic cautions against strong drink: "Careful with that, Meg—it'll go down your throat like a torchlight procession. At least for the first sip or two."

Johnny Otis began singing "Double Crossing Blues." Meg held out her hand. "Give me some coins, would you, Hector? I want to improve the music." At that moment, Hector allowed himself to think she was maybe a woman after his own heart.

He muttered, "You sound like me," and handed Meg some pocket change. He sat back in his chair and considered her voyage to the jukebox, savoring her sway. Hector watched her, and, hell, *every* man in the bar watched her, too, he noted. Meg seemed oblivious to the attention, or long beyond caring. What a sad thing for one so young and pretty if it was so, Hector thought.

She slid back into the booth across from him, sloe-eyed. "I put in a few coins for you, too."

He arched a dark eyebrow. "You think you know my tastes in music?"

"You'll have to tell me how close I came."

Hector said, "Have you thought about what happens once this mess is over, Meg? I mean, once we get you two to Kefauver and he drains you of all that devastating information you offer?"

"You mean *if* you get us there."

"If. When. Either way, what happens to you when the pressure is off?"

Meg sighed. "That's just a clever way of leading me back around to talking about Shannon and I, isn't it, Hector?"

He hadn't meant the question that way, but she was right—he'd staggered into a line of interrogation. He reckoned he could be unconsciously stubborn that way.

Anyway Hector figured it, as long as they were ducking and dodging, Meg maintained her tie to her little girl.

But what would happen once any threat was removed?

Hector didn't see Katy and Meg setting up housekeeping in some Canadian or Mexican backwater and splitting parenting responsibilities for that little blond-haired girl.

He saw no prospect for "happily ever after" for Meg and Shannon.

"I really didn't mean to press," he said, feeling the ogre. "I truly didn't, Megan."

Meg gave him a long look. "I believe you, Hector. Blue eyes don't hide much."

That assertion set Hector back on his heels. It was a line from one of his novels. Meg said, "And you have very blue eyes, Hector. Took me a bit to make the connection. I've read a few of your novels and I liked them a great deal. I've seen some of the movies you've scripted. Read a profile of you in *Movie Fan Magazine* a month or so ago. 'The man who lives what he writes and writes what he lives.' That was the headline." A long pause, then, "There was a lot in that article about you being a skirt-chaser, or ladies-man, too."

"Slander stuff." Hector took a shot of his fiery rum. "Studio public relations bullshit." He said it through the booze's burn.

"Maybe some." Meg smiled. "But the life you've led, the risks you've taken? All the theaters of war and the revolutions you've raced into according to that article? You're still standing and looking not the much worse for wear. I mean, you look… I don't know, almost, boyish. Game for anything. You've got the kind of reputation and charisma that might give a girl some crazy kind of hope." Meg smiled. "I mean, if I wasn't such a cynic."

"It's safe enough for you to hope," Hector said. "Even to believe in the two of us, I mean. If I blow it, Jimmy won't. In all the world, he's the one I'd most want to have my back in a scrape like this."

"You've known James a long time?"

"Since before you were born, I'd guess." *Now that was a stupid way to put it*, he thought.

"How old do you think I am?"

"Maybe twenty-two. But an old soul." That last was a bit disingenuous on Hector's part. Meg struck him as somewhat less than worldly, despite some of the lamentable varnish she'd acquired in her relatively short life.

"Your math is close enough," Meg said.

"You're certainly younger than Kate."

This look. "Mistresses are always younger than the wives, aren't they?"

"Touché."

"I was watching you two through the window of the diner," Meg said. "James and you both looked very serious, Hector. And Hanrahan? He looked badly shaken. Don't lie. What's happened?"

"You shouldn't read so much into Jimmy's expressions and the like," Hector said, trying for a dodge. "He revels in all that Irish cynicism. Claims he has an abiding sense of tragedy that sustains him through temporary periods of joy."

Meg wasn't having it; she pressed. "What's already gone wrong, Hector?"

He thought about it, sipping more of drink and savoring the way it warmed his gut. He impulsively decided he trusted Meg, and couldn't put much by her anyway, even if he didn't. She already seemed adept enough at reading him. He said, "We've lost some potentially valuable allies it seems."

"What allies?"

"The Cleveland police force."

Meg looked stricken. "*All* of it?"

"Enough of it to make picking and choosing potential partners too treacherous to try. Your former friend, Vito, his reach is long and very deep. Limitless blood money can do that." Then he thought, *You sure know how to pick 'em, Meg.*

"No revelation there. It's like what you said about God and money." She sipped her water-weakened wine. Meg made a face at her drink. "This isn't going to get me there."

"It isn't going to get you where?"

"It isn't going to get me to that place where I'm numb. Closer to beyond caring."

"Then bottoms up." Hector passed her the rest of his cocktail and held up two fingers for reinforcements. The waiter saw, nodded. Hector noticed Meg's lipstick on his glass. It made Hector want to kiss her, to taste her pouty mouth, softly bite her bee-stung bottom lip. He said, "We're not beat yet, Meg. Not even close. We'll see you all through this, I swear."

She smiled and briefly laid her hand over Hector's. "You are some kind of crazy, Hector Lassiter. You and your Irish friend." She smiled, shaking her head. "That sometimes accent of yours, am I right that you come from Texas?"

"That's right. Galveston. I hear some Missouri in your accent. Don't look at me like that—it's nearly ground out, but I catch flickers."

"You called it," she said tucking hair behind an ear. "From around Moberly, or thereabouts." Hank Williams on the juke-box now, "Long Gone Lonesome Blues".

Hector said, "So you think this tune is to my tastes?"

Meg shook her head. "I played this one for me. The next one is yours."

His song came around eventually, a cover of "I've Got It Bad (And That Ain't Good)" given a mild Texas Swing treatment. A few couples took to the smallish dance floor. Meg slid out of the booth and offered Hector a hand. "C'mon, cowboy, dance with me. I'm finally feeling the liquor. Might just be able to forget for a dance or two how sorry and hopeless our situation probably is."

Situation? That was a fifty-cent word for what they all faced.

Still, they danced to that tune. That one, as well as "You Took Advantage of Me"… "I Can't Give You Anything but Love," "After You've Gone" and "Exactly like You."

Someone behind Meg had dropped coin for Bing Cosby's "White Christmas." They danced to that one too, Meg draped around Hector, hanging on him, more like, at the end. She was clearly more than a bit blitzed by the rum.

She said, "Holiday plans, Hector? Hate to have all this cost you Christmas with some comely honey back in New Mexico. That's where that article said you live now if I remember it rightly." Meg's Missouri accent was coming through thicker now. "Any big New Year's Eve plans, Tex?"

"Depends," Hector said, deciding to let a little more Gulf Coast and Galveston into his own tones. "You have any notions about maybe headin' south for the New Year? Maybe flirtin' with being a Snow Bird? I've got a little place in Key West I'm still holdin' onto."

She gave him a knowing smirk. It was there in her eyes; maybe because it had been in his eyes for so long, he figured.

Hector took a chance and leaned in close. Meg smiled and closed her eyes, tipping her face toward his. Her lips tasted of rum, catsup and coffee. Her tongue was suddenly there in his mouth, and now there was the taste of white wine, too.

Slowly opening her eyes, Meg, a little breathy, said, "Thanks again for everything you're trying to do for us. Please tell your friend how grateful I am."

"You can do that yourself," Hector said, "but just don't kiss him like this when you do that."

Hector leaned back in, found her mouth.

They kissed a last time in the parking lot, clinging to one another under the light above her hotel room's door. Hector coaxed her to the door of the room that he and Jim were sharing. "You can use the connecting door," he said, fumbling with the lock, his fingers stiff from the cold.

Her hand was suddenly at the small of his back. "Hector, that gray Olds from before is sitting across the parking lot. I can see two men inside."

Son of a bitch.

Meg said, "How'd they find us again?"

"Sometimes FBI work in trailing teams," Hector said. "Didn't think to look for another car, or perhaps even two. But there must have been, and they must have switched off again for the graveyard shift. There'll likely only be one car watching us now. They'll figure we're bedding down for the night."

"How do you know all of this, Hector?"

"Sometimes my life seems eternally confounded by the goddamn Bureau and old J. Edgar," he said. "Swear that sometimes I can't swing a dead cat without smackin' the head of some Hoover stooge. Either way, I know their moves."

"So what do we do now?"

"Go and get everyone packing to leave, pronto. Tell Jimmy what's up. Tell him to join me outside in six or seven minutes."

"What are you going to do?"

"I'm thinking about going and talking to them."

"*What?*"

"Really—I've decided it's time for a conversation. What Jimmy might call a *colloquy*."

Meg's eyes widened. "Is that wise?"

"Guess we'll see, directly."

"Just talk?"

Hector shrugged. "At least at first."

Hector made a show of lighting a cigarette while looking around for a burst of inspiration. A vending machine glowed in a lighted alcove about twenty yards from their motel rooms. A water spigot jutted out of the wall next to the soda pop machine. On the ground near the spigot lay a length of coiled garden hose.

The Olds was maybe twenty yards behind Hector; he reckoned the hose looked long enough.

He bent down as if to tie his shoelace, his back between the Olds and the water spigot. Hector threaded the end of the hose onto the spigot, then tried the handle. It finally gave with a groan. Water began to trickle from the end of the hose. Hector turned the spigot off again. For cover, he dug out some change and then bought a bottle of Orange Crush, popping the lid off on the opener on the side of the machine. Steam rose from the lip of the soda bottle.

A vagrant was wandering the parking lot, leaning on the hoods of cars a row behind the Feds. The juicer looked to be struggling to stay upright against the slick pavement and a profound state of drunkenness.

Hector walked out to meet the vagrant, knowing the Feds were watching closely. The snow was picking up and visibility dropping. Hector called, "Hey there, old pal!"

The wino turned and grinned. There were more teeth missing than left in his head. He had rheumy eyes, wet from the cold. His back to the Olds, Hector pulled out his roll and shucked off a ten-dollar bill. "Hamilton is yours," he said to the vagrant. "All you have to do is walk up to that gray Olds there and tap on the window. Make a nuisance of yourself. It's a gag on some friends."

The old juicer's brow wrinkled. Dubious: "Yeah? Make a nuisance? Then what? Then what happens to your *friends*?"

"Nothing. You just be persistent until I send you on your way. Just get 'em to roll a window down. Passenger side would be best. Once that window goes down, you just walk away."

"Do just that for ten bucks?"

"You do just that for ten bucks." The bottle of soda was cold in Hector' hand. "Say yes now, and I'll throw in a bottle of Orange Crush."

The juicer grinned his gummy grin. "Hell, I'll do it."

"Then do it right now, old sport."

The snow was falling harder, starting to freshly accumulate. There were big, wind-driven flakes twirling down. Hector shook some snow from his hat and brushed more off his shoulders. Then he crouched down behind a Buick, staying low and making his way back to where the Olds sat parked.

The old wino was banging on the passenger side window of the Olds and yelling. The man in the passenger seat was yelling back at the juicer. The old man kept a hand cocked at his ear, like some demented and deaf duffer.

The Fed finally rolled down the window. Hector heard him say in a loud voice, "All right pops, I'm going to give you two dollars, then you go the hell away."

The wino said, "Bless you, brother." When he went to reach for the bills, the juicer accidentally dropped his bottle of Orange Crush. It bounced off the window and tumbled into the Fed's lap. The G-man yelled, "Shit!" then, "Stupid rummy dumbass!"

The old wino backed away with his dollar bills, feet slipping and sliding on the ice.

Hector sidled up and put his Colt to the Fed's ear and cocked the big old Peacemaker. "Easy there, amigo."

"You just put your feet in deep shit, Lassiter," the driver said.

"Wouldn't be the first, nor likely the last time," Hector said. "You boys get your guns out now, 'tween thumbs and forefingers. Then you reach over your shoulders and drop the rods behind the front seat."

The driver said, "Screw you, Lassiter! We're FBI!"

"Big so what? I'm the hombre with a gun to your partner's noggin'. Roomy as I suspect it is in there, a head shot is not something your buddy's going to bounce back from, righto? With this weather, there's also no prospect of anybody identifying me later as the shooter if you piss me off more than you already have."

The guns went over the seat. Hector figured his inter-Bureau reputation preceded him.

Jimmy stepped up alongside me then. He had his own gun, a forty-five, out. "What have we caught ourselves, Hector?"

"Just about to ask these boys for identifications," I said. "But I think we already know."

Jimmy pointed his gun at the driver's crotch. "Let's have those wallets, lads. We're not going to waste time here, or even pursue the possibility, that you're both likely bought-out sons of bitches on the pad for that Dago Youngstown hoodlum Vito Scartelli. But we will have your wallets, boyos."

Hector said, "Everybody almost ready to roll, Jimmy?"

"Ready when you are, Hector. Lasses are finishing loading the car now."

"You've got these two in hand, then?"

"I can handle 'em," Jimmy said. "These are barely fit to mind mice at a crossroads." He tossed Hector the car keys. "Couldn't bring myself to trust the ladies with those yet. Shame on me for being the suspicious sort. I sincerely rue that sad quality in myself. Something else to add to my catalogue of character flaws."

Hector said, "These boys' guns are on the floorboards behind the front seat."

"I'll retrieve them," Jimmy said.

"Then I'll be back in a minute," Hector said.

On the way to fetch the garden hose, Hector stopped by his Chevy. He said to Meg, "This is a gesture of trust." He handed her his car keys. "Keep that little darlin' warm. We'll be leaving in about three minutes."

He scooped up the garden hose and turned the water all the way up.

The temperature was well below freezing, but with the wind off the lake Hector guessed it was probably closer to single digits, it surely felt that way. He turned the hose's spray on the Olds' windshield and let the ice begin to build up across the windscreen, maybe a solid quarter-inch of it forming on the driver's side in just a few seconds. It would take nearly a half-an-hour to hack-away-at and scrape off all that ice.

After he had a good veneer of ice covering the windshield, Hector went to work on the door hinges, seams and car door locks. The Fed on the passenger side of the car yelled, "Please don't do this! We'll be trapped in here. We'll never live it down. You're shaming us."

"Better put that window up," Hector hollered back, moving around to that agent's side of the car. Jimmy, grinning said, "This is pretty cruel, Hec. They'll be made for major assholes by their Hoover chums. They are indeed FBI, by the by. Wonder how long it will be until they figure a way out of that car?"

"Hell, they can simply kick out the windows once they think of it," Hector said. "Got their guns?"

"Got those, and their IDs."

Hector fished out his pocketknife. "I don't know, Jimmy. These two seem somewhat crafty. Better take the stems off at least a couple of their tires. Figure even Feds don't carry extra spare tires."

The passenger side window wasn't quite rolled up all the way; the agent on that side was still screaming obscenities at Hector when he wasn't imploring Jimmy and Hector to give them back their guns and IDs. Losing those would put them in deep Dutch with Hoover of course.

Hector hesitated for about half-a-second, then thrust the hose through the window crack. He savored the ensuing screams.

8

It was Jimmy's town, so Hector rode shotgun.

They stayed to backstreets and carefully made their way downtown.

The city's skyline was a flickering haze through the falling snow. Through that sheer white curtain, there was just the hint of the lights of the Terminal Tower poking through the pale gloom now and again to assure them the landmark skyscraper still stood.

Meg said, "What's the plan, boys?" Hector looked back over his shoulder at her. Shannon was asleep, stretched out, her head on Katy's lap and her legs resting on Meg's thighs. Passing streetlights caressed Meg's face. Megan had taken off one glove and was stroking Shannon's skinny little leg.

"Hotels are out now," Jimmy said, voice sound hoarse from fatigue. "Too easy to be found out in those. So I want to make a phone call." He palmed over to the curb in front of Halle Brothers Department Store. The store's various windows were decorated with gaudy little displays depicting Christmas in other countries. Hector was almost tempted to wake Shannon and show them to the little girl, but she needed her sleep. And anyway, it was so bitterly cold.

Jimmy said, "Wait here." He trotted across the icy side-walk to a phone booth. He closed himself inside and a light came on overhead inside the booth. The phone booth was iced over on one side and slush splashed up from the curbstones stained the street-side of the phone booth.

"Who's he calling?"

Hector detected a new edge there in Katy's voice. She kept looking back and forth between Meg and Hector, like she sensed some connection between them, now. Something going a good bit deeper than simple rumors of Hector's tabloid-touted libido. *So credit Kate some kind of harrowing intuition*, Hector thought to himself.

"His partner is a bit older than Jim and looking toward retirement," Hector said. "So Jimmy's partner invests in property. Mostly rentals. Jim's calling to see if he has a spare unit or two he can put us up in for a day or two. At least until we can make contact with Hoover or Kefauver directly. 'Til we can see about getting you a proper and reliable praetorian guard."

"Holidays aren't going to help with that effort," Katy said.

"That's the spirit," Hector said. "Do try to hold fast to that hopeful outlook of yours, darlin'."

Jimmy swung back into the Chevy, his cheeks and nose red. He rubbed his hands briskly together, then got the car in gear. "We're in luck. We've got us a nice little brownstone three blocks from here, with attached garage. One unit, but two bedrooms, furnished. We can have it for a week, if it takes that long."

Katy said, "And you truly trust this man?"

True ice in Jimmy's tone: "Told you, I trust him with my life. He's my partner." Jimmy put it out there like that said it all. Softly he said to Hector, "That woman's got a tongue on her that would clip a hedge."

"Thank you, Mr. Hanrahan," Meg said softly.

Jimmy smiled at Meg in the rearview mirror. "Jim," he said. "Do please call me Jim."

The women had their own room. Hector promised Jimmy the single bed in their room and vowed he'd take the couch.

Hector carried Shannon up to the bedroom from his car—the little girl never stirred.

Now the two old friends were sitting at the kitchen table, sipping spiked Sanka. Jimmy had turned on the radio to cover their talk. The Cleveland Orchestra was playing Christmas music. The orchestra wrapped up their Tchaikovsky tune and a commercial came on:

> *Mr. Jingeling*
> *How you ting-a-ling*
> *Keeper of the keys...*

Hector spun a chair around and straddled it. "What now, Jimmy?"

"You said you know a Fed or two you trust, Hector."

"That is to say, up to a certain point," Hector said. "A little. And I'll try and reach them tomorrow morning. But as Katy pointed out while you were calling your partner, it's close to Christmas. Afraid D.C. is likely to be a ghost town about now. Senate's on recess, and so the world is safe once again for democracy. But who knows where that damned Kefauver is? Toothy son of a bitch could be back in Tennessee, maybe holed up in a cabin in the Smoky Mountains somewhere. You have any ideas, Jim?"

"As it happens," Jimmy said, "I do. I think we should reach out to Eliot."

Hector almost sighed. He had to resist rolling his eyes. Eliot. *Ness*. Jimmy's regard for the man ran so much higher than Hector's own. But he couldn't fault Jimmy. The cop knew Ness when the man was, by all accounts, more of a force to be reckoned with. And they'd probably shared plenty of their own tight spots.

Eliot and Hector? Not so much. But Hector just couldn't hide his reaction to his friend's suggestion. Jimmy grunted and said, "I know Eliot's a long time out of the life, but he still has…you know, connections. And he might get us a line to Hoover quicker than anything we can come up with on our own. I want to see him tomorrow."

A door clicked: Meg had taken off her heels. Her party dress was swiftly going from enticingly slinky to looking a shade too lived-in.

Hector said to her, "Kate being Kate, I figure she bolted with a roll of dough and can see to her and Shannon's wardrobe. Have you got a trusted friend who could pack some stuff for you? I'll get someone to pick up any suitcases. We could run the luggage through some paces that'll fox anyone trying to follow your bags back to you."

"I'll make a call in the morning," Meg said, closing the bedroom door behind her. She looked back at the door and said, "They're out cold. Are our prospects looking any better? Please don't lie, because candidly, I couldn't bear it."

"Sure," Hector lied. "They're much better. I'll get my federal friends on the phone in the morning. We're also going to pay a visit to a pal of Jimmy's. You ever hear of Eliot Ness?"

"Eliot who?"

Jimmy's cheeks reddened.

Hector said, "A famous treasury agent, but from before your time, kid. Eliot ran a detail in Chicago during Prohibition. Ness took on Al Capone and smashed his bootlegging business' infrastructure. Eliot kept Big Al distracted so some bean-counters could build a tax beef against Capone. Later, Eliot became safety director of Cleveland, the youngest man in the country to hold such a post. The Cleveland police department was corrupt as a hell in the wicked Thirties. Ness fixed all that. Ness was formidable, a can-do sort. In Chicago, he and his squad had a reputation for incorruptibility. Couldn't be bought off. They called him and his crew 'the Untouchables.' He's a goddamn American hero." Of course Hector said all that as much for Jimmy as for Meg. Hector's current misgivings about Eliot aside, Ness had been formidable in the early going in Cleveland.

"Sounds like the kind of help we need," Meg said.

Jimmy gave me a nod. "'*Tis.*" He stood and stretched and draped his suit jacket over the back of a kitchen chair. He shrugged off his shoulder holster, and swinging it in one hand, said, "Night, children. Please do not stay up too late. Tomorrow looks to be another frantic day."

Hector nodded. "Night, Jim." Jimmy waved over his shoulder and closed the bedroom door.

Meg sat down on the couch next to Hector. "I can tell I made your friend angry. I'm truly sorry for that." She took his coffee mug from his hand and sipped some, then made a face.

"He's just very touchy about Ness," Hector said. "Eliot's had some bad turns in recent years. He got picked up a few years ago for driving drunk and fleeing the scene of a fender-bender. That pretty much cost him his top cop post in Cleveland. Then, not too long ago at all, some folks talked Eliot into a run for mayor of Cleveland. The Republicans tried to get him to run for mayor in the 1930s. Back then, Ness would have well walked away with the race. But after that DUI? And he was too many years away from Cleveland when he finally agreed to make the political run. Eliot's independent run for mayor was a debacle. He got trounced."

Meg said softly, "So all that nice stuff you just said about this Ness was for Jim's benefit, right?"

"Ness just made some bad decisions. Chose some wrong moments. As Jimmy once put it to me, Eliot was always in the field when luck was on the road." Hector squeezed his neck and rolled his head side-to-side. "So much in this life is mere dumb timing, kiddo. Stuff you can't plan to make happen in your favor or sway in any way at all. Eliot may yet have his time again. Maybe he'll do that helping us. Hell, it could happen. Lord knows he's long overdue for a break."

"So Ness isn't really going to be much help at all? Isn't that the bottom line?"

"I aim to be pleasantly surprised."

Meg nodded slow and deep. "We're really up against it, aren't we, Hector?"

"Been in better spots, but been in worse ones, too." He smiled. "At least one of those was with Jimmy. Few years back, he and I tried to get another little girl to safety. She was being chased by same as the whole Nazi empire. We were running crazy across the width of France that time. This seems somehow easier."

Meg searched his face. "And that time in France, how'd that come out?"

"You're with both of us now, aren't you? You seen any Nazis, lately?"

Meg gave him a knowing smile and took his hand. Her hand was warm and soft. "Honestly, Hector, why are you doing this? I don't see any benefit in this for you. Nobody ever really plays Good Samaritan, not like this, at least. Not against these sorts of odds."

"Jim's a cop, to the bone. A great one. Vito is a stain on Jimmy's town. For him there's no choice."

"I get Hanrahan doing this, it's his job, just as you say. But you're... well, you're just a writer."

That almost hurt.

"Just?" Hector shrugged and said, "Maybe I'm just that thrill-seeker you were noodling about earlier."

She brushed that stubborn comma of hair back from over his right eye. The damn thing was untamable, despite the ministrations of so many others, Brinke, Molly, Duff... too many more. None of 'em ever tamed that damn cowlick.

"I can't sleep yet," Meg said. "There's that diner around the corner. Think we could go down there? Eggs-over-easy and some toast? Screwdrivers?"

"Be honest," Hector said. "You're just trying to stretch out the evening, aren't you, Meg? Don't want to be alone with your head in the sorry dark? Trying to distract yourself? You must have gathered by now, you can run from a lot of things, but never really from yourself."

Meg said, "Sure, but... *still*..." A faltering smile. "I can try to dodge myself for a moment, here and there, right?"

Hector had been there. Hell, he'd been there a lot. He just gave her a sad smile.

"Suppose that's it," she said. "You're right that I'm not really hungry."

"There are so many better ways to distract ourselves," Hector said. He pulled her close.

Meg drew back, nodded at the closed door. "What about Jimmy?"

He stroked the curve of her bottom lip with his index finger. "Of course, Jimmy went in there so we could be out here."

9

Hector woke up very early, as he always did, rising well before dawn in order to write. He tried to slide out from under Meg, but she stirred. Seemed she was a very light sleeper. Or maybe he was losing his touch 'tween the sheets, Hector thought ruefully. Maybe his gift to exhaust a woman with passion, too, was going somewhere far away along with his ability to put a man down with a single punch as he reached his half-century mark.

Fifty: it didn't feel so old, not really. But his twenty-five-year-old self still stubbornly lurking somewhere inside might argue that point.

Brushing hair from her face, Meg whispered, "What time is it?"

"About four, probably. My body clock always wakes me up about that time."

"Your famous writing time," she muttered, feeling around the floor for her dress. "I mean, I seem to remember that being so."

God, but that freshly grated on Hector, this notion that he was known in advance to so many people—to so many women—known through news clippings and those crummy movie magazines because he'd courted a round-heels actress, here or there.

But Hector was also known to any who read them through his novels. He stood naked in his fiction, despite protests to the contrary. All of his desires and dreads were confided there in his books. All of his disappointments and dreams were tucked between those covers.

Of course, he had only himself to blame for that last. He'd chosen his profession.

No, that wasn't true. Not really.

His craft had chosen him. Hector never believed he really had a choice about any of that. He was born to write and wrote to live. It all came together for him as a kid after a chance encounter with another writer, dying alone in the desert. The man who'd bequeathed him his precious Peacemaker.

But what had the trade cost him? Rarer and rarer was the time Hector met someone who got to know him through simple time spent together. That was the real rub: that too many came to the table with their notions of Hector firmly fixed by others before he really got to *know them*.

It was a sorry-ass way to live, sometimes. Now Meg was looking to be another of those who had ideas about Hector.

His eyes were already dark-adjusted. He scooped up her dress and handed it to the pale-skinned, platinum blonde. He decided to confirm his worst suspicions. "How do you know about my writing time?"

"It was in that *Movie Fan Magazine* article." Meg smiled and kissed his cheek. "Going to try and get a little more sleep." She padded over to the bedroom door, whispered, "Good luck with your typewriter."

Hector waited until the door clicked shut, then dressed and whipped up some instant coffee. He didn't want to wake anyone with the clatter of his portable Royal typewriter, so he got out a notepad, opened the kitchen window shade to let in a little street light, then set to it with a pen.

It was like he'd told Jimmy: Hector had turned over two books in New York on a new contract. His publisher already had three others awaiting publication. But that didn't mean Hector could afford not to write. Not in terms of the condition of his own head.

Hector had been in a kind of recent *belle époque*: feverishly producing something like four sixty to seventy thousand-word manuscripts a year, each of the past twelve months. He was stockpiling so much material his editor and his agent were both trying to persuade Hector to adopt a penname or even two—to pull a Cornell Woolrich and become his own pseudonymous cottage industry.

Despite his recent prolific period, Hector had not even a flicker of a story speaking to him at the moment, so for no particular reason he wrote "Better Angels" at the top of the page and started in on an account of what was happening with the two women.

In his first draft, Jimmy was "Danny Kennedy." Hector was "Jack Linder." Hector let Meg keep her own first name.

About six, there was a tug at his sleeve, pulling Hector back into the real world from the more enticing one he was constructing.

He was so deep into his writing he'd never heard the little girl's approach and so was momentarily startled.

Shannon stood there, bleary-eyed, still in her little party dress.

One tiny knuckle ground at a blue eye filled with sleep; her other arm was wrapped around her dolly.

She said, "My tummy's hungry." On cue, there was an impressive stomach growl and Shannon winced a little. She pressed a stubby-fingered hand to her belly. Something in the moment pierced Hector.

He closed his notebook. "I'll leave a note for the others," he said. "Go fetch your shoes and coat and we'll get us a hot breakfast. Right-o?"

Shannon beamed. "*Right-o!*"

The sidewalk looked treacherous, so Hector carried Shannon in arms to the diner.

They ducked into the eatery from the cold and Hector stomped slush from his boots. Grinning, Shannon stomped her own dry feet after he set her down.

Because they were the morning's first customers, they had the run of the place. Shannon selected a wraparound booth, hard up against the radiator. It was very cozy, but shrugging off some strange chill, Hector said, "How do you like your eggs, kiddo?"

"Scrambled."

"Me too." He ordered those, some sausages and bacon, plenty of toast, a flask of coffee for himself and chocolate milk for the little girl. As he ordered, Shannon sat flipping through the selections in the little chrome jukebox mounted on the wall above their table. He handed her a coin. Hector doubted she could read much yet, so God only knew what tune would issue from the little music box.

They ended up with Sinatra, a seasonal cover of "Have Yourself a Merry Little Christmas."

Shannon bounced her legs under the table, occasionally accidently kicking Hector in the shin with her high-gloss, patent leather shoe. He took it cheerfully, ever the hard case. He nodded to Francis' Christmas tune. Sinatra sang it beautifully, eventually even reaching Hector on this lonely, encroaching Christmas.

Shannon said suddenly, "Are you a daddy?"

"No," Hector said, shaking his head. "Afraid I'm not."

"Oh." A beat. "So that makes you sad?"

Hector wet his lips. He said, "Doesn't faze me. What's your daddy like?"

"He works a lot."

"So you don't see him much?"

"Hardly ever."

Call me a bastard, Hector thought. He asked, "So you don't miss your pap much, then?"

Shannon shrugged. When she did that, something in the way she moved reminded him of Meg.

While they waited, Hector unfolded a napkin and gave it to her along with one of his pencils. Shannon promptly set to drawing on the napkin.

This voice: "How *dare* you leave with her?"

It was Katy, of course, and all anger.

Hector waved a hand. "Kid was starving as kids are wont to do. Hunger pangs you could read on her face. And I left a note, hence you being here. Take a load off, Kate. I'll buy you some eggs."

Kate scowled but slid into the booth next to Shannon and began fussing with the little girl's hair. "You're a mess," she said to Shannon.

Hector almost said, "Looked in a mirror this morning?" Instead, he pulled from behind the napkin dispenser a menu sticky with old syrup and passed it across the Formica table-top. "Make your selection now and you might not have to sit there and watch Shannon and I eat."

Katy did that. When the waitress left them, she said, "Someone came in very late this morning."

"Don't make something of it," Hector said. "Meg couldn't sleep and I wouldn't go out in the cold for another drink. So we sat up, talking." He waited a beat, then said, "Mostly about me if it matters." Hector figured she'd figure him for that kind of narcissist. Hell, the movie mags said it was so. Nearly every woman who knew him first through his books thought it so. Those women often even spoke to him in echoes of dialogue Hector had put into the mouths of the femmes fatales in his books. Or they spoke in echoes of the voices of the better and all-too-real women Hector had immortalized between the pages of his novels.

All of those sorry lines between fantasy and reality just seemed to get fuzzier as the years ground on. And hell, what writer *wasn't* a narcissist, at base—a kind of artistically inclined sociopath? Every fiction writer he'd known was the same—always outside the moment, living in their head.

Katy smirked. "Playing truth or dare, were you? I mean, as Meg came in late, carrying her dress."

Hector shot her a look and dipped his head a fraction in Shannon's direction. "Watch your mouth, lady," he said.

Katy said, "You know everything, now, I can tell. She's won you over to her side confiding it."

"I know it all, sure," Hector said, choosing his words carefully. He could only hope Katy would do the same for Shannon's sake, it behooved her too, after all. "But I don't know it because anyone told it to me," Hector added. "It didn't take much observation or logic to put it together on my own, and a while back at that. Genes aren't easy to hide. Heredity is a witch."

Katy scoffed. Shaking her head and opening her cigarette case, she said, "I don't believe that at all. Not even a little."

"And I don't much care either way what you believe," Hector said. "But it's true enough. Blonde hair and such rare violet eyes don't lie. And even then, I've got a terrible knack for divining the way things are. It's an occupational hazard. I read between the lines all too well. I drew my own conclusions miles back."

He held up his Zippo and opened it with a one-handed flick.

She leaned in, holding his hand to steady it. Her hand was still cold from the walk over from the brownstone. *Or maybe it's always cold*, he thought.

"Like I said, it was obvious enough," Hector said. "Meg never even confirmed it for me if that comforts you. Megan didn't have to do that. Jimmy tumbled to it, too. We're going to talk more about that topic, you and I, and I promise you that. Because I mean to know more about all of it and Meg isn't sharing *anything* with me. And isn't that ironic, given your wrong suspicions about Meg running her mouth? But you and I will have that conversation later, when it's just us, alone." Hector looked again at Shannon.

The diner door opened, letting in a chilly breeze. It was Meg. She's taken some trouble with herself: her hair and makeup looked fresh. She must have hung her clingy dress in the bathroom while she showered because all the wrinkles had fallen out of it as if it had been steamed.

Meg sat down next to Hector. She smelled nice and enticing. Meg looked back and forth between Katy and Hector. Biting her lip, Meg scooped up a menu and said, "And so what's good?"

Shannon looked up from her drawing and smiled with a little dark milk moustache. "Scrambled eggs and chocolate milk!"

Meg laughed and said, "Then I'll have that." That assertion drew a death stare from Katy.

Thank Christ that Jimmy found them then. Hector slid around in the booth a bit closer to Shannon and Meg followed to make room for the rangy cop.

Pushing his fedora back on his head, Jimmy said, "Somehow colder today than yesterday, I think." He reached into the booth behind them and grabbed an unused, overturned coffee cup.

Hector passed Jimmy the coffee urn and said, "What? *No top of the mornin'?* What kind of Irishman are you?"

"Not the stock or vaudeville kind," Jimmy said dryly. "Let's talk shop, Hector. There's a forty-eight Packard sedan parked across from our hideout, Hector. Two men are inside. They look like more Feds to me."

Hector had missed them; leave it to Jimmy the cop not to have repeated that mistake.

"Not a menace yet, I think, but I wouldn't like to lead them to Eliot, or to others who might get dragged into this along with us," Jimmy said.

Katy said, "You said you could trust your partner, Mr. Hanrahan. But how else could those two men out there have found us so soon unless they were tipped by this trusted partner of yours?"

Hector sipped coffee, watching over the rim of his cup as Jimmy began to seethe.

Fact was, Kate was maybe on to something, Hector thought.

But for Jimmy's sake, Hector said, "Doesn't have to mean more than the Feds do this stuff for a living, Kate. They likely figured Jimmy would contact his partner, the one man Jimmy can trust in this town without reservation. So maybe they tapped Josh Gordon's phone. It's what I think happened."

Jimmy said, "Me too. And these aren't the same ones from last night. These lads look much more the pro."

Sadder news for us if true, Hector thought.

"Let's leave them there, then," Hector said. "At least for a time. Maybe we've been sent help of some kind. Maybe old

J. Edgar Hoover knows about our plight, after all. That frog-faced bastard owes me a favor, or two. Maybe these Hoover minions at least have instructions to have our backs."

"Maybe," Jimmy said. "But my instinct is against that possibility. Just when did you become such an optimist, Hector?"

"Maybe it's just the holiday season," Hector said. "The cold wind of hope blows eternal."

"The rum in the eggnog, more likely," Jimmy said.

Breakfast remained a tense affair: pointless small talk and rehashing of strategies that were less than half-evolved. Some gallows humor that could be pitched safely over Shannon's head.

The waitress brought the bill. Jimmy reached for it, but Hector snagged it and said, "My party."

Jimmy and Meg thanked him, which prompted a mumbled thank you from Shannon, who was bent over her napkin, intensely scribbling away.

After a time, Jimmy slid out of the booth and offered a hand to Katy. She took it and he pulled her from the booth.

Shannon said, "All done!"

The little girl handed Hector the napkin. He held it up and Shannon said, "It's for you."

In the drawing, three stick figures were basking under a smiling sun.

Two had triangles between their waists and feet. Those three-sided shapes represented skirts, Hector guessed.

One of those stick figures was shorter than the other.

The third stick figure was definitely a male. There was a gun in that stick figure's hand. The little male stick figure held the hands of the other two.

Above the three figures were three names scrawled in toddler, Pidgin English, and all of the 'e's were rendered backwards: "Meg, Me, Hector."

Jimmy was drawn in there as a beaming, broken-nosed sun.

There was no Kate in sight.

Hector thanked Shannon and deftly folded up the napkin and slid it into the breast pocket of his sports jacket, slipping it behind his display handkerchief.

Katy hadn't seen the picture, thank God.

But Meg surely had.

The look on Meg's face broke Hector's heart.

10

They were scheduled to meet Ness at noon. The stores downtown opened at ten.

Katy selected Sterling Lindner Davis to replenish hers and Shannon's wardrobes. Hector leaned hard on Katy. "You buy off-the-rack stuff, only," he said. "No futzing around trying things on. We don't have the luxury of time." To insure Kate's compliance, Hector insisted Shannon stay with him.

As they ducked into the warmth of the store, Jimmy leaned into Hector's ear and said, "I'll see to the missus; you see to—"

If he said "the mistress" again Hector thought he might swing on Jim, best of friends or not. But Jimmy said: "—Megan and the little one, of course."

They did that, a grimacing Jimmy and an annoyed Katy briskly wandering off to shop for clothes.

Shannon held Hector and Meg's hands, staring up at the giant Christmas tree looming above them, reaching up several floors toward the ceiling. Meg smiled at Hector and said to Shannon, "Want to see Santa, honey?" As if she had to ask. Hector watched Meg and Shannon together—clearly in the moment, looking to the world like mother and child.

Katy? She didn't exude much maternal instinct, so far as Hector had seen.

They loitered in a short line to see a paunchy old Clevelander who'd taken the trouble to grow his own yellow-white whiskers out, thick and full. Hector thought the ringer a pretty good Kris Kringle, as those big-gutted suckers ran.

At some point, Shannon was taken from them by a dishy, busty young thing in a scarlet and crushed-velvet elf suit to stand in line with other children between crimson velvet ropes. Meg pressed against Hector, still watching Shannon. She said, "I should maybe split off from you all, and quite soon. It's getting tenser between Katy and I. When it was just the two of us, and Katy thought she needed me, it was a little easier. Now it's just very bad. Me leaving would probably be the best thing. And the three of us wandering around up here together with the holidays and all these pretty lights and the season? It feels like…" A long beat. "It feels like the best of home in some ways. It feels like family and that frankly hurts more than I'd have imagined."

Hector felt a bit of the same way, and more so now as he let himself actually think about it. Hector didn't like the sound of his own voice as he said the next: "You running would be the best thing for who, Meg? For you? For the rest of us? Just how do you figure your bolting helps anything?"

"I'd do it for my daughter's sake," Meg said. "You saw that picture she drew of us."

Hector shook his head, emphatic. "You running off doesn't help Shannon in any way I can fathom. Hell, Katy's mothering instincts *aren't*. She thinks providing clothes—providing mere *things*—are the same as giving her love." Hector kissed Meg's forehead. "You stay close to us," he said. "Closer than ever. You don't rabbit on that child. Or on me. Don't you do that."

She pressed a hand to his heart. "You said it yourself, Hector. If you and that Irish flatfoot by some miracle actually pull us through this mess, then Katy is going to take Shannon and bolt on me somewhere not too far down the road. We all know that's so."

Argue that? Hector didn't try. He went for the change-up:

"How did this come to be, Meg? How did Shannon come to believe Katy is actually her mother?"

Meg was watching Shannon who was fidgeting in line. She said, "There isn't time, Hector. I haven't the stomach for it. And satisfying your curiosity will not change anything for me or her. It's all just done."

Christ. He chewed his lip and then lit a cigarette. He gestured at Shannon with his cigarette hand. "What do you think she'll ask Santa for?"

"A puppy," Meg said, smiling. Her eyes were moist. "It's all she talks about. A little white puppy."

Hector nodded, exhaling cigarette smoke though both nostrils. "She's told you that?"

"She talks about it all the time. It's just that I actually listen to Shannon." Meg didn't haven't to say, *Because Katy doesn't.*

She said to him, "You have children of your own?"

"Came very close once. Lost that child a long time ago."

"How old was he—she?" She wrinkled her brow. "And lost the baby, how? Divorce?"

"Never quite really born," Hector said, voice raw. Didn't hurt less for that, not for Hector, but he held his tongue and didn't volunteer that fact to Meg. She was keeping plenty of secrets, so Hector felt entitled to a few of his own.

"Brand new clothes," Katy said, holding up shopping bags. Jimmy was behind her, lugging new luggage. Hector hoped those suitcases, and whatever Shannon had wending its way via cutouts to their brownstone, would fit in his Chevy's trunk.

Shannon looked at the bags and said, "That's nice. Hey, Santa said he's going to bring me a puppy! I'm going to call her Hector."

"That's a boy's name," Katy said. "And there'll be no dogs in our new house."

Shannon said, "But Santa promised."

"That wasn't Santa," Katy said. "That was just some old drunk dressed up like him."

Shannon's lip began to tremble. Hector could tell Meg was about to say something she'd regret later. He squeezed Meg's arm and whispered urgently, "Please, don't."

Katy's other shortcomings aside, she was a fast shopper: they still had an hour before their scheduled meeting with Ness, so Jimmy suggested early lunch.

The cop took them to an Italian joint about five minutes from Sterling Linder Davis. On the way there, they passed a theater. The marquee was touting its offering of the television broadcasts of the Kefauver hearings. The senate hearings were still the biggest show in television, and, according to morning papers, the hearings were spiking Christmas television set sales.

The little girl was again wolfing down her food. A jovial, white-haired man in a chef's hat stopped by their table to inquire about the quality of their food. His voice was heavily accented. The man in the chef's hat had a white moustache and seemed vaguely familiar to Hector. The chef clapped Hanrahan on the back and said, "Everything is okay, James?"

"Aces," Jimmy said. "Better than perfect. Dee-*lish*."

Shannon, pointing at the chef said, "You look like the man on the spaghetti cans." Shannon pronounced it *sketty*.

Jimmy smiled and cupped Shannon's chin in his big hand. "He is the man on the spaghetti cans, child. This is Mr. Boyardee—*Hector* Boyardee."

When the chef left, Jimmy said, "*That* Hector—or Chef Boyardee—opened the Il Giardino Italia an age ago. Made a name for himself around these parts. Now's he's a corporation with his *Chef Boyardee* line of foods. Owns a string of restaurants around northeastern Ohio. Has a production plant in Parma."

Shannon, evidently envisioning some pop culture pantheon of white-mustached burly men somewhere, said, "I wonder if Chef Boyardee knows Santa?"

Jimmy said, "Very cute, that." He bit his lip, suddenly gone all over grave. Jimmy said to Hector, "Be subtle here, Hec. There in the mirror. Regard those two boyos by the bar. Guinea hoodlums if I ever saw any."

Hector grunted and said, "Yeah, I see 'em. And, yeah, they have the look. But it is an Italian restaurant after all, Jimmy." Hector gave them some more consideration, then said, "Yet they do seem to only have eyes for us."

Fearful sounding, Meg said, "How'd they find us? Maybe tipped by those Feds in front of our place?"

"Maybe," Hector said. "But if those Feds are as pro as Jimmy thinks, I don't believe they'd be on any Mafioso's dole. So it must have been something else."

Meg raised her eyebrows. "What then?"

Hector turned to Katy. "You often shop at that store we just left?"

Katy pulled out a cigarette. This time Hector didn't reach for his Zippo. She rooted around in her purse for matches. "I go there all the time," Katy said, not making eye contact. "It's the only place I shop for clothes." She didn't quite sniff as she confessed that last, but Hector thought it was implied.

"They know you there at the store then," Hector said. "Know you all too well. Probably have all your measurements. Shannon's, too."

"Of course," Katy said, rather haughty now. Hector knew why her shopping spree had taken so little time.

Jimmy, now in detective mode, said, "Don't suppose you paid cash for all that back there, did you dear Kate? I kick myself for not more closely observing your transaction, I'll confess."

"Of course not," Kate said. "We'll need what money I have on me when we set down roots."

Hector wanted to smash her on the spot.

"Brilliant," Jimmy said.

The two hoodlums were rising. One's jacket gapped as he stood; Hector saw the butt of a gun poking from under the man's left armpit.

Hector said, "Whether you need to go or not, Shannon, I want you to go to the bathroom and lock yourself in a stall. Wait until Meg or Katy comes to get you. Go right now. Go fast."

The little girl ran toward the restrooms as Meg pointed to them. Jimmy and Hector stood. Jimmy said, "Best meet 'em halfway, eh, Hector? Maybe throw 'em off step? Figure they're headed here to escort us outside to do the wicked deed. Us rushing to greet them just may unnerve 'em."

"Sounds the grand plan," Hector said, letting a little Irish accent into his voice. He watched one of the thugs. The man looked flustered to see Shannon running toward the lady's room. Hector said, "One on the left is mine, Jim."

They walked briskly toward the two thugs who were now moving more uncertainly toward Jimmy and Hector.

As an afterthought, Jimmy said, "You do have your Colt on your person now?"

"I do," Hector said. "I just hope Chef Boyardee doesn't have a hefty insurance deductible. This to come bears all the earmarks of serious mayhem."

11

Hector wasn't too keen on pulling a gun in a restaurant, particularly not in an Italian joint in northern Ohio where you couldn't be sure whether or not significant numbers of other noshing patrons might be packing gats themselves. Cleveland was a Mafia beachhead. This joint was fairly busy, too, and a stray bullet seemed more apt to hit a civilian than to miss one.

So Hector let his man get his hand in his jacket to reach for his piece, then Hector grabbed hold of that wrist with his left hand. With his right, Hector reached between his man's legs, got a handful and squeezed tightly, twisting at the man's genitals and getting him up on his toes. The thug gasped and turned red. His eyes filled with tears and he tried to talk but couldn't find his wind.

It was dirty pool, sure, like back-shooting or maybe even a little worse than that, Hector thought to himself.

But it was also the quickest way to shut down a man's nervous system short of shooting him just-so in the head. This nasty move of Hector's brought full and instant compliance. And hell, this was survivable.

Jimmy was still more direct: he shoved his .45 under his man's chin and held up his badge for the dining room to see. He said, "Stay seated, folks. Eat up and enjoy and please excuse these two hoodlum fools' shenanigans. Low-level police business, this is, that's all. Nothing to write home about. Relax and enjoy the grub."

Servers stepped aside as Jimmy and Hector pushed the two men backward to a dimly lit corridor and on into the kitchen to the sound of excited murmurs.

Jimmy's man made a grab for a pot of boiling water. Jimmy saw it coming and kicked his attackers' legs from under him. The man's arm upset the pot of water as he fell. The scalding water splashed over the man's head. Jimmy cursed and clubbed his man senseless. He grabbed him by the belt and half-lifted him, half-dragged him through a back door. He dropped the scalded man in a snow bank at the back of the restaurant.

Hector hauled his man out and then pushed him down onto his knees and stepped back, cocking his vintage Peacemaker on the draw.

As the man clutched between his legs, trying to catch his breath, Hector took the man's gun and dropped it into his own overcoat's pocket.

While the man was still incapacitated, Hector felt around and then tugged the man's wallet from his right hip pocket. Hector flipped through cellophane panels and found the man's driver's license: Lawrence Burrachi.

Jimmy held up his man's wallet and said, "One Thomas Pinelli." He tossed the wallet onto the chest of the unconscious man. Jimmy thrust his man's liberated gun behind his waistband. "More weapons for our armory," Jimmy said. "We're amassing quite the arsenal, eh?"

Hector said, "Okay, Larry, be a man and stop milking it. What I did to you wasn't as bad as being kicked down there. And it's a hell of a lot more benign than being shot in the plumbing, which is where I mean to put my first." Then Hector pointed his Peacemaker. "How'd you get onto us?"

Larry spit at Hector's boot. This time Hector kicked him between the legs. It took the man a while to catch his breath from that assault. Hector pointed his gun between the man's legs again. He said, "You surely aren't stupid enough to try for the trifecta, are you Larry? You *really* think I'm a bluffer after that kick?"

Wincing, the thug—*Larry*—looked at his unconscious comrade.

"Tom" looked much the worse for wear. Tom's skin was livid red and heat blisters were forming on his face now. Going straight from scalding water to rolling in the snow and slush wasn't going to help with any of that.

Larry said, "The clerk at the store where you shopped called you in when Mrs. Scartelli paid on credit for the stuff. We were in the neighborhood and dispatched to meet you. We followed you from the store to this joint."

"Just like we figured it," Hector said to Jimmy.

Jimmy grunted and stepped up alongside Hector. "How much does Vito know, Lawrence? What have you been told, boyo? Spare no details, lad."

"Not much," Larry said, his voice ragged and thin. He was still clutching between his legs and his eyes were watering from the brisk and icy wind. Hector's eyes were stinging too... he could feel his nose getting ready to run.

Sniffling, Hector said, "Cut to the chase, mister. Tell us what you do know."

"Just that the boss's old lady has turned on him. Her and some other twist close to the boss," Larry said. "Wife is going to canary. Bitch took the kid and ran. We were told to bring her in, whatever it took. Failing that, boss said we could do the wife and the other, too. We were supposed to grab the kid if we could and send her back on to Youngstown."

Jimmy scowled and said, "This all come to you through direct instruction, or did you get wind of some of this via the grapevine, Lawrence?"

"A little of both," Larry said. "Everyone knows the wife is on the lam. Fucking frail supposedly has some stuff on the boss. They say she's going to turn it over to fucking Kefauver. Everyone's looking for Mrs. Scartelli to stop that happening. Being the one to bring her in or down should bring some handsome rewards."

No doubt that seemed a sound enough plan to the likes of these, Hector thought.

"Who's your direct contact, Lawrence?" Jimmy leaned in close, all fury. "And don't lie to me, because I'll know."

"Johnny the Lip."

Hector rolled his eyes. "Jesus, who the hell is that supposed to be? Sounds like some goddamned Dick Tracy character."

"I know him well enough," Jimmy said. "The Lip is Johnny Rimbaldi. Some Chinese cooze he was running was flying on opium one night back in the late Thirties and cut Johnny, and I mean cut him *good*. Doc's sewed the lips back on but they didn't heal so well. Nerve damage. Bastard ends up wearing a portion of every drink." Jimmy holstered his forty-five and pulled out a pad and pencil. "Give me a phone number, an address where Johnny can be found or reached."

"What are you going to do with it?" Lawrence voice sounded stronger, like he was recovering from what Hector had done to him.

"I don't know if I'm going to do anything with it," Jimmy said. "Just good to have stuff like that, 'cause you never know, you know? And what possible fecking business is it of yours what I do with the information?"

Larry shrugged. Jimmy said, "What are we gonna do with you now, Larry?"

Scartelli's stooge licked his lips, looking around. "Not kill me?"

"No, that would be cold-blooded, if no less deserved," Hector said. "I mean, particularly given what you were prepared to do to us. That all puts you in line for killing. But lucky for you, it's not our way. Least ways, not yet." Hector smiled meanly. "Best that you not put us to the test."

Nodding, Larry said, "Maybe you could just give me one shot. Leave me with a black eye or maybe a bruised cheek."

"Something you can show poor Thomas," Jimmy said, "is that what you mean? Something to tout you took some grief, too? Something to assure Thomas and your bosses you didn't rat anyone out to spare yourself more damage than just those aching bollocks?"

"Yeah," Larry said, "something like that. Say, a black eye."

Pretty thin stuff, in other words. "I can certainly help you with that," Hector said, making a fist. But Hector thought to himself, *Anything worth doing…*

After, Jimmy said, "A bit gratuitous, all that, wasn't it, Hector?"

Hector's barked knuckles tended to agree.

But Hector scoffed for Jimmy's sake: "After what Old Larry pulled back in the restaurant there? I think he got off too easy. Besides, maybe I'm still a little sore about how my two got back up at the hotel when yours stayed down. I didn't want to make that bloody mistake again."

Jimmy stooped and grabbed Thomas by the wrists and dragged him over closer to Larry, who was now also unconscious. Hector figured Jimmy's would surely be the first to rise this time. Hector had certainly done his worst to Larry to see to that.

"Here, Hector, get yours and let's get 'em over closer to the fire escape," Jimmy said. "We'll cuff 'em to the angle-iron support. Eventually someone will find them or call the cops. Either way, it'll look bad to their boss for these two boyos. Then we need to hustle, I don't want to be late to meet Eliot."

When the duo got back to the dining room, Meg was alone at the table, looking worried. She said, "Kate is in the restroom with Shannon, waiting to hear word the coast is clear—and yes, I checked, there's only one way in or out."

Hector said, "Go and fetch her then, won't you, darlin'? Food is going to get cold and we need to eat up and scoot across town."

Meg said, "You mean to keep eating? But those men...?"

Massaging his red and now swelling knuckles, Hector said, "You can put those particular fellas out of your mind, I swear it's so."

12

"A bookstore? This incorruptible friend works in a bookstore?"

If Katy had said it, it would be bad enough, but coming from Meg? That clearly hurt.

"It's not his usual gig, not his day job, *per se*," Jimmy said, looking wounded.

A man stood behind the register. He was not particularly tall. He was also rather stockier than he remained in Hector's memory.

In the 1930s, Ness was lean and hungry and focused. Also very dapper, rather like Scott Fitzgerald.

Now he was pale, puffy and unremarkable looking, rather like F. Scott Fitzgerald at his *end*. Eliot's jacket was frayed at the cuffs. His shirt collar, too. It made Hector feel worse for the way he felt about the man. It made Hector feel still worse for Jimmy.

Eliot was carrying drinker's weight and his fuller face made his chin seem weaker than maybe it really was. The ex T-man's gray eyes were bleary and his eyelids were red-rimmed— looked to Hector like it hadn't been so many hours since he last tied one on.

Jimmy shot Hector a look that warned him to hold his tongue. But Hector wasn't disposed to be that mean, not to as dear a friend as Jimmy.

The big Irish cop hugged Ness to him. "It's been too long, Chief."

"Much too long," Eliot said. He clapped Jim's back. As he did that, Ness held out another hand to Hector. The rangy writer's hand engulfed Eliot's. Ness smiled and said, "Hector, it's good to see you again. It's really been a long time for the two of us."

"It has." Hector gestured at the bookshelves around them. "I hope to God you aggressively hand-sell my oeuvre, Eliot."

Ness smiled and shook loose of Jim's bear hug. He said, "Look over here."

The former Untouchable led them to the mystery section and pointed to a long shelf set at eye-level. There were hard-covers and paperbacks—first editions and reading copies of Hector's myriad novels.

Whistling, Hector pulled down a hardcover of first novel, *Rhapsody in Black*. He looked at the dedication inside to Brinke Devlin and smiled.

The book was in excellent condition despite being a quarter century old. Hector next checked the price penciled faintly on the flyleaf. Frowning, he said, "They ask, and they get, about thirty dollars more for this book in New York City."

"We're not in New York," Eliot said. "And I really only work here a couple of days a week as a clerk. I don't set the prices, Hec. I'm just here to make some extra money for Christmas, you know?"

Eliot looked embarrassed. Jimmy had confided to Hector that Ness—as he had been off and on since leaving his post as Cleveland's safety director—was between various ill-fated business ventures. Hector smiled and said, "I know how it is, buddy. It's always money, for all of us. Always on the scratch. You married again?"

"That's right," Eliot said. "I believe this one will go the distance. And you? Married again, too, Hector?"

Hector shook his head. "Not this year."

"We adopted a boy," Eliot said. "His name is Bobby. He's a great kid. It's great having a child."

"I'm sure it is," Hector said.

Jimmy cleared his throat, said, "Is there a place we can talk? Our situation is showing no signs of improving with age. Quite the reverse, actually."

Eliot nodded. "Heat is still on you then?"

"As recently as ten minutes ago, and furiously so," Jimmy said. "Bastards were prepared to shoot up Hector Boyardee's place to get at these two ladies. No worries about them following us here, that's not going to happen. Hec and I saw to that with those ones. But, yes, our problems are actually mounting, Eliot."

"Then we'll talk in back," Eliot said. "Just let me put up the out-to-lunch sign and lock the front door."

Megan was browsing over the shelf packed with Hector books. "I'll catch up you back there," she said. She pulled down that vintage copy of *Rhapsody in Black*, checked the photo of a smiling, twenty-five-year-old Hector on the back of the book. Eliot led them to a storeroom dominated by a long, battered table surrounded by chairs. Crates of books were stacked around the walls of the room. Shannon sat next to Hector. She picked up a piece of stray paper and bummed another pencil from the writer.

Eliot said, "I hear the Kefauver focus, in so far as our region is concerned, is on targeting Vito's Scartelli's under-bosses. Those would be Morris Kleinman, Louis Rothkopf, Sammy Tucker and Moe Dalitz. Nearly six-dozen subpoenas are out 'round these parts. Maybe a sixth of those are proving hard to serve. Notion seems to be to fire at everyone and maybe put pressure on some weak link to get at Scartelli himself. So far, that doesn't seem to be producing results."

"His minions will never turn on my husband," Katy said. "He pays them far too well. And he rules by fear. He's a sadist. And he knows too many things about his men, things he's ordered done, and not always because they needed doing. He ordered those things done because they would bind his men to him. Make the cost of betrayal too high, inevitably self-destructive."

"It's always the aim of these sorts," Eliot said. "Snorky ruled his organization the same way. I mean, before he started losing his mind to the…" Eliot looked at Shannon and said, "To that disease."

Snorky—Ness meant Al Capone. Glory Days stuff, Hector thought. And "that disease" was a virulent dose of Syphilis that left Big Al a shuffling drooler at his end.

Ness continued, "Kefauver's guy here now, doing the groundwork for the great Lakes Region, is a lawyer named Joseph Gibson. He's the committee's counsel. If we can get you two ladies to him, well, he should be in position to get you some official protection. The kind that won't sell out."

"That would maybe do," Hector said. He lit a Pall Mall. "But I like going to the very top. You have any truck to get us a connection to Hoover, Eliot?"

"No chance with the FBI," Ness said. "Hoover's got resentments about me and my squad that go back to Chicago and Capone days. Besides, Jimmy said you might have some trustworthy federal connections of your own."

"Time will soon tell," Hector said.

"I do, however, have a few last strands stretching back into the treasury department," Eliot said. "I might be able to reach out to the senator through those channels. Maybe get some reliable escort for you that way. I mean, if you want me to try."

"Anything at all," Katy said, imploring him. "I just want this over so Shannon and I can disappear to somewhere safe to start our lives over—" Hector recoiled at that as she said it (and did he notice a sudden tonal shift for the last?): "—*just the two of us.*"

Hector was glad Meg was still out in the stacks, browsing over his goddamn books for secondary-market sale out there.

Eliot said to Katy, "We'll see what we can do, Ma'am." He opened a filing cabinet and pulled out four shot glasses and a bottle of gin. He raised his eyebrows, "Katy?"

"Yes, thank you," she said.

Eliot looked to Hector, who resisted meeting eyes with Jimmy. Hector said, "Sorry, I'm just not a gin drinker. Actually detest the stuff." In fact, Hector had always been distrustful of those who drank gin. Some of his life's deepest grief had been fueled by avid gin-swillers.

The former treasury agent who'd first made his name shutting down bootleg gin mills said, "And for you, Jim?"

"Uh, none for me either, Eliot," Jimmy said. His voice sounded pained. "You know me," Jimmy said, pulling out his flask and pouring a little dribble in a shot glass. "I'm strictly a whiskey man." Then Jimmy nodded at Hector. "Except when this heathen entices me with that Scottish single malt stuff." Jimmy winked. "You know—the whisky with no 'e'."

Shannon had finished her pencil sketch, this one of a castle.

Hector saw a stack of plain white paper and said to Eliot, "Mind if I snag a couple of sheets?"

"Help yourself," Eliot said. Hector took a couple of sheets of paper and handed them to Shannon.

The little girl said, "Thank-you."

Hector remembered then and pulled out the small box of crayons he'd bought in a brief stop at a pharmacy where he'd detoured to restock on smokes and get a new flint for his vintage Zippo. Shannon squealed when she saw the box. "What should I draw now?"

Hector feared that if Shannon was left to her own devices some other sketch of Meg or himself might ensue, so he said, "What about a puppy?"

Shannon set to the task, her tongue screwed out one side of her mouth.

Meg found them then. She was carrying two hardcover copies of Hector's novels. "Haven't read these yet," she said as Hector pulled out a chair for her.

"It really isn't necessary you do read those," he said to her.

Meg said, "But I want to read them."

Katy was listening to them; she held her tongue. She gestured at Shannon's drawing and said, "That's very nice, honey."

Eliot poured himself three more fingers of gin. As he drank, his voice grew a little louder; his gestures broader. He said, "Would really help the campaign if you could give me some notion of what you have to share, Mrs. Scartelli. I hear, also, that you have some incriminating documents secreted somewhere."

"I'll only give those directly to the senator, in person. And only when I have a written assurance of new documentation of mine and my daughter's identities, and some financial provisions guaranteed to help the two of us establish and maintain our new lives, Mr. Ness."

Hector couldn't bear to look at Meg as those selfish words were uttered.

Katy—that self-centered sorry piece of work and witchery. Some small part of Hector, one deep inside, was sorely tempted then to do Vito's bidding, *pro bono*. It was a fleeting urge, but it was surely there. Realizing what was inside him left Hector feeling a little shaken, a little ashamed.

"I will not turn over my papers to anybody else," Katy continued. "I simply will not do that. I'll only give them to the senator, and only once he's agreed to my terms."

"She's quite indomitable on that point," Hector said, his voice was low and raw.

"'Tis true, Eliot," Jimmy said. "My patience with this lass on that front is exhausted."

Eliot sat back in his chair. He ran his fingers through his graying, sandy-brown hair that was parted slightly off-center and slicked back. "I get off at three. I'll make some calls and see what I can do."

Hector said, "We'll call you?"

"No," Eliot said. "Let's set a meeting, somewhere with lots of people to discourage anything else like you hinted happening at that Italian restaurant. How about five o'clock? We'll meet at the Kent Hotel. Do you know the place, Jim?"

Hector felt bad for Jimmy—he looked a little sick. Jimmy had earlier told Hector the Kent was reputed to be Ness' favorite current watering hole. Jimmy had been fleetingly heartened when he heard Ness hadn't chosen it for the place for their present meeting.

Jimmy said, "Yes, Eliot, I know it well enough. Five it is then."

Jimmy nodded at Hector as he rose. The writer sensed the cop wanted out of the bookstore and away from the stench of Eliot's cheap gin, *fast*.

Hector scooped up the copies of his novels that Meg had selected for herself. He tossed Jimmy his car keys. "You all go ahead and warm up the car," I said. "I'll see to paying for these."

Meg sighed. "Pay for your own books? That won't do. I'll get them."

"No way, and anyway, I'll receive royalties on these on the backside," Hector said. "That's the beauty of me buying them, it's a kind of a wash." That was a lie—no author ever made a cent of money from books sold on the secondary market, not on those copies sold by rare bookstores and the like. But Hector figured Meg wouldn't grasp any of that. The writing life was an arcane and closed little world far outside Meg's reality. Lucky her, Hector thought.

Eliot and Hector were alone at the cash register. Eliot was opening each book and keying in the price. He said, "Have to say, it's good to be back in the game, even it it's only for a day."

"Some of us are shaped for one job," Hector said. "Seems to me your talent and forte is to enforce the law, El."

"Too long away from it," Eliot said. "I'm too old to go back to the treasury department. And Hoover would never have me in the Bureau. He blocked me back in the day when I tried. And I would never work well under that bastard even if he'd have me. Do you have any sense of the grief that prissy little monster gave Melvin Purvis?"

"I've heard the stories," Hector said. There were some children's books stacked by the register. Hector found one about dogs that looked about Shannon's speed and added it to his stack.

"What brought you to Cleveland in the first place, Hector? Just visiting Jimmy?"

"Actually, I was in Youngstown," Hector said. "That's where I hooked up with Jimmy and met these women. Jimmy was there, still chasing the Butcher. He said there was a similar torso killing committed this past July in Cleveland. He was chasing clues about that in Youngstown."

Ness said, "I've been following that murder a bit. I don't think it's the Butcher. Jimmy and I had a good suspect back in the day. Now he's in a mad house down in Dayton. Checked himself in a while back to escape the possibility of prosecution. Near as I can tell, he's still there. He sends me crazy, taunting letters sometimes. Postcards that read like the ramblings of the bloodthirsty mad man I know he is."

Somehow, that admission made the hair stand up on the back of Hector's neck. "No kidding?"

"No kidding. I won't let my wife or child fetch the mail anymore because of the possibility of another sneering letter or postcard coming. They're well-beyond sinister, Hector."

"So what do you make of this latest killing of this Robertson fella who Jimmy's been on about?"

"An homage to the Butcher, maybe," Eliot said, placing the books in a brown paper bag. "A retrospective on the Kingsbury case ran in one of the slick magazines not too long before the body was found. May have excited some other psychopath. Or maybe it's just… something else. The victim was a low-level criminal. Who knows what kinds of enemies he may have made for himself? The mob has elevated dismemberment to a kind of trademark in these parts."

Eliot's movements seemed fairly loose now, like he was pretty strongly affected by the booze. Something about the way the spirits took Eliot reminded Hector of watching similar transformations come over Scott Fitzgerald during café crawls along the Left Bank decades before.

"Why are you doing this, Hector? Jimmy's a cop and so he has little choice. I mean, being the born cop he is. But you're a civilian now." Eliot smiled. "I mean, more or less."

Hector shrugged. "No particular reason other than they need help. And I'm solo lobo this year and so hard to touch in that sense. Hard to really hurt."

Eliot smiled, eyes unfocused. "It's like the old saying goes, 'The man who doesn't want anything is invincible.' It's like me, when I took down Capone."

Accountants did that, not Eliot and not his squad of "Untouchables." At best, Eliot and his crew were harriers to Capone. In military terminology, Eliot and the Untouchables were dispatched to Chicago to provide "harassing fire" against Capone, a headline-generating distraction while the tax accountants did their arcane but truly devastating work against Big Al.

Eliot's real glory had come in his first years in Cleveland. Nobody could take those triumphs from him.

Except maybe for the Kingsbury Butcher. Eliot's failure to catch the Phantom Headhunter—his inability to publicly close the pattern killer case—had eclipsed his successes in cleaning up the corrupt Cleveland police department, in subduing the feral youth gangs that plagued the city and in neutralizing the Cleveland mob's circa-1930s expansion.

"Maybe we can deal another body blow to Costa Nostra again," Eliot said. "What do you think, Hector?"

"That'd be swell," Hector said, passing Eliot some bills. Too many bills. Hector meant to be gone before Eliot maybe caught the error. He shook Eliot's hand. "Until the next time, buddy."

Hector turned his overcoat's collar up and stepped out of the bookstore into a snow squall. The driver's seat of his Chevy was empty, so Hector slid in. He passed the parcel of books back to Meg.

"Let's get the hell out of here," Jimmy said.

Hector got his car in gear and muttered, "Sure. Let's do that, Jimmy."

They rolled a couple of blocks and Hector said, "Notions on a destination?"

"Doesn't really matter, the brownstone, I suppose," Jimmy said, surly. "Time to pack up again and be ready to roll to the next hiding place."

Katy said, "What about those men parked out front?"

Jimmy shook out a Lucky Strike and struck a match on a thumbnail. "For all we know, when Eliot pulls the strings, those boyos will maybe be your new escorts."

13

Hector sat at the kitchen table, typing up the early morning's output.

Katy wandered out from one of the bedrooms. She held up her hands and said, "Sorry, I would hate to interrupt a working man."

"You're not doing that," Hector said, tugging the sheet of paper from the typewriter. "I've caught up to myself."

Katy smiled. "Must be a kick, *hmm*? Remaking the world the way you want it to be. People forever saying just what you want them to say. Making them do what you want them to do."

"You might be surprised," Hector said. "You might even be wrong. And *forever*? That's just pretend. What's on your mind, Kate?"

"I wanted to thank you for all you've tried to do for us," she said, pulling up a chair. "You despise me, I can tell. Positions reversed, I'm sure I'd hate me, too. But you keep fighting for us, and I don't think Meg's the whole reason. Not Shannon, either."

Hector stacked up the sheets of his manuscript. He slid them into a leather valise he'd converted from an old saddlebag he'd retained from his days with the Pershing Expedition, back when he was mounted cavalry and chasing the rogue Mexican revolutionary general Francisco "Pancho" Villa.

Hector sat back in his chair and picked up his pack of Pall Malls. He knocked one loose and held it out to Katy. She took the cigarette and he shook loose another one for himself. He held up his Zippo and she leaned in. She looked at the engraving on the lighter. "Who is E.H.?"

"Another writer I knew."

"Knew?"

"Know. Knew. It's the same thing, in some ways. People are never really gone from your life or at least your mind. Least of all if you're a writer, to boot." They both exhaled some smoke. Hector said, "You truly want to show your gratitude? Tell me what you know about what I want to know."

She looked back over her shoulder at the bedroom where Shannon and Meg were. The door to the room was closed—Katy had shut it. She said, "My husband always had other women, pretty much from the time of our honeymoon. Whores and hangers-on. Round-heels trash who cadged drinks in the clubs he owns. Then there was Megan. She sang in one of Vito's clubs. She sang standards and torch songs. Most of his women came and went. Megan somehow endured. And she seemed maybe just a cut above the rest. Kind of a corn-fed Veronica Lake." Katy stared at the end of her cigarette. "That sounded uncharitable. I mean, she *is* a cut above the rest. A little anyway, you know? At least that's true now." More damning with faint praise: there seemed to be a lot of that going around these sorry days.

Hector blew smoke, said, "How do you know, or how did you come to know, about Meg and her lingering thing with your husband?"

"I hired a private investigator. He was a sleazy, terrible drunk of a man who liked to act like he was doing me great favors taking my money and performing the tasks I was paying him to execute. But he proved effective enough." Katy blew some smoke his way. "He wasn't like the private investigators in the mystery novels and movies. Not like Marlowe or Sam Spade."

Hector almost snorted. "Hammett is a lushed-up commie and goddamn Ray Chandler is an anglophile romantic fool who's unwittingly light in the loafers. Old Ray and his goddamn tarnished knights of an ilk that never walked this wicked earth? Sentimental bullshit. Ray married a woman old enough to be his mother. Anyway, P.I.s are all bottom-feeders and parasites. In the real world, private eyes make their money on domestic strife and snapping incriminating photos. They're little better than ticks or leeches. Only way they can make money is on others' suffering." Hector's cigarette was pretty much down to a smoldering stub. He got out another cigarette. "What about Shannon?"

Katy tipped her head back, blowing smoke out both nostrils. "I was barren. I am barren. Megan? Not so much. She got pregnant by Vito. So he paid her to go ahead and have the child. He thought it was important that he have a son. I should say at this point that Megan was a serious heroin addict. Vito put her in a clinic for the duration of her pregnancy to try and keep her clean."

"She's clean now, I see no signs of an addiction." Like Hector really knew. He'd always disdained drugs, dodged them and their users. Liquor was lone Hector's vice of choice. Well, that and nicotine.

Katy said, "Now, yes, she's clean. Then, not even close. Thank God Shannon wasn't ruined by her birth mother's addiction."

"Yes... thank God." Hector wasn't sure he believed Kate about Megan's alleged addiction. Not sure at all.

Katy helped herself to another of his cigarettes and he lit it for her. "When Shannon was born, Vito arranged to have her birth records reflect both of us as her natural parents. Then Vito promptly lost interest in our baby. He only wanted a son. When Shannon's sex was known, he washed his hands of her."

Hector blew smoke out both nostrils. "And Megan?"

"About the time Shannon turned two, Megan really got herself straightened out. She finally got clean."

"So how'd you two end up allied?"

"Another private investigator," Katy said. "I learned Meg broke it off with my husband when she kicked her habit. I now suppose, for Megan at least, it took narcotic influence to sleep with my husband. That may give her an edge over me, wouldn't you say?"

Hector just looked at her for a while. Then he asked, "What made you run, Katy?"

"My husband is going insane. I told you the truth about that. It's a congenital thing. God, I hope Shannon's spared *that* legacy. But Vito *is* losing his mind, there's no doubt about that. His memory is failing faster all the time. He's become violent. Coarse language in front of our daughter, *all* the time, now. He raised his hand to Shannon, twice. So I ran to the one person in the world I knew would care about his threat to Shannon maybe almost as much as I do."

At least as much, Hector thought. "Thank you, Katy," Hector said. "Thank you for sharing this."

She half-smiled, the essence of skepticism. "What does your knowing really change in the end, Hector? What difference does it truly make?"

He stubbed out his cigarette. "Honestly? It makes no difference at all," he said.

"But you feel better for knowing?"

"Wouldn't put it that way either," Hector said. "Let's say my curiosity is at last satisfied."

"Your friend's friend is a lush, you know. Mr. Ness, I mean."

"Sure," Hector said. "Eliot has been an alcoholic for years."

"This Ness guy really used to be somebody?"

"He did. Hell, he may be somebody again. Don't write him off yet." Hector sighed. "We're all somebody, Kate."

That drew an unbecoming and harsh laugh from the woman. "Now who's slinging sentimental bull?" After a time, Katy said, "What odds do you give all of us, Hector? Honestly—what odds do you give us for surviving this mess?"

"At least fifty-fifty."

Katy narrowed her eyes. "That high? Really?"

"Absolutely." Hector had given, now it was time to take it away: "It's the cold, even odds of a simple either-or, darlin'. We either come out on the other side of this thing, or we don't."

Hector was sitting on the couch, browsing over one of his older novels that Meg had selected for herself.

God, but the memories those pages of pulp paper stirred, the heat of that island and the scent and taste of that woman… the silvery sound of his grandfather Beau's voice.

Meg's hand was suddenly on the back of his neck. She said, "Does it read as good as you remember it, Hec?"

"You assume I finish each book satisfied with the work."

"Don't you? And maybe if you're away from it for a long enough time?" Meg arched an eyebrow. "Maybe then you can approach your own book as a reader?"

Hector said, "Fella once said that no book is ever truly finished by its author, only abandoned."

It had been years since Hector looked at that particular one of his novels. "Reads better than my memory of it, actually," he said. "Damn, I could nearly write then."

"You can write now, I'm loving your newest one," Meg said. "But it's stressful, as you clearly intended. Why don't you take me to a second lunch, Hector? Someplace swanky and romantic. Well, as much as any place can be in this town during lunch rush."

Hector closed his novel. "We can certainly do that. Just thought you might want more time with Shannon."

Meg tipped her head, searching his face. "You say that based on the premise that this Eliot Ness might get us our protection today and Katy may bolt before nightfall and I'll never see Shannon again? Is that how it is?"

"I hadn't thought that through quite as explicitly as you have, but yes, I suppose that is what I meant," he said. He did so reluctantly.

Hector reached out and took her hand and coaxed Meg over the back of the couch and onto his lap. He kissed her. Meg curled up in his arms and said, "Time spent with Shannon now, knowing there may be hardly any time left, is almost too hard. It makes any time with her at all nearly unbearable. Some crazy split, huh?"

Hector had no good answer for that one so he squeezed Meg's hand. "I'll tell Jimmy you and I are stepping out for a bit."

Hector rose and dipped his head into the next room to alert Jimmy to their leaving.

The Irishman just smiled and shook his head. "They just get younger, don't they, Hector?"

Ouch.

Hector scowled. "She's in her early twenties. They're always in their early twenties." He could hear the defensive tone in his voice.

Jimmy said, "But *we* just keep getting older. So the sea just gets wider." Jimmy sighed and said, "Hell—go, *enjoy.*"

14

Hector was fed to the teeth with Italian food so he drove to a little Chinese hole-in-the-wall joint a couple of miles from the brownstone. On the way, Hector kept an eye peeled for tails. Their federal friends were indeed back there; Hector decided to let them stay.

As they pulled up in front of the restaurant, Meg said, "This place one of Jim's recommendations?"

"I actually remember it from old days," he said. "You like Chinese?"

"Love it."

Hector came around the back of his Chevy and opened Meg's door and then wrapped an arm around her waist. She said, "You told Eliot you're not married this year."

"That's right. But that's not how I remember saying it."

"Is some woman who is not your wife waiting on you somewhere? Some woman with an eye to being next year's wife?"

He smiled. "You mean like that 'New Mexico honey' you were theorizing about the other day?"

"Right. Like her, yes."

Hector thought of Jimmy, about his friend's acid remark about Hector's increasingly younger flames. Damn Jimmy, anyways. Hector just shrugged at Meg.

"Just checking," Meg said, gripping his arm harder as they made their way carefully across the icy pavement. "I mean, I have nowhere to go anymore, so anywhere will do, I guess. Maybe I should think about New Mexico for my new next place. Sun would be hell with my complexion, but after this fall's weather, I could maybe do with the desert heat and air."

"There's plenty of room," Hector said. "You could come there anytime you like." To his own ears, his voice lacked a certain conviction.

Meg shivered a little, wrapping her arms around herself and running her hands up and down her bare arms. Hector slipped off his sports jacket and draped it over her shoulders, then sat back down across from her. He scooted his chair around closer to hers and tugged his placemat around to where he now sat.

A pot of hot tea arrived and he poured them both some of that while they browsed the menu. In the low light, something in Meg's looks, something in her bone structure, reminded Hector just a bit of another woman he'd known, a darkly creative painter.

Not looking at Hector, trying instead to look engrossed in the poultry section of the menu, Meg said, "Katy said she had a heart-to-heart with you."

"No, that's not so," he said bluntly. "Not at all. Kate did all the talking." Hector sipped his hot tea and then ran his fingers through his hair. "She told me some things."

"So you finally got all your answers?"

"Let's say I heard some things."

"And you're still talking to me?"

"You must be very strong," Hector said. "Very strong, deep down inside yourself. They say it's the hardest of the addictions to overcome."

Meg narrowed her eyes. "Addiction? What on earth are you talking about, Hector?"

Hector narrowed *his* eyes.

Her voice going hard, Meg said, "What did Kate tell you?"

He told her.

"That's not how it was," Meg said afterward. There was real hate in her tone.

"Kate seemed to believe it."

"I'm sure she does, Hector. It suits her needs. She required a story like that one to rationalize taking another woman's child. It's all a monstrous lie."

"You and Kate never talked about this?"

Meg's eyes flared. "No." She sipped her hot tea and pulled his jacket closer around her. "I spent maybe six hours with Kate before you and Jim saved us at the hotel. That's all. Even in that short time, it quickly became clear to me the last thing to do would be to confess any weaknesses to that witch."

"Then what's the real story?"

"I suppose you have to know that just to ensure you don't detest me."

Hector stretched his legs under the table, pressing his calf against hers. "I don't have to know, darling."

"Yes, you do. You certainly must know, now. I have to have you know if only to offset what you've been told by Kate." She sipped a little more tea then pulled the pot closer and pressed her hands to its sides, warming them. "At first, when Vito learned I was pregnant, he urged me to see what he called a 'pin doctor.'"

Hector suppressed a wince: that was indecorous gangster slang for an abortionist.

"I'd foreseen that demand," Meg said. "So I waited before telling him. I broke dates, canceled club gigs. I waited until an abortion was out of the question before I let Vito know I was carrying his child. Waited until it was too late to kill our baby. Too late even for a monster like Vito." She shivered a little. "Well, I suppose he could have decided to kill us both at that point, but that was my gamble."

Hector admired her for it. He said, "Katy said her husband decided he wanted an heir."

"That was a fall-back position on Vito's part," Meg said. "When he saw I was committed to having the baby, he began praying that I'd have a son. It's every man's dream, isn't it?"

"I don't know," Hector said. "All that rivalry and Freudian bullsquash? Who has the damned time?" And Hector had evolved a kind of arrogant pride about ending his line in that sense. He'd tried to kid himself he had a hankering to be the last to carry the decidedly vexed Lassiter surname. He figured on being the last Lassiter. And anyway, he'd always proven better at destroying than creating things.

Except for the writing, of course.

Hector said, "There is a lot to be said for doting daughters. Little girls to pamper who'll become dutiful daughters in a man's dotage."

"But what about carrying on the family name?" Meg seemed indomitable.

He shrugged. "Lassiter is no pretty handle. The man who really raised me, my grandpappy, Beau, hates the name." He held out a hand. Meg hesitated, then took it. Hers was warm from the tea pitcher. Hector asked softly, "How'd this man end up with your child, Megan?"

Meg looked up at the paper lantern hanging above their table. Her eyes were wet. Raw voiced, she said, "I sold her, God forgive me. My father was quite ill. He needed a surgery no Missouri farmer could afford. Not even selling the farm—which he ruled out—would have paid that bill."

Fair exchange of trade. Right.

Hector felt sick inside. He said, "Your old man, did he pull through?"

Meg's head was bowed. "*No*. He died on the table. But a deal is a deal. Vito made that clear enough. Those two years Katy described as my drying out period, those two years immediately after my baby was born and taken from me? I had a complete nervous breakdown. I was in an institution, eating myself alive from the inside out for giving away my daughter."

Hector didn't know what to say to her. Fidgeting, he eventually asked, "What would you have called your daughter, Meg?"

"Shannon is the name I chose. I got just that much. In the hospital, they brought the paperwork to me for her birth certificate. So I gave her the name I wanted. My little gesture."

She worked at her eyes with a napkin, trying not to wreck her makeup.

"It's a beautiful name. Very Irish."

"My grandmother was from County Antrim."

"You do actually sing, professionally?" He was awkwardly trying to lighten the mood. "If that's true, you could duet with Jimmy. Put a few shots of Jameson in him and Jimmy can belt out a killer version of "Carrikfergus". And his "Minstrel Boy"? That one'll tear your heart out."

"That much is true, I did sing in many of Vito's clubs." One of Hector's still beloved ex-wives, Duff, had been a sometimes singer, too.

"You sang standards and torch songs, Kate told me. Like those tunes you selected the night we danced in the bar."

"I know 'em all," Meg said. "Are you truly hungry, Hector?"

"Not so terribly much," he said. "Not truly."

"Then what do you say we get out of here? We have a couple of hours. Spend the money you would have spent on dinner and get us a room somewhere."

"Meg…"

"Please, Hector. Depending on what happens in the next few hours, I may not have long left with you, either."

15

"I'm leaving to go to the rendezvous early," Hector told Jimmy.

"To lose those FBI boyos across the street?" Jimmy cast down his cigarette. It sizzled in the snow at the foot of the steps leading up to their loaner brownstone.

"Well, that is one notion," he said, still tasting Meg on his mouth.

"What's another?"

"I desperately need a drink." Flashing on an image of bloated old Eliot, Hector added, "Or really maybe just some fresh, cold air."

Jimmy said, "You're getting quite close to Meg and doin' it fast. That scares me a bit for Katy in some ways."

That brought Hector up short. He said, "What do you mean by that, Jimbo?"

Jimmy tread carefully. "Just that I get this growing sense that if things really blow to pieces, if the bullets are flying, I begin to think I'll be the only one trying to keep poor hapless Katy safe."

Deny it? Hector really couldn't.

This other thing about Jimmy that made things a little frightening for Hector at times—Jim seemed sometimes to have what you might call second-sight.

16

The bartender was slicing up lemons and limes. The keep said, "We didn't believe. All the time Ness has been coming here, we just thought he was some blowhard—a boastful, deluded lush. All that crazy stuff about Al Capone, about how he helped bring 'Snorky' down, we thought it all so much bullshit."

"Ness fought Capone, for sure," Hector said. That was face-saving vague and the least Hector could do for Eliot, or more exactly, for Jim. He'd be leaving town soon. He might never get back this way. But Hector figured Eliot would be parking his broadening ass on these very barstools long after Hector was back in New Mexico. It seemed that in confirming Eliot's exaggerations he would buy Ness some face in his favorite bar, maybe at least earn him some budget-extending, free drinks.

"Sometimes he puts away ten, twelve drinks a night," the keep said. "You know, like it's water. Never a sloppy drunk, though. Have to give him that."

That seemed not a lot to give. Rubbing his jaw, Hector said, "Eliot has a lot to forget." As if he really knew. But hell, it might well be true. What else could there be?

"He also has a lot to lose, sounds like," the bartender said. "I mean, he wears a wedding ring. He talks an awful lot about this son. Kid's adopted I think."

"Eliot does have one of those," Hector said. His stomach was sour. He checked his Timex. "Keep my drink here and my stool open, would you, pal? I've got to hit the phone booth in back for a quick chat. Shouldn't be more than five minutes."

Hector bee-lined for the phone cabinet in the back. He fished out his little black book and flipped through it until he hit "F" and a man's name.

Not "F" for the man's last name… no, not that.

"F" for "FBI."

Agent Edmond Tilly said, "Holy Christ, Hector, it's been a spell. When was the last time we talked? That Los Angeles mess, back in forty-seven, wasn't it? The Short murder?"

"Maybe," Hector said, not sure himself. "Probably. January, 1947. The Dahlia."

"That mess with Welles was something. You know that cocksucker is still hiding out in Europe?"

If he was smart, Orson would stay there at least several more years, Hector hoped. Quietly, intently, there were still those in the Bureau who wrongly suspected Welles of the Black Dahlia murder.

"I have a new issue for you to consider," Hector said. "It's another big one."

"That shoot-out in Times Square last week? Rumor has it you were on the scene. Jesus, the berserk life you live, Lassiter."

"No, not that," Hector said, grimacing. "And shoot-out is grossly overstating that stuff. There weren't all that many shots fired."

"There's another rumor too," Agent Tilly said. "About you having some mob boss's wife and moll you're trying to get to Kefauver."

Holy God, Did someone take out a double-truck ad in the *Times*?

Hector said, "Would those be rumors spread by tails your fussy boss has on me?"

"Could be. I can't say much, Hector. Not even to you. You've always enjoyed a certain special relationship with the Bureau, because of Spain in thirty-seven and that crazy stuff in Los Angeles in January of forty-seven. You know that the Director has a rare soft spot for you, at least presently. Hell, you're one of the few non-lefty writers of record out there, and that counts for something here. You're one of the few we're not presently eyeballing with intent. You should see the file on that Red Hammett that Mr. Hoover has built. But if you're calling for help now, well, I'm afraid the answer is a regretful no way."

Tilly suddenly lowered his voice; Hector strained to hear it: "You know what the Bureau's position has been on the mob, Hector. Mr. Hoover is not inclined to do anything to help that grandstander Kefauver's committee. Every time that bastard serves a subpoena to one of those Dago hoodlums, it's like a swift kick in the Director's balls." Tilly rushed to add, "And don't you dare try to make a joke out of that last statement."

Hector said, "So why do I have these two agents camped out in front of my hiding place now, amigo?"

"Because we also don't want a total debacle that can hurt us. You tend to be a lightning rod for certain kinds of mayhem, Hec. You're also a public figure with a penchant for writing about things you don't so much invent as much, these years. Those two guys out front are Mr. Hoover's insurance policy, good men with instructions to involve themselves only under certain circumstances and where they might do so without official entanglement or media presence. Containment is Mr. Hoover's term for it."

"They're honest, these agents? Not bought off help?"

"That's right. So I wouldn't try to lose them if I was you, Hec."

"You seem to know a lot about them and my current situation, Ed," Hector said. "Almost like you maybe anticipated my call."

"Mr. Hoover foresaw you making a contact," the FBI agent said. "He's nothing if not a strategist, and he says the same of you. You're up against it, after all. It was logical you would reach out to the Bureau via me."

Bastard.

Bastards.

Hector said, "Well, tell old John Edgar he may want to strongly re-evaluate his current policy of non-intervention. I've got the IDs and service weapons of a couple of your confederates. They're on Vito Scartelli's dole. So this nonexistent mob and its reach extends right down into your hallowed Bureau's ranks. Run that one by old J. Edgar, won't you, pal?"

Silence. Hector sensed Tilly might have his palm pressed over the receiver. There was some rustling and he said, "When you get back to your place, take the guns and the IDs and walk across the street and hand them to the agents there, if you would. We'll see to those rats."

"Sure," Hector said, "After all you've done for me in this time of need, why wouldn't I want to help you out like that, Ed? After all the favors I did you and damned HUAC three years ago? Why the hell wouldn't I want to grab ankle again?"

"Hector, I wish I could do more, I really do, Lass. But the politics of this situation are complex and the possibility of a public relations disaster are unthinkably high. Particularly with a maverick like you testing the fences. Speaking strictly personally, I hope to hell you make it, Hec. I hope you ram it down that Buckeye Don's goddamn throat, sideways."

"Thanks loads, Ed," I said. "Your support means the world to me." Hector racked the receiver, seething.

He checked his watch again. Ten minutes until Ness and the next meeting was to begin. He exited the phone booth and called to the bartender, "I'm claiming this table over here." Hector then thought of Shannon and said, "Say, do you know how to make a Shirley Temple, pal?"

17

J immy and the ladies arrived first. Hector pulled out chairs
for the girls and scooted 'em in, then moseyed to the bar
where Jimmy was ordering drinks. Jimmy nodded and said,
"Is it too much to hope our situation has improved in some
inexplicable way, Hector?"

Hector leaned in, elbows on the bar. "Wish I could surprise you, brother. I talked to my FBI guy."

"And there's no help coming," Jimmy said, "that's what
you're going to say, isn't it? It's in your eyes." The bartender
passed Jimmy his whiskey.

"Right," Hector said. "*Nada.* FBI's not gonna lift a finger for us, sounds like. Hoover's got some hard-on over being
keistered by Kefauver."

The Irish cop shotgunned his Jameson and said, "Given
the rumors I've heard about Hoover's sexual proclivities, you
may want to rethink that phrasing, Mr. Author." He made a
sour face. "And I've heard, as I'm sure you've heard, that John
Edgar only has eyes for sorry Clyde."

"Hoover's sex drive aside, either way, the upshot is we're
left twisting in the wind."

"Let's see what Eliot can do for us," Jimmy said. He checked his watch. "He's late. But then it's snowing again, and it's evening rush hour to boot."

Hector forked over some bills to the bartender and carried Katy's gin and Shannon's Shirley Temple to the table. He made a second trip to pick up a couple of glasses of rum St. James for Meg and himself. Their rum drinks represented another bid on Hector's part to recapture something by chasing the taste and fire of his old winter-in-Paris favored libation. For some reason, the sentimentalist in Hector seemed to be stirring with a vengeance these past few days. Brinke Devlin loomed large in his dreams.

Jimmy was still drinking at the bar, perhaps shortening the duration between refills, Hector guessed. "We should think about what we might do if Eliot can't bring us any assistance," Hector said.

"Let's not get ahead of ourselves," Jimmy said, tapping his shot glass with two thick fingers to signal his desire for a refill. "Eliot's not so far gone as to not have a few surprises for us."

Maybe that would prove out. "You should go easier on that stuff," Hector said.

"I can handle it," Jimmy said. "And let's face it—if we don't get some light thrown on all this from Eliot, I see two options. We either make a blind run to Tennessee, or we go to D.C. in hopes of somehow finding the senator. Or we simply run off for parts unknown. We do that until we sense the chase has stopped and we find a place to squirrel those three away. Let 'em live underground, from here to forever."

"If you call that anything like living," Hector said. "I'm the running kind, of course, Jim. A nomad and a rambler at the best of times, sure. But even I couldn't live all of my life like that. And it's no way for that little girl to grow up."

The little rubber stopper with a bell inside strung over the bar door jingled and some snow squalls swirled in through the widening crack. Eliot brushed snow from his shoulders and shook out his hat. He grinned and said, "Hey there, boys."

Sour-faced, Jimmy gestured at the bar and said, "What'll it be, Eliot?"

"Gin and tonic," Eliot said. "What's the latest news, fellas?"

"The latest is the FBI officially telling me we are squarely on our own," Hector said.

"I wish I could say I'm surprised," Eliot said. "Huddle close, I've got some news."

They walked to the end of the bar: Katy and Shannon had their backs to the three men. Meg watched the trio. Eliot said, "I've talked to Joseph Gibson, the counsel for Kefauver's committee. He's in Dayton presently, and will be there for the next several days. I've explained to him what you have and what the woman purports to have. Made it clear that the wife is willing to turn committee's evidence. Gibson was quite excited by the prospect, as you might expect."

"Precisely how excited, Eliot?" Jimmy dipped his head, searching Eliot's eyes. "How deep does this shyster's enthusiasm run? We frankly need real and meaningful exuberance."

"He's not excited enough to send you an escort," Eliot said. He took a sip of his drink and shook his head. "He doesn't want to risk the black-eye of this star witness being shot or blown up in route. But he agrees that if you can get to Dayton, he'll then take over security—contingent upon seeing whatever paperwork this woman is carrying."

Eliot shrugged. "If you can reach Dayton with them, and turn them over, then they'll have their protection and you two will be effectively in the clear. Wouldn't be any percentage in Scartelli's outfit messing with the two of you any further."

Eliot drained his drink and nodded for a refill. He said, "Damn, I wish I still had a badge. I'd take six of my best men and we'd make that Dayton run. We'd get you there, safe and sound, by God. But it looks like it's just me."

Hector scowled. "What the hell are you saying, El?"

"I'll come along with you, of course," Eliot said. "If the weather clears a little, we could make Dayton before sunrise. I'll follow, be extra muscle and help grease the grooves with Gibson when we get there. I speak those bastards' language. The sorry tongue of bureaucratese, that is to say."

Jimmy said, "Eliot, you have that little boy, now. A wife. You have things to lose you didn't have to risk back in the bad old good days."

"It should be a milk run, Jimmy," Eliot said. "No arguments. Just tell me when we leave. I'll follow. Trust I have your back covered."

It was clear to Hector that Eliot wouldn't back down. Hector said, "I think we get one more night's sleep here"—one more night with Meg, he was thinking—"then we make the run at dawn. Roads are treacherous enough without driving 'em at night. Be a sad irony killing ourselves on slick pavement when there are so many other options for a violent death in the twenty-four bloody hours ahead."

"I agree," Jimmy said. "First we recharge our batteries. *Then* make that run south." He winked at Eliot. "While we're down there in Dayton, maybe we could visit our old friend. Make sure he's still locked up in the loony bin, eh?"

Hector guessed Jimmy meant their Mad Butcher suspect from the old days: the deranged and drunken doctor who had booby-hatched himself years before to evade possible prosecution for the string of torso killings, according to Eliot. Jimmy went and confirmed it: "We'll make sure our boyo was accounted for when Robertson was slain and cut up."

"We'll do that, Jimbo," Eliot said. "Maybe I can at least scare him enough to stop writing me those crazy letters and postcards." Ness nodded at Katy in the mirror. "We're being eyeballed. Guess we better get over there." He looked from Jimmy to Hector and back again. "We're agreed then on the generalities?"

"Think so," Hector said. Hell, what else could he say?

Jimmy said, "Eliot and I will work out the rest by phone, later. Now I think we need to start working on Katy. Get a better handle on what she can turn over to this shyster lawyer. I'd hate to make this Charge of the Light Brigade-style suicide run only to learn she can't deliver the goods." He stood up and stretched and said, "We better tell them how it is."

"You two do that," Hector said, keeping to my barstool. "I haven't the heart." That was true, so far as it went. He hadn't the stomach to sit at a table with selfish Kate Scartelli right now, not as Meg and Shannon's time together was clearly drawing to a close.

Meg joined Hector at the bar, her drink in hand. She slid onto the stool next to him. He closed a hand over her knee, stroking it through nylon. He said, "Don't you want to hear the plan?"

"Not really," Meg said. "Honestly, it's all beginning to seem appallingly academic to me. I have nothing to give that senator. I have nothing to trade for protection. And Katy's use for me is all but finished. Katy knows I know it and she doesn't even bother to pretend anymore." Meg sipped some of the belly warming rum. "All that aside, I heard Dayton mentioned."

"We'll start down that way tomorrow morning. Very early."

Meg looked back over her shoulder. She put her hand under the bar and pressed it to the back of Hector's hand, pushing his hand from her knee up and inside to her inner thigh. She pressed it hard there. It was very warm—her hand and that other place. "Part of me says let them start," she said. "Let them make their trip to Dayton without us. You and I could run the other way. Run away from it all. I've always been the kind to run away from the bad."

"You didn't run from Youngstown after Shannon was born," Hector said, searching her eyes. He brushed a wave of blond hair back from her right eye. "You hung in there solidly enough."

"Waiting for something," she said. "Waiting for something, but I hardly knew what. Still don't know. And I don't hold out hope for any future at all with my baby, now."

"A part of me feels like running away with you, too," Hector said. "But we have to see Shannon through this. See she's safely cared for and provided for by this damned committee. I couldn't care less what happens to Katy, but Shannon's fate concerns me almost as much as I know it does you. And I started down this bloody road with Jimmy. Can't just leave him, and now Eliot, holding this sorry bag of misery."

"No," she said. "You're too loyal a friend, so you couldn't do that. You're that rarest of things, a finisher." She drained her drink and tapped her fingers to signal she wanted a refill. The keep nodded. She said, "You wouldn't consider a kidnapping, and then the three of us running, would you, Hector?"

"You almost sound serious," Hector said.

"For my part, I am," Meg said. "But for you? *No.* Though I've heard some important books were written in prison."

Hector smiled. "Important books, yes, but not particularly lucrative."

"You write for money?"

"God yes," Hector said. "I do this for a living. This is my trade. My preferred epitaph: 'He did it for the art, but he wasn't above the money.'"

Meg smiled. "Because the pile was too high?"

Hector laughed. "It's going to mean a bigger bill from the stonecutter," he said, "but I much prefer your version. I'm amending."

"Think we might drift off for a time again tonight? Some little dark place where we can dance?"

"I'm sure it can be arranged," he said.

After they pulled up in front of the brownstone, Hector went around to the back of his car and popped the trunk. He rooted through a cardboard box filled with weapons they'd confiscated from all the bent officials and would-be torpedoes the past couple of days. Jimmy and Hector had amassed quite the little collection of handguns for themselves. Jimmy peered under the lid of the trunk to see what Hector was up to. Jimmy said, "What's this?"

"Though I don't feel it is owed, I promised my FBI guy something," Hector said.

Hector dug out the guns they'd taken from the FBI agents outside their hotel. He slipped those in his pocket, along with the agents' identifications. "Back in a jiffy," he told Jimmy.

The Feds watched Hector cross the street. The driver rolled down his window. He said, "Agent Tilly said you'd have something to give us."

He was careful pulling the guns from his pockets, holding them by the barrel between thumb and forefinger. Just in case, Hector wiped down each one and let the Fed behind the wheel lift them from his handkerchief.

"You're a careful man," the driver said.

"Your agency hasn't done much to distinguish itself, nor breed trust, not this sorry trip to the well," Hector said. "Mr. Hoover's frankly pissing me off."

The one on the passenger side said, "And their identifications?"

"Here," Hector said, handing over the little leatherette cases. The driver opened each one, then showed them to his partner. The other agent partner grunted. "I don't know 'em," he said.

The driver said, "Me either. And thank Himself for that."

"Whoever the head Bureau honcho is here in this goddamn city, he's allegedly a problem for you boys, too," Hector said. "The women were working through that fella to get protection for themselves. Near as I can tell, the bastard sold them out for a cold, hard hit."

The Feds looked slight queasy then. That gladdened Hector's heart. He said, "Now, having done you boys all these unreciprocated favors, tell me—exactly what will it take for you two to exceed orders?"

"What do you mean?"

"I mean when do you, you know, *do* something? What's *enough* to make you raise a finger for us? What's it going to take, hombres? Say a car rolls up and three thugs with guns climb out here." Hector gestured across the street at the brownstone. "*Then* do you get off your asses?"

"Hard to say," the driver said. "We have a broad charter. Oodles of autonomous discretion. You know, *mucho latitude.*"

"You must be very proud to engender such high-flying trust from J. Edgar," Hector said. "So what happens now? You two just keep shadowing us? Stick to us like goddamn remoras?"

"Not sure I like that comparison, but that's about how it shapes, Lassiter," the driver said.

Hector shook his head and lit a cigarette. "Nice guy that I am, I'm going to give you two a tip. Why don't y'all call it a night then? I may take the prettier of the ladies there out for drinks and a dance in a bit, but we're all more or less *in* for the night. Having said that, we'll be hittin' the road, bright and early. Got a little road trip ahead of us. You may want to prepare for that."

The driver almost groaned. "Holy Christ. Where to?"

Hector smiled. "I can't really say. See, I'm exercising mucho latitude. Let's just say you boys best have a full tank of gas."

"Shit," the driver said, sour-faced. "How exactly early is early?"

Hector shrugged, backing away from the FBI agents' car. He half-turned, then stepped back quickly as a green Plymouth whipped by. Several men in the car: the guy in the backseat on the passenger looked back at Hector with dead eyes.

He looked to Hector like a stone killer.

18

Meg swayed against Hector, dancing to *Star Dust*. She'd been softly singing the lyrics in his ear, but that sultry serenade had tapered off a stanza or so ago. She said, "Jim tells me you spend a lot of time on the road, that you're a well-traveled man. He says your passport is a thing to behold."

"I just bore too easily," Hector said. "I'd hate to leave this life wondering about anything. And I've got to feed the muse. It's also an interesting way to live. Never settle, and you're new every dandy place you go."

"But you're a stranger, too."

Funny: Hector had long ago said a similar thing to another writer who had traveled even more widely than he had, to his first wife, Brinke Devlin. "There is that perspective, as well," Hector said.

"I have nowhere to go after tomorrow," Meg said. She gripped his hand. "Were you serious about me coming down to New Mexico with you?"

"Not if you're doing it only because you have no place else to go," he said. "I'd like to think there are deeper urges than no better options motivating you."

"You can trust that to be true," she said. "I mean, if you're not bothered by our age difference."

Jesus, had she been talking to Jimmy about *that*?

Hector pulled back a bit to search her face. "Are you— bothered by that? You should know, up front, in a few days, I turn fifty-one. I came in with the New Year. Hell, with the new century."

Meg didn't flinch, bless her. "So when's your birthday?"

"January 1st," Hector said. "Landed at midnight. Like I said, I came in with the bloody present age."

"I'm fine with it. Does me being younger bother you, Hector?"

"I'll find some way to cope."

She smiled and leaned back against him. "I'm going to be a mess tomorrow, Hector. I just want to prepare you for that, up front. When Shannon is spirited off to whatever place they've found to hide her, I'm going to blow to pieces, you know."

"I'll see you through it," Hector said. "I promise you I'll do my best to do that."

"I wish I'd known you six years ago," she said. "I might have talked you into that kidnapping. Or you'd have talked sense into me. Kept me from that devil's deal I made. Vito will never stop hunting any of us, you know that, don't you? Not as long as he thinks there's some threat. And I'm not sure he'll be any less dangerous in prison."

"Don't borrow trouble," Hector said. "You're thinking too far ahead, darlin'. Remember: man proposes then God promptly disposes. Or so the downcast believers say. Anyway, I hear old Vito's slipping away upstairs. He may well forget us in time. Hell, to hear Katie talk, he may forget himself, inside next week."

Hector felt her head nod under his chin. "I don't suppose you would spring for another hotel room? Too risky making love on the couch again," she said. "I don't want to be worrying about who might hear or walk in on us."

"I've already got us a room reserved. Figured we see that posh old Hollenden joint."

"We can't be away more than another couple of hours," Meg said. "The expense of that place for just a little bit we can be there? You're crazy!"

"Right," Hector said, smiling. "So we should probably go there right now then, don't you think?"

19

Five o'clock in the morning: the sun wasn't yet up and city was sleeping, except for the fugitives and those two Feds parked across the street with their engine running.

The agents sipped coffee from thermos lids and stared all hell at them as Jimmy and Hector loaded the Chevy. It took the two men some time to wedge Meg and Katy's suitcases in around Hector's own luggage, his portable typewriter and their box of confiscated firearms. Meg, thankfully, was traveling light: it wasn't as much trouble wedging in her single suitcase Hector had run around the city via cutouts on its way to them.

Jimmy rubbed his hands together, his breath coming like smoke from his nose and mouth. "Godless goddamn weather," he said. "We should be at your place in New Mexico about now, Hector. Nice and warm and flying on tequila or agave. Nibbling tortillas, staring off through the cacti. Away from all foolish young women and their silly little girls' problems."

There Jimmy went again.

"Days are still pretty warm down that way," Hector said, "but the nights can be brisk there, too. It's the way in the desert, you know."

"Well, Hector, the world turns the right way, this time tonight, we could be well shed of this mess," Jimmy said. "Should have this one cleanly behind us. What *were* we thinking getting twisted up in this calamitous knot of misery?"

"You ask that like we had a choice," Hector said. "Once that kid tugged on my sleeve, we were both goners. Hell, you were the driving force behind this escapade on the front end."

"On that note, I'll go get the wee one and bring her down first," Jimmy said. "Car should be warmed up by now. Eliot should be by in about ten minutes. Maybe I'll ride with him, see if he'll let me drive. He's never been much of a wheelman."

And chances were Ness could use a sober driver if he'd kept up his drinking at the same pace he had been putting them away at the hotel bar. Hector didn't venture that opinion aloud, of course.

Jimmy carried Shannon out and put her in the center of the back seat. The tyke was sleeping through it all. Meg followed them out. She said to Hector, "Katy's fussing with one of her new dresses. I'd figure on at least five more minutes."

"Then you best get in the car with Shannon," he said. "She might be afraid if she wakes up and finds herself alone and in some place other than the one where she fell asleep."

Eliot pulled up in front of the brownstone then. He drove a dark green Mercury. He rolled down the window and Hector walked over to Ness. Eliot smiled and said, "Those FBI agents aren't exactly subtle, are they?"

"I think we passed subtle with Hoover and his cronies at least two days ago," Hector said. "You have a gun, Eliot?"

He looked a little sad. "No."

"Then just a second." Hector fetched a spare gun from the box in the trunk of his car and passed it to Eliot. "It's got a full clip. And here's another couple." He folded the clips into

Eliot's other hand. "It's far off the books, so keep it if you don't need to pitch it after use."

Ness beamed. "You can really spare it?"

"We've got plenty of extras," Hector said. "Jimmy's planning on riding with you. He has the route. If we get separated, we've picked about five points along the path where we'll hook up again. He has those written down, too."

"Sounds good," Eliot said. "When do we roll?"

"As soon as Mrs. Scartelli decides she's ready for the road. Any minute, probably."

As they were talking, a milk delivery truck rolled up the street and parked on the wrong side, about a quarter block from the brownstone. The milkman got out and started fussing around the side of the truck. It looked like he had someone riding shotgun.

A bird screeched and a couple of black crows took skittish wing from the roof of a building across the street. Hector thought he heard metal-on-metal from somewhere above and behind. He found himself getting jittery.

Goddamn Katy: Hector just wanted to get the hell underway, lickety-split.

The front door opened and Katy came out. She held tightly to the wrought-iron banister as she navigated the slick stairs down to the sidewalk.

Cursing, Hector went to help her.

That's when the gunfire started.

Bullets flew from every direction—even the flare of a couple of Tommy guns from the back of the milk truck.

Hector gathered up Katy and pushed her down behind the concrete staircase, sheltered from the fire from the milk truck. Other bullets were almost finding them, though.

Hector looked up and saw two men on the roof across the street. Both leveled high-powered rifles. Jimmy and Eliot began firing back; the latter from the cover of his car, already pocked with bullet holes.

Eliot shot one of the men off the rooftop; Hector took down the other. Both fell four floors and made moist, cracking sounds as they slammed into the pavement behind the FBI agents' car.

Those FBI bastards were ducking down in their seats, the agents using their "latitude" to refrain from helping, Hector saw, gritting his teeth. *Craven sons of bitches.*

The Feds' attention seemed to be focused on the machine gunners who'd driven in on the milk truck. While they were looking that way, Hector fired three shots straight into the Feds' car.

Hector put one shot just an inch or two above the driver's head, shattering his window. The Feds fell out of the passenger side door of their car then, cursing and firing at the men who'd come in on the milk truck. The FBI boys were all tiger now that they felt personally threatened.

Eliot opened the passenger's side door of his car and beckoned. Hector saw Jimmy run around to the back of Eliot's car and begin shooting at the roof of the brownstone. Jimmy yelled, "Heads up, Hec!"

Hector pulled Katy closer as a man fell off the roof of the brownstone and crashed at their feet. Hector grabbed Katy and manhandled her over the dead man's ruined body, propelling her into Eliot's car. She slid in and Jimmy yelled, "Over the seat, Kate!" She awkwardly skidded over and into the back seat as Jimmy slid in next to Eliot. Jimmy yelled, "High time we fled, Hec!"

Hector waved back at him with his gun, then looked up over the concrete staircase. One of the machine gunners was making a run toward Eliot's car.

Either Hector or one of the Feds put that man down. Hector thought about making a dash for his dropped machine gun—he sure would have liked to add that wicked security blanket to their weapons cache. But it would have been suicide.

Hector had been counting his shots; with his old Peacemaker, that was a vital thing to do in a gunfight. He figured he had one bullet left. So he shot out the front driver's side tire of the milk truck, then ran to his Chevy. Hector got her in gear, backed out of the driveway and tore off.

Meg's voice from the backseat: "I moved Shannon to the floor when the shooting started. She didn't even wake up. Are you okay, Hector?"

"I'm fine," he said thickly. Eliot's car was coming up fast behind them. The Feds were still shooting it out with the remaining machine gunner.

Meg said, "And Katy?"

"Okay. She's in Eliot's car with Jimmy."

"How'd they find us?"

Hector sighed. "Don't ever tell Jimmy I said this, but I'm beginning to trust his cop partner a hell of a lot less than Jimmy does."

20

The path they'd chosen was a fairly obvious one—the only sensible road open to them: they'd pick up Route 42 and ride it down to Route 40—the Old National Trail—two hundred seventeen miles of slush and snow and two-lane roads lending themselves to all-too-easy ambush. Milk run? Sure.

They stopped around eleven at a mom-and-pop place for some meal between breakfast and lunch, most of them opting for eggs or the like.

At their second stop for a proper lunch, Jimmy, Eliot and Hector decided to spend the night in Yellow Springs, a college town not far from Dayton. Once there, Eliot and Jimmy would contact the lawyer, Gibson, and arrange the final details for turning the girls over to the attorney for federal protection.

As they may their way to Dayton, Hector felt this little stab of pain as he saw signs for Springfield, Ohio. That was the town where Brinke was born, the wide-spot-in-the-road she'd fled in terror and disgust and never returned to. Hector had never been there, and even if he wasn't pressed to be elsewhere now, he doubted he could bear to see it.

They found a small inn on the outskirts of Yellow Springs, sitting at the fringe of the Antioch campus, some joint that mostly catered to the visiting parents of college students. Because of the holiday break, the inn, like the rest of the town, felt deserted.

Jimmy and Eliot shared a room; the ladies had a room and Hector took one to himself—a move he justified by citing his need to write and the early morning clatter of his typewriter. They put the women in the center room that had an adjoining door with Hector's. Potentially useful, of course, that extra door.

They took their dinner in a place downtown. Jimmy and Eliot clearly saw a night of drinking and boozy war stories ahead of them. Hector figured writing in his room was probably out of the question: Eliot and Jimmy would insist he participate in their spirit-stoked reveries if he was close at hand.

So Hector envisioned finding a bar in which to write. He was just getting ready to put on his overcoat when the door between their rooms opened. Meg said, "Could you use some company, Hec?"

"Absolutely." He smiled regretfully. "But not just *yet*, okay? Missed my writing time this morning and that's very bad luck and a bad habit that's far too easy to sustain. I truly hate to break my routine. But trying to write here is going to be a problem with the boys in tow."

Not to mention the distraction of having Megan merely one wall away.

She nodded. "Understood. Just in case things go haywire, where should I look for you?"

"There's an old stagecoach stop on Main Street," Hector said. "It's a pub these days. I'm told the college literati congregate there to write, so I'll maybe blend-in there in my rickety way with pen and notebook. Hell, maybe some of that youthful zeal and literary inspiration will rub off."

"You don't need any inspiration," Meg said. "Not that kind."

He kissed her. "I'll come back and fetch you around nine, okay?"

A sad smile. "Oh, it's surely a date, Mr. Lassiter."

The three block's walk to the inn was eye-watering cold. The snow had become brittle and crunchy underfoot.

The pub's clientele was a mix of old locals and sullen-looking undergrads who hadn't made the run home for the holidays. A mangy Christmas tree stood in the corner by the jukebox, decorated with beer bottle caps and promotional coasters for seasonal ales and hard liquors. A Bing Crosby LP of Yule tunes was cranked up *loud*.

Taken together, it all almost made Hector yearn for a proper Christmas tree.

He bypassed the bar and made his way into a slightly quieter backroom that offered tables and booths. Several solitary younger types sat in various booths, crouched over notebooks and legal pads, scribbling away.

It was Hector's kind of place for certain: the flavor of watering hole that in his youth he'd have burned down the hours, filling the pages with ink. The place brought back vague memories of the Closerie des Lilas, or Le Select in the best of the old days.

He snagged a corner booth in the back that gave him a line-of-sight shot back to the bar area and right on to the front door—a place where he'd have plenty of time to prepare if any unfriendly types happened in.

After ordering a beer and whiskey back, *and* being brought a complimentary bowl of thirst-bolstering pretzels, Hector got out his notebook and fountain pen and knuckled down to work.

No warms ups, no preludes and no false starts.

Hector resumed by completing the sentence he'd left unfinished the morning before—a trick he'd long ago evolved to kick-start his composition process. That and never writing himself out were the vital secrets of writing to Hector's mind. They were what made him seem so much more prolific to peers who bitterly admired or acidly rued Hector's compositional speed.

That and not over-thinking it.

It wasn't about *W-R-I-T-I-N-G* for Hector.

It's was just writing, lowercase, no italics.

His trade.

Or so he told myself each time he sat down to do it.

Hector wrote longhand for more than an hour, lost in the country of his story. When he sensed he was close to writing the well dry, he stopped cold, once again at mid-sentence.

He read back all that he'd written, making just a few small tweaks along the way. He figured to get back to Meg a good bit ahead of schedule. He closed his notebook and smiled.

Someone cleared his voice and said, "Excuse me, Mr. Lassiter? Mind if I join you for a few minutes? Could I please stand you another beer?"

It was a youngish man. The stranger had thick black hair, dark eyes and a likeable enough smile. He looked a bit too old to be a student. But he was no federal agent, and no thug, either. Of that much Hector was certain.

The man held a fresh pitcher of frothy beer and his own frosted mug. Hector scented *writer*.

Hector nodded. "You know me?"

"So you *are* Hector Lassiter. I was pretty certain of it. I've read your books for many years." The stranger arched one of his dark, bushy eyebrows and smiled. He had a dimple in his left cheek. His diction was crisp and precise. He ended his sentences by placing stresses on the last word of every sentence. "I know you from your dust jacket photos," the stranger said.

"Please, call me Hector." He gestured at the empty bench opposite. "Snug in and take a load off, Mr.—?"

"Rod," the stranger said. "My name's Rod." The younger man filled Hector's mug, pouring down the side of the glass to tamp down the head. As he did that, Rod said, "I'm a student here at Antioch. Studying on the G.I. Bill. Or I was. Graduated earlier this year. Took a radio job in the Queen City. But our friends are all back here, so with the holidays...?" A sheepish shrug.

That explained his age—Rod was a brainy Vet. "What exactly did you study, Rod?"

"Writing."

So he was right. Hector said, "Poet? Aspiring novelist? Short stories? You know, the kind of stuff they print in the *Antioch Review*?" God, but Hector surely hoped not.

"It seems I may be too populist for that," Rod said. "More of a commercial writer. Or so I'm told." This rueful smile. Hector had seen it before, right there in the mirror.

"Books, plays... screenwriting, mostly," Rod said. "There's a difference between living as a writer—what most around these parts seem to want to do—and making a living as a writer. I want to do the latter. I need to do that. I see this as my career. I've got a family to support. I want to go at television, and I mean to do that, full bore. It's like a new frontier for writers, I think."

The boy was on a roll: Hector just smiled and sat back, watching Rod go.

Something in Rod's ensuing monologue reached Hector.

"I want to be intellectual *and* commercial," Rod said, intense eyes and gravel-voiced. "I really believe it can be done, Hector. It's not conforming, either. Not at all. I've never written beneath myself, *never*. Friends from school taunt me for my interest in television. They sneer and say I'm selling out. But I'm not some meek conformist. I'm a tired non-conformist." He grimaced. "Like it or not, television is here to stay. Of that much I'm certain. These Kefauver hearings and the interest in watching them on that strange tube are just another sign I'm right."

Rod smiled and shook his head. "And I'm motor-mouthing like a star-struck jerk, aren't I? Sorry, but it's just kind of overwhelming to meet a man I so admire as a writer. The career you've charted, Mr. Lassiter, is just the kind I aspire to. Popular writing, but *smart*."

So writing was indeed his intended *trade*.

Rod was doing it for the art, but not above the money. Hector loved him already.

"We're just folks, so you call me Hector," he said. "And sounds to me like you've got the winning attitude."

"Well, I've already sold a few things."

"That's great, Rod." Hector hoisted his mug and they toasted. "To *working writers*," Hector said.

Rod licked his lips as he lowered his glass. "As it happens, I've been studying some of your scripts these past few weeks," Rod said. "I notice in interviews you disparage your own film work, but you're a natural screenwriter, Mr. Lassiter. Really one of the best screenwriters currently going to my mind. Your dialogue is nearly always pitch-perfect. Very naturalistic, yet character comes through in your dialogue."

Hector waved a hand. "That film stuff pays the freight for what the book advances don't always cover," he said. "You know, things like cars… clothes. Food and libations. That sort of necessary stuff."

Rod said, "Have to say, I was pretty stunned to look up from my notepad and see you sitting here, writing. Didn't know you ever made it up this way. And so close to Christmas? You have family around these parts?"

Hector winced a little. "God, tomorrow *is* Christmas Eve, isn't it? I'd completely lost track."

"So, do you have family around these parts, Hector?"

"No, I'm sort of out this way on unexpected business," he said. "A favor that keeps growing in scope. Headed to Dayton tomorrow, then probably back down to New Mexico."

"Shame it's holiday break," Rod said. "I'm sure the university would love to have you speak to the English department. I'm sure they'd *pay* you to do that."

"I'll be long gone before school resumes," Hector said. "And I don't cotton much to that kind of public speaking, Rod. I'm happy to sign 'em when some reader like you puts the arm on me along the way and hands me back a book I wrote. But talking about my writing in front of people? Just don't enjoy it, between us. It's best, I think, just to keep well out of way of your own writings. And from what you said about your classmates, I'd irk the ones at the university every bit as much as you do, my friend. Hell, probably more. I'm a writer, not an author—you know, full caps with swirly serifs."

Rod smiled and lit a cigarette. "How do you expect the young ones studying writing to learn if the seasoned pros like yourself don't share the knowledge?"

"Studying writing?" Hector smiled and shook his head. "Must confess, that I don't get, either. Sorry, but you're talking to the wrong hack writer, Rod. I never even graduated high school, kid. I lied about my age and ran off to the wars, first down in Mexico, then over to Europe. Stayed on there a time, living in Paris while teaching myself to write—one true sentence. I had no writing teachers like you mean. Not even mentors, per se. Hell, Gertrude Stein taught me flat nothing about crime writing. In the end."

Hector was overstating, of course. He'd learned some important and valuable things about prose, about echo and repetition, from Gertrude. The most important things he'd learned from that other female writer—the far more fetching Brinke Devlin.

Through a haze of cigarette smoke, Rod said, "What are you working on now? A novel? A screenplay?"

"Been in a kind of novel phase lately," Hector said. "The film stuff coming my way hasn't been compelling and I'm okay for cash presently. Most of the film stuff lately offered me has been punching up dialogue for lackluster melodramas or requests to adapt the works of other crime writers." Hector waved a hand. "Only thing worse than adapting your own work is chewing the cud of some rival writer. What are *you* working on, Rod?"

"More scripts. I'd like to have my own television series some day soon. An anthology kind of thing, but dark. Slightly macabre. Shadows and substance." Grinning sheepishly, he said, "It's my pipe dream."

"You Ohio writers are a breed apart, you know," Hector said. "Ambrose Bierce… O. Henry. You Buckeye boys like your twist endings and gothic settings, don't you? You are a dark but enticing crew."

"I was born in New York." Rod's brow furrowed. "O. Henry was from Ohio?"

"Started writing here, anyway," Hector said. "In the state pen in Columbus. One of those prison writers, like Cervantes, maybe. Fella name of Chester Himes got started in the Ohio State Pen, too. That one's a prickly son of a bitch in person, but I like Chester well enough in small doses."

And Bierce? Hector couldn't tell *that* story. He'd sworn an oath of secrecy to Bierce himself.

Talk of prisons and writers reminded Hector of Meg and a similar conversation. He felt an obligation to get back to her. He pulled out his pen and opened up his notebook. Hector slid them across the table to Rod. "Here, please scrawl your address down there and I'll keep you in mind, friend. I don't say yes to every film project that comes my way. Maybe I can send you some work. I'd dearly love to do that."

Rod half-smiled. "But you haven't read any of my stuff."

"True, but I like your attitude and poise," Hector said. "I'm going to trust my instincts that you're worthy and capable."

The younger writer inscribed his contact information in Hector's notebook and passed it back to the older writer.

Hector checked his name, read aloud: "Rod Serling—it's a good name for a by-line."

"Thanks. You looked like you were headed out, Hector. I truly didn't mean to detain you. But I'd have kicked myself *forever* if I didn't take the opportunity to have a drink or two with you. To chat a little."

"I *really* enjoyed it, kid," Hector said. "You headed out yourself?"

"Not quite yet." Rod grimaced again and lit another cigarette. He offered Hector one of his smokes. Hector took it and fired them both up with my old Zippo. "I have trouble sleeping from time to time," Rod said. He shifted uncomfortably. "How to put it? You see, since the war…"

Christ's sake, that said it *all*.

Rod looked more than a little embarrassed. Hector smacked the younger man's arm and stretched some hard truths. "Holy Jesus, you don't need to say a word more, buddy. Hell, I don't think I slept through a single night after World War I until about 1923. My best ex-friend Hemingway, either.

I was so groggy with sleep deprivation those years I don't even remember much about 'em."

That was all true enough.

It was about 1924 Hector finally started to put it all behind him.

Sultry, exquisite Brinke had helped with that, though Hector had never told her so.

His best nights' sleep in those haunted years came tangled in her arms.

More bitter regrets.

Hector hoisted my glass. "Thank you for your service, son."

They toasted each other. That's when Hector saw the stranger—a swarthy, husky man in a tight-fitting wool overcoat and gray fedora. He was seated at the end of the bar where he could keep Hector in line of sight.

Hector guessed he had gotten so engrossed in talking to Rod he hadn't seen this new bastard drift in. The goon was hired muscle, there was no question of that.

Hector poured Rod and himself a little more beer. He looked around and saw there was a back door opening onto to a dimly lit beer patio, currently closed for the season. The door looked like a still-working exit. Hector said, "Rod, that business I told you about?"

Rod smiled, knowingly taking his measure. "You mean that favor that keeps growing in scope?"

"That's just the one," Hector said, smiling. "You mentioned those Kefauver probes…"

"They *are* the talk of the nation," Rod said. "They're selling beaucoup televisions, I hear." Rod blew some smoke up into the light above them, considering Hector. "Why do *you* raise 'em?"

"Because I'm trying to get a couple of women to Dayton, to the Kefauver counsel," Hector said. "They're going to testify against some northeastern Ohio mob types."

Rod smiled, incredulous. "God, how in the hell did you draw *that* duty?"

Hector shrugged. "Like I said, a favor kind of went cross-wise on me."

"Where are you going with this, Hector?"

"We've been pursued these past few days, chased hard and by some pretty rough trade," Hector said. "Now, please don't turn around, Rod. Let me just say since you and I started talking, one of *them* wandered in and took up a seat at the bar. I'd dearly love to know how they found me here. I thought we'd shaken all our tails."

Rod nodded. He looked tense, but maybe game. "You figure together we can take this guy?"

"Not precisely the direction I was heading, buddy," Hector said. "I was merely going to ask you to leave with me. We'd stand up, put on our coats and hats and exit through that back door. Once we got out there, you and I would swap coats and hats. You'd trudge on through the snow a ways, letting him follow. I'd follow him, then take him down, pronto."

Rod didn't hesitate, bless him: "Sure. I'll do it."

Bravado there in his voice... *and* a little fear.

But Rod was game for it.

Hector had a knack for inspiring that kind of impulsive loyalty and intrepidity in a certain kind of man—usually younger men who foolishly admired his writing.

Hem had the same flavor of dark gift.

"I can't lie to you, kiddo," Hector said. "Bastard is almost certainly armed. I can't deny there'd be some real risk to you in doing this favor for me, buddy."

Rod nodded. "I've read *a lot* about you, Hector. I trust you to see nothing happens to me. Just tell me you *are* armed." A jagged smile: "Really, you are, right?"

"Very." Hector pulled back his sports jacket to reveal his holster and Colt.

Rod drained his beer. "Then let's do this before I lose my reckless buzz," he said.

Hector smiled and said, "I'm going to owe you, and I mean *deep*, my friend."

Rod shook his hand and said, "Then just don't lose my address. Remember to send some of that precious script work my way. That's how we even this out."

"Swear, kid."

The younger writer moved across the room to fetch his coat and hat. They both dressed to go outside, taking their time so the torpedo at the bar could get a good look at Hector's hat and coat. Rod wasn't near enough Hector's height, but the older writer figured out there in the snow with the bare trees and twilight and no familiar reference points Rod would pass well enough.

The two writers slid out the back door, snow squalling in through the crack. Outside, they quickly swapped coats and hats. Rod set off alone across rear lot. Hector crouched behind a big old pin oak and waited.

He closely watched Rod: the aspiring screenwriter walked with a pronounced limp. That gimpy tread was the vestige of a war injury Hector guessed.

If Rod still had the insomnia, he must have seen some pretty nasty action.

The back door of the pub opened and a shaft of light slid across the iced-over lot.

That crunching sound of heavy, determined steps on the crisp snow.

Hector didn't want to take any chances of getting Rod hurt and there would be no sneaking up on the bastard, not on that damned, hard-packed snow. He slid out his old Colt and raised the Peacemaker over his head.

As the man passed by the tree where the novelist had taken shelter, Hector brought his gun down. He heard bone crunch and teeth fracture. Hector swung the butt of his Colt down again against the back of the stranger's head and the man went down, hard.

Hector had fleetingly hoped to question the son of a bitch. He turned the man over and the low light from the moon didn't reassure him. Hector felt for a pulse.

Nada.

Uh-oh.

It must have been that second blow to the base of his skull, Hector figured. It always looked *so* easy in the B-movies, always seemed so straight-forward and reliable in the lesser pulp novels to knock some son of a bitch out cold with a blow to the base of the skull.

Rod crunched back through the snow toward Hector, favoring his injured leg. "That went well, yes?"

"Very well," Hector said, trying to act nonchalant. Hector slipped the man's gun into his own waistband and rolled him over onto his face so Rod wouldn't get a good look. "Let's switch back," Hector said, standing and shrugging off Rod's too-small coat. Rod pulled off Hector's coat and hat and passed them back. Hector put them on and said, "Thanks a million, Rod. You've really done me the hell of a favor, buddy."

Rod said, "Let me help you get him. Where are we taking him?"

"Uh, *nowhere*. I'm just going to sit here with him after I duck inside and call my contact with the Kefauver committee.

They'll send someone to pick him up. They will, you know, *process* him."

"Must be real nice to have friends in high places," Rod said, rubbing his arms.

Hector smiled. "Friends? That's quite overstating it."

"You better phone those men then," Rod said. "Otherwise he might freeze to death."

"And we surely can't have *that*. Let's get back in there, and I'll make that call." Hector paused and squeezed Rod's arm. "Oh, and one other thing, Rod, you earn yourself major points with me for not saying something like, 'God, this is just like one of your books.'"

Rod smiled. "Never even crossed my mind to say that." Definitely Hector's kind of writer. He said his good-byes to Rod and then borrowed the phone behind the bar and placed a collect call to D.C.

Agent Tilly answered his desk phone. "Jesus," Hector said, "what lousy hours you keep."

"Doing a little OT," Tilly said. "Trying to get some money scraped together to help lighten the damage of the holidays. My wife spoils the kids rotten at Christmas."

"Let's cut to the holiday chase: I just killed another mobster," Hector said. "I'm in Yellow Springs, Ohio. The body is behind a pub—the *only* pub—on the town's main drag. It's some old stagecoach stop. The bastard was seen following me and another fella out. You do *not* want the local cops poking around this mess and pinching me."

"And why is that, Hector?"

"'Cause I'll work my mouth to save my sorry ass. I'll do that enthusiastically, Ed."

"No threats needed, Hector. Can you secret the body away somewhere, Lass?"

"It's snowy here. Tell your guys to look alongside a big old oak for a fresh drift."

Hector hung up and went out back again to toss snow over the dead man.

Of course, calling Tilly insured they'd probably recover their FBI tails.

At least this next crew, if tied to Tilly, would likely be straight arrows.

Fucking J. Edgar Hoover.

One day, Hector swore to himself, *there'll be a reckoning with that toad-faced monster.*

21

Before he left the bar a last time, Hector talked the bartender into selling him a few bottles of spirits: Jameson, Dewars, Gordons and Bacardi. Sounded like a heady, hi-tone law firm to Hector as he rattled off his booze wish list to the tired-eyed keep.

His arms full, Hector kicked at the door of his friend's room.

Jimmy unhooked the chain, holstered his forty-five and took the bag from Hector's arms. The big cop set it on a bed and rooted around inside the poke. After a low whistle, Jimmy said, "Jesus, Hec, what have you done this bloody night that needs this much forgetting? I'm all atremble awaiting word."

Hector told Jimmy and Eliot what had happened with his now-deceased shadow.

Eliot said, "Katy wouldn't tip anyone to come and find us. Meg wouldn't have reason to tip them either, would she?"

In some ways, Hector could almost believe that of increasingly desperate Meg—except for the threat that kind of move would pose to Shannon.

Hector shook his head; Jimmy just watched, chewing his lip.

"It's possible we could have been tailed," Hector said to Jimmy. "There's a lot of holiday traffic now. People on the way to visit granny and gramps or distant parents. Kids returning from college for the holidays. We were always in pretty heavy traffic coming down here."

"True enough," Jimmy said. "So I choose to believe we were tailed from this morning's gunfight and just failed to spot 'em."

"Me too," Eliot said. "Let's go to your room, Hec. The door there opens to the women's hotel room. We can't drink all this stuff alone. And we should all stay close now in these last hours. Tactically, it'd be better to barricade and defend a single space. I mean, if that man you took out isn't alone in town." Sound enough strategy from an alcoholic. Hector wrapped a hand around the back of Eliot's neck, squeezed fondly and said, "Let's go do that."

Katy and Meg sat and drank with them for a while before retiring to get Shannon ready for bed. Meg soon enough drifted back their way. She stretched out on Hector's bed, crossing her legs at the ankles, nursing a rum and cola. She'd been reading his Key West book, *The Last Key*. That particular novel was cured in rum, passion and loss. Hector wondered if his writing gave Meg her sudden taste for Cuba Libres.

Eliot said, "After this other, we're going to go over to the Veteran's Administration Center and visit our old friend there."

Their *old friend*: Jimmy and Eliot's prime Mad Butcher of Kingsbury Run suspect.

Jimmy said, "You'd be welcome to come, Hec. Your company would even be appreciated. Case is so stale, it could use a fresh perspective. Some... well, *friendly* dark imagination."

Hector glanced at Meg. She shrugged.

He said, "We'll see, Jimmy. God only knows how tomorrow will sort itself out, brothers. Hell, given what we've been through, you and Eliot and I may find ourselves subpoenaed. Forced to testify about all these killing runs made at us these past few days."

"It's a real possibility," Eliot said. "I checked my car," he said suddenly. "I was pleasantly surprised to find fewer bullet holes than expected."

"Mine came through okay, too," Hector said. Hell, his car was unscathed.

Eliot said, "It was good luck for us those hoodlums took a shot at those Feds this morning."

Hector was finally himself a little drunk. He confessed, "Actually, I shot at those FBI agents to invest them in our fight. Figured they'd never know where the pivotal shot came from." Meg bit her lip, considering that and assessing Hector in some new way.

Jimmy roared and slapped his thigh. "Isn't that grand! Almost makes the whole bloody hurly-burly worth it." Jimmy suddenly put a hand to his belly and made a pained face. "All this boozing on a near empty stomach, it's sorry strategy. Time to call it a night, lads. And *lassie*." He held his glass up and winked at Meg.

She raised her glass and said, "I've heard an Irishman is never drunk so long as he can grasp a single blade of grass and keep from falling off the face of the earth."

Jimmy laughed again and struggled to his feet. "Come Eliot, last call has come and gone." Ness stood and they all tapped glasses. "To tomorrow and all the vile things it may bring," Jimmy said. He shot-gunned his dregs.

Hector passed him his overcoat for the short walk back to their room. Eliot said, "I'm to call Gibson at nine. We'll work out last details then. I've committed to nothing at this point. That results in less time for any plans to leak to the opposition."

"I like that thinking," Hector said. "Very shrewd." For a juicer, Eliot was proving eerily effective now that the chips were down. Ness was what they called a "high-functioning alcoholic," Hector guessed. Or maybe it was a kind of muscle memory. And this was Eliot's former *métier* after all, the sacred calling Ness never should have abandoned for the sorry business world.

Hector closed the door behind them and slipped on the security chain. Through the door Hector could hear Jimmy laughing and singing in the snow:

> *The minstrel boy to the wars has gone*
> *In the ranks of death you will find him...*

"I love that man," Meg said. "He's wonderful."

"Jimmy?" Hector smiled. "Me too. He may well be my best friend in the world." Well, the best of Hector's still-talking friends at any rate.

"Eliot's okay, too. I bet he was something in his prime."

"Yeah... sober." Hector wanted to kick himself for that too easy, too mean joke. *Christ but you can be a mean, cynical son of a bitch,* Hector thought. *Especially when you're drunk yourself. How do people put up with you? Why on earth do they do that?*

Meg ducked her head into the next room and then softly closed the door. She left the lock off. "All is quiet." She began fiddling with the buttons of her dress. "It's okay if I spend the night here, isn't it? I mean, most of the night? Need to be back there in the morning when Shannon wakes up."

"It's fine," Hector said. "I'll be up at four to write. I can wake you then." He stepped up closer to her and cupped her chin in big hand. "You holding up fine?"

"Don't know about fine, but I'm doing okay."

"You're sure?"

"Just finish taking off my damn clothes, Hector 'cause my fingers aren't working so good presently. Get me naked and love me hard. Make me tired enough to sleep without dreams. You can do that, can't you?"

Meg rolled off Hector and onto her side. She propped her head on one hand. Panting, she said, "This place you live in New Mexico, what's it really like?"

"Rambling, white stucco and a covered second floor porch that wraps all the way around the house," Hector said, his voice hoarse. "Far too big a place for one man. It sits up against the Rio Grande. I dug an irrigation trench a couple years back. I just lift a board and flood my front yard with run-off from the river to water the grounds."

"Sounds like you don't spend much time there."

"But what time I'm there, I do really love." That was a mild lie. Place held bittersweet memories...

She rested her head on his chest, raking her fingers through his graying chest hair "I've been counting the men you've killed for us since Shannon found you in that hotel bar. I'm so sorry for making you do that."

Hector closed his eyes. "I've been to a few wars, Meg. These recent ones I've put down, they're far from my first. And these recent men needed killing long before they crossed my path. They're far from my conscience, in that sense. So there's no real sense of guilt. After all, this hasn't been first blood." Hector bit his lip. He sighed, deeply. "First blood is a terrible thing, sweetheart. A fierce burden. That's the killing you spend real time getting over, or maybe being taken down by, slow and hard. Your first kill is a thing you can't outrun and so you have to conquer."

"But you were killing for the state, Hector. Soldiers like you were, back in the day, they killed under orders, right? That has to take a toll, too, of course. But I wonder if maybe it's different if one kills for revenge. Maybe it's different if one kills for oneself and kills for righteous reasons."

"Maybe it could be," Hector said, though he thought he knew better.

"I talked to Jim some more while you were out writing," Meg said. "I've been trying to reconcile things he told me against articles I've read about you. Profiles. This novel of yours I've been reading, *The Last Key*, how much of that isn't made up? The woman in there, was she real?"

The Last Key... a.k.a. *Never Send 'Em To the River* in some countries, in the UK, for instance. It was *Forever's Just Pretend*, elsewhere: some book titles simply didn't "travel."

"I don't care for talking about my writing that way. Don't much like wagging a finger at what's invented and what's drawn from all this." Hector waved a hand in the dark at the bad old world. "It's not fair to expect a writer to conduct tours for readers through the country of his own work, you know. It really isn't fair at all."

"The woman in that book, though, Brinke, was she real? I mean, I can kind of tell she might have been."

"Have you finished reading that novel?"

"A few hours ago."

"Yes, Brinke's real. She was my first real love. My first wife."

"And the ending of that novel? Did that really happen as you describe it, too?"

"Sure." Hector combed her yellow-white hair with his fingers. *It happened just like that*, he thought. *No invention needed, terrible as that was to face.*

"My God." She kissed his throat softly and stroked the comma of hair back from his forehead. "I'm so sorry, darling."

"All that happened same as your lifetime ago," Hector said. "Time does help with the loss." He paused, revised, "Helps with the pain, anyway."

"I'm still so sorry. And sorry to have dragged you into this bloody mess." She kissed his chest again. She tried to make a joke. "Maybe you will at least get another sad, sexy book out of all this."

"No. I envision a different ending to all this. Know this, Meg: Whatever happens, if old Vito doesn't end up spending all of what's left of his daffy waning years in jail, I swear to you, I'll drive back up to Cleveland and I'll kill him myself. Either way, he's not going to be in any position to ever come back at you, or at Shannon. Hell, in most ways, he'll be even easier to see killed in jail. That can be hired done for a carton of smokes. Whatever it takes, we're shooting for some kind of happy ending this trip to the well."

Meg traced his mouth with her fingernails. "And Katy?"

"He won't be striking back at her, either."

"Tomorrow, will you give me back my gun, Hector? I mean for just in case?"

"Let me think about that."

"This isn't a good way to spend this night," she said. "Talking about all this, I mean."

"You're right." He urged her up next to him and kissed her, his fingers tangling in her pale hair. His lips grazed her throat and he said, "Do you know any border ballads? Spanish love songs? *Canciόns?*"

"What?"

"Mexican love songs."

"Suppose I could learn 'em," she said, leg twisting around him. "I could do that for you."

"Do that, and we'll get you some gigs across the border in the Kentucky Bar. Once in a while, Francis—Old Blue Eyes—actually gets down that way. Talent scouts, too. You might even be discovered in the good way. Maybe get yourself a recording deal in the bargain."

She bit his chin, playful now. "Trying to put me to work already? And who is this Francis?"

"Sinatra. Frank. You've got a pretty voice that needs to be shared, Meg."

"You haven't really heard me sing, Hector."

"I've heard you talk. You have a beautiful, lilting and contralto voice."

"You have any happier books that I could read? At least happier than *The Last Key*, I mean? Maybe one that really does have a happy ending?"

Hm. Hector stroked her breast. After a time he said, "Let me get back to you on that."

A few hours later, Hector heard the bedsprings squeak. (Those cheap, goddamn motel box springs and their infernal noise—they'd driven the lovers to the floor, earlier.) Meg whispered, "Sweet dreams, Hector."

"You, too," he muttered back. He must have slept again for a time. Yet it seemed moments later he was roused from sleep again. Groggy, thinking it might be trouble, he slipped a hand under his pillow and wrapped it around the butt of the Peacemaker. A tiny voice said, "Mister Hector, if we keep moving around, how will Santa find me?"

"Santa knows everything, Shannon," Hector said, cotton-mouthed, but smiling. He propped up on one elbow to see her better. "And maybe Santa can ask Chef Boyardee."

"*That's* a good idea. So you do think Santa will find us?"

"I'm sure of it, honey. Please don't fret about that." Given the success her father's minions were having, some supernatural elf should be able to locate Shannon without breaking a sweat.

"Mommy hasn't left me much room in bed. Think Megan would mind if I got in bed with her?"

"I'm sure she wouldn't mind," Hector said. Take that, Kate.

"I hope I get what I really want," Shannon said. A puppy.

"I hope so too," Hector said. "I hope we all get what we really want."

22

A knock at the door. Hector fetched his gun from under the pillow and stepped to one side of the door, cocking his revolver. He said softly, "Who is it?"

That tenor voice: "Jimmy and Eliot." Hector eased down the hammer on the old Colt.

He opened the door and the duo shouldered in, stamping slush from their feet. It was just a tick warmer this morning because of the sun and a thaw looked to be taking hold. Hector figured the flooding threats would resume soon as all that snow turned to run off and freshly swelled the Ohio River and its myriad tributaries. The parking lot and sidewalks around the hotel were already turning to slushy soup.

"Gibson is starting to irk me," Eliot said, sitting at the foot of Hector's bed. "We're what, forty minutes from Dayton, something like that?"

"In that vicinity," Hector said. "Certainly less than an hour."

"Well, it's too far for Mr. Gibson to drive that distance evidently," Eliot said. "I wanted him and a security detail to come here to pick up the girls. To guard and deliver them, properly. But Gibson is adamant we run them to the police headquarters in downtown Dayton instead. I don't rule out the prospect Gibson has contacted area press, either. Maybe even television cameras. He probably wants a newspaper photo of the ladies turning themselves in to stick in Vito Scartelli's eye." It was ironic to hear a notorious headline chaser like Ness rue press coverage.

And Hector figured the damned journalists would probably paint Meg as some scarlet woman to sell papers. *Dammit all.* And Eliot was likely right about the other, too: about television. Hell, Meg was made for the camera.

"Christ sake," Hector said, furious now, "if the Dayton cops are like Youngstown and Cleveland flatfoots, then a fair percentage are going to be in Scartelli's hip pocket. We might as well save a step and shoot down Meg and Kate ourselves."

"Well, I'm not pleased either," Eliot said. "So I'm trying to offset that, to give us back a little cover, Hector."

Wetting his lips, Hector said, "How do you mean to do that, exactly?"

Jimmy and Eliot exchanged wary glances. "Rather hold back on that for a time," Eliot said.

"This help, such as it is, may not come through, Hec," Jimmy said. "Rather have you pleasantly surprised if it does."

"Terrific," Hector said. Leaps of faith—taking those had never been Hector's style. But he wasn't spoiled for options. "Then here's to your plans coming through," Hector said.

Eliot and Jimmy rolled out of the hotel parking first; Hector's Chevy followed.

Seven miles east of Dayton they slowed and pulled over behind a dark blue Buick. Kate said, "What is this?"

Meg was seated up front next to Hector. She said, "Should I get some guns?"

"Hold off on that," Hector said, palming the wheel and rolling to a stop behind Eliot's car. Eliot walked over to the Chevy and Hector cranked down the window. "Our support has arrived after all," Eliot said. "C'mon, I'll introduce you, but we'll keep it very short."

Two men lumbered out of the waiting car. The stockier of the trio stalked toward Jimmy, spreading his arms wide. Jimmy said to Hector, "That's Pete Merylo, one of Cleveland's honest finest."

Merylo and Ness pointedly avoided one another; Hector sensed some bad blood there. The second man vigorously pumped Eliot's hand. Ness pointed at that one and said to Hector, "This is Arnold Sagalyn, one of my key people when I was safety director. I trust him and you can do that too, Hector."

Hector shook Sagalyn's hand, then Merylo's. Eliot said, "Arnold and Pete are old hands from the Butcher case. Pete's still on that one, in fact. They'll see us safely into Dayton and the precinct house. After we've handed over the ladies, the four of us are going to pay a visit to an old friend."

Hector said to Merylo, "I've been hearing about you for years from Jimmy."

"Likewise," Pete said. "Wish the circumstances were better. Hell of a way to meet."

Jimmy said, "I'll ride with Pete, if you don't mind, Arnold."

"No sweat," Sagalyn said. "Me and Eliot have a lot of catching up to do. Been too long."

"Then let's get going," Eliot said. "Hector, you ride in the center position. Pete and Jim will cover your tail. Let's get this wrapped up now boys." Then Ness actually said it: "Let's do some good, men."

Corny as that last sounded, Hector had to smile.

Thirty minutes later, they whipped by an interurban car and rolled up in front of the Dayton police headquarters.

Katy's voice sounded strange to Hector, fear constricting her throat, he guessed. She said to me, "Will you stay in the car with Shannon, Hector? Just until we get safely inside? I don't want to take any chances. I know you'll do whatever it takes to keep her safe."

"Surely, Kate," Hector said. He pulled his Colt out and rested it on his lap. "Hanging back, Meg?"

"She knows things too," Kate said. "Meg best at least try for some protection as well. My husband is not going to let her just walk away after all this, you know. He's not the kind. Not so long as he remembers anything."

Probably that was too true. But Hector figured he could hide Meg well enough. He figured he could get lost down around the border somewhere where even mob money couldn't cut through language barriers and places that had no names. Where maps didn't mean much.

They'd let things cool down for a few months, then set Meg up close by Hector's hacienda.

"I doubt I'll be long," Meg said to him. "I have too little to offer them." Meg reached across the seat and squeezed his knee. She leaned across a little closer and kissed his cheek. Whispering in his ear, she said, "You wait for me, Hector. I want to leave town with you. You'll keep me safe, I know."

Hector hesitated, then opened the glove compartment and pulled out one of the myriad liberated guns stowed inside. He checked the forty-five's clip, pulled back the slide, then handed it to Meg. "Just in case. If anything goes wrong, you point it like a finger and you aim for mass."

Meg weighed the gun in her hand and nodded. She looked sick, more than a tad scared. Then she kissed Hector hard on the mouth. She said softly, "Thank you, I think."

"Just get inside that damned building, and do that fast as you can," Hector said. "Really run. They won't try anything inside the place. The public relations' stink of a shooting inside the station would be too much for even them to handle or cover up. Once you're through those doors, I'm sure you'll be safe."

Any attack would have to happen on the street, Hector was sure of exactly that much.

He looked up: at the top of the steps of the police headquarters there was a guy in a three-piece suit. That was Gibson, Hector guessed—the angling son of bitch. Gibson was flanked by uniformed and plain clothes cops. Some newsboys stood on the steps sure enough, top and bottom, their cameras poised. And there were indeed a couple television crews.

The right thing for Gibson to do was to stomp down those steps and swamp the three cars with his men—to get Katy and Meg out, keeping them low and lost in a sea of bustling bodies. But Gibson clearly wanted his goddamn photo opportunity. He wanted the women to come to him, standing posed and mighty at the top of that damn flight of stairs like some damned Moses or Zeus.

Katy said, "Are you two finished talking?" More edge in her voice. Hector thought then about how little he was going to miss Katy. He twisted around in his seat to face her. "*Bonne chance*, Katharine," he said. "Run it through that bastard good, won't you? I know you're well capable."

Her blue eyes flared, but then Kate half-smiled and said, "Thank you, sincerely, for risking so much for us, Mr. Lassiter. All things considered, you're some kind of man."

Hector said, "Just go now. Go fast and keep your heads well down." He smiled. "Was me, I'd kick off those heels and run barefoot into there, cameras and how it might look be damned. Speed is your best and truest friend on your trip up those stairs and through the doors."

Meg slid out of the front seat and opened the back door for Katy—did it like she was some chauffeur to Kate.

Jimmy, Eliot, Pete and Arnold were waiting by the Chevy, trying to surround the women as Gibson and his men should have been doing. Hector saw Jimmy look at Meg's gun and scowl.

When the back door closed, Hector said, "Shannon, honey, I want you to slide down onto the floor and stay there until I tell you. We're going to play a game, sweetie."

That little voice from behind the seat: "Okay, I'm down here. What kind of game?"

"I spy with my little eye. You know that game, kiddo?"

The child sounded delighted. "I've played it!"

"Great," Hector said.

"Why do you want me on the floor?"

He could say, *Intuition.* Instead he told her, "I don't want you to see where I'm looking. I don't want to make the game too easy for you. You're too smart, that way."

A giggle. "Okay! Let's play!"

"I'm going to step out of the car for a second first," Hector said, "but I'll be right by the door, honey. I want a better look around. I want to find something really extra good to spy."

Of course he was getting out of the car so he'd have a clear line of fire if needed. And Hector feared it likely would be. The air was thick with the possibility of ambush.

Hector first saw the cop—his bearing was all *wrong*. The man was too swarthy and gaunt for Ohio police.

Then Hector got a really good look at the man's face.

Those too-familiar dead eyes: It was the man in the green car that had nearly run Hector over on the street after his talk with the Feds.

Taking aim at the man, Hector yelled, "Jimmy, it's going south!"

The dead-eyed man looked Hector's way then, pointing his gun at the author.

Hector emptied a chamber of the Colt into the man's face, killed those dead eyes.

From there, it turned into a war zone. Bullets flying every which way. People screamed and glass began breaking. Reporters dashed for cover to save their own sorry asses. One of 'em turned in the wrong direction and actually got shot in the ass.

Still standing behind the cover of his car, its open driver's side door to his back, Hector fished the pocket of his overcoat for more bullets and started thrusting them in chambers. He was up to four when he felt something rush close by his face. No time to finish. Hector took aim at another ersatz Dayton cop who was shooting at him. Hector shot that one in the forehead, yelling, "Shannon, stay down honey," then, "I'll be right back!"

Hector ran in a crouch toward the front door of the police H.Q.

Gibson was already ducking inside to seek shelter with a couple of his cops. Hector was sorely tempted to shoot the cowardly lawyer in the back. Hector hadn't spotted her yet in the melee so he hollered, "Meg, kiss the ground!" Hector then shot a man in the throat who was about to shoot Jimmy in the back.

Hector saw that Kate was already stretched on the ground, sprawled on her back. Hector got a closer look and winced. Her face was obliterated. Katy had almost made the lobby door. Well, it was over for Katy now, and forever so.

Vito had neutralized that threat to himself. The bastard's fate now rested in Meg's hands.

A couple of cops—maybe honest ones—were huddled close by Katy's corpse. One of those fellas had taken one in the pump. The other was clutching his belly.

Hector saw Meg, pressed up against the wall of the police HQ.

There was blood on her skirt. She wasn't moving. Hector's stomach kicked.

Two men in black hats and overcoats were running toward them, opening their jackets and reaching: two more torpedoes.

Jimmy yelled, "Hector, you get Meg. Those two lads coming are mine."

Hector trusted Jimmy to know his own lethal capabilities, so he thrust his Colt down his waistband and slid an arm behind Meg's back and the other under her knees, rising with her.

Good as his word, Jimmy shot both men between the eyes. Two machine guns clattered to the damp sidewalk from under the dead men's overcoats. Jimmy fetched up one of the Tommy guns and began firing at a rooftop across the street from the police headquarters. It was full-scale war, now. Those TV cameras were unmanned, pointed uselessly at blood-stained concrete.

Hector could see Meg had caught a bullet in the thigh, just above the knee. Crouching low again, he ran with her back to his Chevy, running through a hail of lead. He screamed, "Shannon, it's Hector honey, open the back door, baby!"

Fifty-fifty the tyke would open the right door, the rear passenger's side door. She did just that, bless her tiny heart.

He slung Meg into the back seat, covering her body with his own. Hector said, "Shannon, stay down there on the floor honey and cover your eyes."

Hector had been an ambulance driver and a kind of a medic in the waning days of the Great War, so he knew some things.

The hole in Meg's leg was close enough to her femoral artery—the bleeding hard enough—that it left Hector spooked. He looked around for something, anything, then focused on the seatbelt strap. He wrapped it around Meg's thigh and cinched it just tight enough to slow her bleeding— he didn't want to cost Meg a leg. He slammed the back door then and pulled out his Colt again to rejoin the battle.

Jimmy, Eliot, Pete and Arnold were still standing. Some presumably honest cops were backing them up. Jimmy and Pete were both making good use of the Thompsons. Jimmy locked eyes with Hector. Jimmy looked down at Kate's corpse and then back at Hector. He read Jimmy's lips:

Run.

Hector shook his head.

Hector read Jimmy's lips again:

Run, now. Please. Go boyo! Jimmy jerked his head, indicating the road.

Do it, Hec, the Irishman's lips said.

Torn, Hector shot at two more men. Then he ran around the back of his Chevy and slid behind the wheel.

Jimmy pointed down the road with his machine gun:

Go boyo! Run goddamn ya!

Hector didn't want to go. Then he saw all the blood all over his back seat, Meg's blood.

Shannon said, "What's all that noise?"

"Fireworks, honey," Hector said. "That's all. Crazy fireworks for Christmas."

Hector stamped the accelerator and peeled off the curb.

PART II

— ON THE ROAD —

Christmas Eve to New Year's Eve, 1950

*"If you don't know where you are going,
any road will take you there."*

— Proverb

23

Shannon said, "What's the matter with Megan?"

"She hurt her leg," Hector said. He checked the rearview mirror: a red coupé slid off the curb in pursuit of his Chevy. Hector could still hear shots being fired in front of the police station. A gray sedan, something anonymous-looking and therefore possibly federal, pulled into the path of the red coupé. Now there was the sound of crunching metal and breaking glass behind them.

Damn. Hector blessed Ed Tilly, figuring him for the federal back up... such as it was.

Hector took a corner at speed and felt his Chevy almost go up on two wheels. He checked the rearview mirror again and saw no tails. He drove three blocks, then skidded into the parking lot of a Sinclair station.

"Slide over the seat, Shannon," Hector said. "Come up here with me, sweetie."

The tot did that. Hector locked her in the car and said through the window, "Won't be a minute. Watch me through that front window there."

He dashed inside the station. Hector said to the old grease monkey inside, "Got me a little problem with my car. Can I borrow a pair of needle-nose pliers, pal?"

The attendant waddled into the bay and then tossed Hector the pliers. He said, "Sure you don't want me to handle it, fella? Won't cost you much at all."

Hector shook his head. "Nah, it's chronic and I know the drill. Second nature for me, now."

Hector climbed into the back seat, hovering above Meg—she was still unconscious. Shock and blood loss to blame, he figured.

Shannon said, "When are we going to play 'I spy,' Mister Hector?"

"Right now," he said. "You keep your eyes off the back seat and try and figure out what I spy," he said. Hector whipped out his Zippo, opening it with a one-handed snap and then lighting it. He teased the ends of the pliers over the blue edged flame of his Zippo. He said, "I spy something red."

So much blood: A terrible choice. "I mean green," he said.

He closed his lighter and fished the cuff of his boot for his flask. He splashed a little single malt whisky over Meg's wound. That set her a bit astir.

Despite the cold, Hector was sweating: it had been a long time since he'd last played emergency doctor, and years since he'd dug out a bullet. He twisted Meg's leg around for better access and ripped her skirt up higher on her thigh to get it out of the way. There was some scorching on the fabric so Hector guessed she must have been shot at close range. He felt the back of her leg for another hole and found no exit wound.

Hector bit his lip and eased the needle-nose pliers into the wound. The ends of the pliers parted just enough to grab the bullet when he found it.

Shannon said, "That tree!"

"What? *No*." Remembering their game, Hector said, "No, not that tree. Try again."

Meg frowned and twisted her head, evidently feeling what he was doing. That was a good sign, Hector hoped.

He felt something hard inside there now. There was some give—hopefully it wasn't simply a bone fragment.

Shannon said, "*That* tree, then."

"No, not that tree either," Hector said. "No trees." His voice didn't sound good to his own ears.

The slug came free from the wound. Hector figured it came from a forty-five. The bullet still retained its shape and looked to be intact, thank God. That was some kind of a break.

Hector dashed a little more whisky in the bullet hole, then fished out his pocket knife and heated the blade so he could cauterize the wound. It was going to leave a scar on Meg's long and pretty ivory stem, but weighing the alternative?

He frowned and looked at his fingers, flexing them. Hector's left hand was sluggish now, tingling a bit. Christ, he hoped it wasn't a heart attack or stroke, or something of the sort. Hell, he wasn't nearly that old, not really. He flexed the fingers of his left hand again. His hand had something of that numbness that comes with sleeping on an arm wrong.

"That car," Shannon said.

"What? What car?" Hector was suddenly alarmed—had they been tailed after all?

"That green car," Shannon said.

Hector's mind was racing: Eliot drove a green car. Maybe Ness had found a way to follow them. He said, "What green car?"

"That empty one across the street. Is that the green thing you spy?"

Their silly game. Damn, he'd lost the thread. "No," Hector said. "Try again, honey."

"That light it's green—no, wait, now yellow. No, wait, now red."

"It's not the traffic light, either," Hector said.

He tore off some more of Megan's dress and bandaged her leg as best he could with his increasingly useless left arm.

There. Done. Now what?

He glanced over the seat: Shannon was craning her neck, looking up through the windshield. She smiled, "I know now!" She pointed at something Hector couldn't see, smiling at him. "The dinosaur up there! That's the green thing, isn't it?"

"That's right, honey."

"Is Megan going to be okay?"

"I think so."

Then she asked it. "Where's my mommy?"

He couldn't do it yet. Hector said, "With some men. We'll check in on her in a little bit." Hector slipped the bullet he'd taken from Megan's leg into his shirt pocket. He reached for the door latch to let myself out of the backseat. The fingers of his left hand felt like sausages—thick feeling and unresponsive. His arm was nearly dead.

What the hell?

Hector looked at his left hand again. His fingers were bloody. He first assumed it was of course Meg's blood. Then he saw the sleeve of his shirt was stained with blood too. A little blood ran down from under his sleeve and across his palm. Frowning, pulse starting to race, Hector felt around his left arm with his right hand.

Goddamn it! Was that a hole in his coat sleeve? He patted around and then felt the pain as his finger slid into the hole a shade.

Hector had been hit back there when all those bullets were flying! He was shot high up on the arm, just a couple of inches down from the shoulder. He felt the inside of his arm and found no exit wound. The slug was still in his goddamn arm! Holy Christ, but this was a bad development. Maybe the worst.

Shaking now, Hector opened the back door of his Chevy with his right hand. He shucked off his overcoat and then his sports jacket. He slid in behind the steering wheel and slammed the door behind himself with right hand.

"My turn," Shannon said.

Their infernal game...

"Sure, honey," he said thickly. "But listen, before we do that, there's something else I have to do and fast. I kind of hurt myself back there. Got hit by a firecracker or something. I'm going to have to take care of it myself. I may yell and maybe *loudly*. If I do, please don't let it scare you, sweetheart. Don't worry, darlin', okay?"

"Okay." Shannon didn't look too worried. Well, she probably hadn't heard a grown man scream yet, Hector figured.

"And if I should go to sleep suddenly, it's very important you shake me until I wake up again," he said. "Maybe pinch my earlobe hard with your fingernails if you have to." He showed her where to squeeze on his ear. "Pinch right here and pinch me hard as you can with your nails. That should wake me up if shaking me doesn't work."

Hector figured he'd probably pass himself out at least twice trying to dig the bullet out of his arm, once when it came free and perhaps again when he pressed that hot knife blade over the wound. He turned up the car's heater and then ripped off his shirtsleeve at the shoulder. He rolled down the window and reached out with his right hand and twisted the driver's side mirror around to give himself a better look at the wound.

It was an ugly but small hole, maybe made by a thirty-eight. Something smaller than the slug that hit Megan, that much was certain.

His left hand was all but useless now. He realized he was going to have to use Shannon, a bit. He said, "Really, Shan, if I pass out, if I go to sleep, you're going to have to wake me up, and *right away*, okay?" Hector might bleed out, otherwise.

"Okay."

"Promise me?"

"Pinky promise," she said. She held up her right hand, her pinky sticking out. They wrapped their little fingers around one another's and shook. Been a while since he'd done one of those. That other time had been with that little girl in Europe, the one Jimmy and Hector had defied the Nazis to rescue.

Hector handed Shannon the pliers. "I'm going to have you hold the ends of these over a fire," he said. "It's to kill germs. Be careful not to burn yourself." He got his Zippo going and she held the pliers over the blue-orange flame. He closed his lighter with a click and dropped it in his pocket a last time. "Careful, honey," he said. "Don't touch the ends or burn yourself."

Then he poured some whisky on his wound—*that stung*—and took a little drink for himself. That swill sharpened him up a bit. Or it felt like it did, anyway. He took the pliers from Shannon and took a few deep breaths. He waited for his right hand to steady.

Shannon was watching him with those big and luminous blue eyes. They were like Meg's eyes, but innocent. He said, "We still have a game to play, right? Still want to do that?"

Poor kid looked pretty worried, now. Hector figured he must not look too good to her. She said, "You still want to play? You're sure? It's freezing but you're sweating. Are you sick? Why are you bleeding?"

He said, "Take a good long look around out there. Find something really good and tricky to spy. I won't watch where you're looking. I'll just fix myself up while you do that."

Hector took another deep breath. He took a look in the mirror, then set to it. He started to root around the wound and tears came to his eyes. He stopped long enough to get his wallet out and slip it between his jaws. He was determined not to scare the little girl with any screams from the agony of what he was trying to do to himself.

24

Hector was dreaming of the war, his first more or less, down there in Mexico, chasing Pancho Villa. He was dreaming about the first time he was shot. That had happened the same night Hector lost his virginity.

This voice: "Wake up, Mister Hector! Please, wake up! You're scaring me!"

Hector opened his eyes. Shannon's face was in his. Her tiny fingers were pinching his right ear lobe. His ear hurt like hell, just as it was supposed to. It had brought him back around like her shakes hadn't, he guessed. He said thickly, "Good girl. You can stop squeezing now, honey. How long was I out?"

"I don't know how to tell time," Shannon said. "You screamed, then dropped these on the seat." She held up the bloodstained pliers and a bloody bullet.

Hector took the bullet from the little girl and looked it over. The slug seemed to be in one piece. "There are paper napkins in the glove compartment," he said. "Wipe your hands and then wipe off that tool, won't you, honey?"

He dropped the bullet into his shirt pocket along with the one he'd pulled from Meg's leg. He looked back over the seat. Meg was still breathing, thank God. There didn't seem to be too much fresh blood coming through the makeshift bandage bound 'round her thigh.

Hector didn't have the stomach to cauterize his own wound—it would almost certainly put him under again if he attempted it. As it was, he already felt nauseous. He couldn't bandage the arm himself, not with one hand. He handed Shannon the sleeve he'd torn from his shirt. "Do you know how to tie your shoes, honey?"

"Not very well."

"Time to start learning then," he said, trying to smile. "You're going to tie that around my arm, over where it's hurt." He pulled loose the knot from his necktie and then tugged the tie from around his neck. "We'll tie this over it, too. We'll make a game of it, to help you learn how."

Shannon gave him an uncertain smile. "A new game?"

"That's right," Hector said thickly. "Make bunny ears. The quick rabbit…"

"I did a good job?"

"A very good job," he said. "I'm very proud of you, Shannon. You've been a big help through this. You're a good nurse."

"I had to wake you up again."

Jesus, he hadn't even known he'd blacked out the second time.

"Thank you," he said. "You're very brave and very smart. I'm so proud of you, kid—you don't know how proud."

"Megan's been talking in her sleep," Shannon said.

"That's good—a good thing, really." Hector figured it was good in the sense that Meg was still in the game. He pointed at the pliers on the dash where Shannon had evidently placed them. "Do me a favor, honey. Take those things in there to that building and give them to that man in there behind the counter. Thank him, please. Can you do that for me, Shannon?"

"Sure." He watched her struggle with the door latch, then slide out and run head down through the whipping snow flurries.

While she did that Hector checked his face in the mirror. His eyes didn't look too good. They were bloodshot and it was hard to focus. He still felt dizzy. Nauseous, too. His arm had gone from numb to throbbing.

There was motor lodge just across the street. After Shannon slammed the car door he said, "Put on your lap-strap, honey. We're going to try and cross the street." God willing, he wouldn't get them killed making what should be a simple crossing.

It should be plenty easy enough to do. Yet in his present state?

Hector steered one-handed in front of the motor lodge's lobby. He had Shannon cover Meg's legs and all that blood on the seat with his overcoat, then leaned on his car's horn.

A surly young bellboy came out. Hector draped his sports jacket over his wounded arm to hide the damage. He rolled down the window with his right hand and said to the boy, "Can you have the clerk come out here and check us in? We've been on the road all night coming down from Canada. Just too tired to make the Indiana border. That's where we live. I don't want to wake my wife or leave my little girl alone. Really, I'd come in if I at all could, but it's been nearly thirty straight hours of driving in the snow. I'm plumb beat to the wide, sonny."

Hector's sorry and haggard looks must have convinced the kid he meant it about being exhausted. "I suppose we can do that," the kid said, seeming not at all sure.

He went in to talk to the clerk and Hector shucked out some bills from his roll.

Hector parked directly in front of their room and handed Shannon the key. "Can you go open the door to the room honey? Can you keep it open for me? I'm going to have to carry Meg inside."

"Sure I can."

"Good girl." Hector smiled: the kid was a brick.

"I hope Meg will be better soon," she said, looking worried now. "Tomorrow is Christmas."

"She'll be fine, I swear it," Hector said. "Go get that door open, honey. I'll bring Meg."

He waited until Shannon had the door open, then Hector climbed out of his Chevy, feeling very woozy. It was quite a struggle getting Meg up and over his good shoulder. He thought he'd black out a third time from the effort.

Weaving, Hector carried Meg in and laid her out on one of the room's two full-sized beds. Hector had a little movement back in the fingers of his left hand, but any attempts to move that arm hurt like hell.

Hector swayed there, seeing spots. He sat down quickly on the foot of the bed and got his head down between his knees, taking deep, slow breaths until he felt something close to steady again. When he thought he could make it, he limped over to the door to watch Shannon as she went out to close the rear door of his Chevy and lock it up.

Hector waited until his dizziness subsided, then, went back out, opened the trunk, and pulled a car cover from the trunk. With his one arm, he managed to get the Chevy under wraps, at least enough to hide the plates and distinguishing features of the new model car.

Hector then locked up the hotel room door and fumbled with the phone. He let the operator do all the work.

A police dispatcher answered. He asked her to find Jimmy Hanrahan.

It seemed to take forever for that request to be fulfilled. Hector cursed each passing click of the clock: he knew time was not on his side.

That blessed tenor: "You're alive, then, Hec?"

"Alive, yes. You too."

"I'm fine and about to blow this cursed place," Jimmy said. "Worthless cretins here have all they're getting from me."

"I need help, Jimmy. I badly need a doctor. Megan and me both."

Jimmy's tone shifted. "Oh, Christ. Where are you, Hec?"

Hector told him. He said, "I don't know what you can do, Jimmy. A real doctor is going to have to report these wounds. We're both shot. I've got the bullets out myself, but I think Meg may need a surgeon. Slug dug in close to an artery in her leg. My wound isn't closed yet. I'm bleeding like a son of a bitch."

"Christ," Jimmy said. "You hang in there Hec, damn ya, you reckless idgit. Let me worry about finding you help. Stay strong, brother. I'll be there in jig's time."

25

Hector heard Jimmy's voice through a kind of haze. "That seems to have it," he said. "And the woman?"

A silky voice—lyrical even—answered. "Oh, she'll be just dand-*dee*. Your friend did quite a respectable job, under the circumstances. He's much man, as the saying goes. Digging that bullet out of his own arm like that? Some very tough guy... Just like you, yes, James?"

"Just finish patching him up, freak," Jimmy said, all acid.

Hector opened his eyes. He mumbled, "I'm not dead yet?" His mouth was dry. The fingers of his left hand tingled.

"Not *yet*," Jimmy said. "You and Meg will be okay. We're just finishing up with you."

"And Shannon?"

"She's perfectly fine," Jimmy said. "The lassie let me in."

"Thanks, buddy," Hector said. "You're still the best in a tight." Jimmy waved a meaty paw in forget it fashion.

The other man said, "Don't thank him—thank me, you *bruiser*. Who's the doctor here, after all? James is just a meddlesome copper—a water-carrier for Mr. Headman Ness."

Hector looked over his physician, then swallowed hard. The guy was ungodly gangly: maybe stood six-five. Something effeminate there, despite all that size. And there was something very off-putting about the stranger. Hector hoped Jimmy knew what he was doing recruiting him to patch them up.

Their strange doctor smiled and winked. Something in the man's expression made Hector squirm. The man said, "The good news is that neither of you suffered artery or nerve damage. Isn't that lucky?"

"Lucky like aces over queens," Hector said, wary. "Thanks for coming in a pinch, Sawbones."

That last elicited a giggle from the doctor. Hector shivered.

"I'll write a script for some pain medication," the big stranger said. "Some penicillin, too. You should probably have a tetanus shot, as well. Bullets are filthy things, wouldn't you agree?"

"Yes." Hector frowned. Something about this giant had his radar fully up now.

"Had me one of those shots a few months back," Hector said. "There was a knife fight in a cantina in Old Juarez I got swept up in. Figure the dose from that shot is still doin' its job."

"Oh dear," the doctor said. "A *knife* fight?" He wiped his hands down with a hotel towel. "You seem perilously prone to these things, Mr. Lassiter. But yes, that shot should still take care of you now. Well, I'll just go and wash up now, righty-o James?"

Jimmy nodded, turning to face the bathroom door once the man closed it. The big man locked the door and they heard water running.

"Jesus, Jimmy," Hector said, "where'd you find that one?"

"Like you said, couldn't go to any *upstanding* sawbones," Jimmy said, frowning. "Not with those bullet wounds they'd phone in to the cops. So I had to improvise, and I do mean furiously, boyo."

"That guy really a doctor?"

"Sure, Hec. I mean, more or less." Hector noticed then that Jimmy was holding his gun at his side. Hector guessed Jimmy had had the forty-five out the whole time the man was tending to their wounds.

"Who the hell is that odd duck?"

"You really don't want to know," Jimmy said. "Trust me on that."

"Now I really *do* want to know," Hector said.

Jimmy wet his lips. He whispered, "He's the man Eliot, Pete and Arnold and I are here to visit. That's our Kingsbury Butcher suspect."

Hector's stomach rolled. He tasted bile. "Holy Jesus, Jim! The one from the madhouse?"

"I know, I know. Keep it low, Hec. I've got this thing contained. Just need to get him back to the Veterans Center before my three friends get there and learn what I've done. I'll drop him back there and beg off the planned interrogation. Get back here as quickly as I can. I'll want to move your lodging when I return." Jimmy paused then shrugged sheepishly. "Our friend in there was far too attentive regarding where we were going and how we got here."

That made Hector's skin freshly crawl.

The water shut off and the man came out, smiling. "Take it easy on that arm, Mr. Lassiter," he said. "It's going to be stiff for several weeks. No more knife fights for you!"

Hector said cagily, "Could I drive? Say in a day or two?" He was thinking more in terms of minutes.

"I suppose you could, though it'll smart like the dickens." Another strange smile. "You're lucky, sir. An inch to the left and you might have lost that arm. I might even have had to am-pu-*tate*." He winked at Jimmy. The doctor said, "That's a little private joke, isn't it, Jimbo?"

Once again, Hector swallowed hard. He said, "And my lady friend? What about her leg?"

The "doctor" looked at Jimmy and smiled again. "That'll hurt about like your arm will smart. No baths for her for a while. Not until it heals more. But she should be able to walk on a cane in a day or two. Of course, your rather hasty treatment is going to leave her scarred."

Jimmy said, "C'mon, Doc—time to travel, ya bloody degenerate pup, ya. Put out your paws, doc." The doctor sighed and extended his hands behind his back for Jimmy to apply the cuffs.

The doctor paused at the door. He was looking at Shannon. She was fussing with her doll and avoiding eye contact with the man.

Kids and dogs—they know, Hector thought.

The stranger said to Hector, "Now don't hesitate to call if you need anything else, Tex. I should maybe check back with you in the morning. I'd be so happy to do that. I can take a cab here. You know, save our dear friend Jimmy the trouble of driving me back?"

"You've done just plenty," Hector said. "Really. Just all that's needed. And we'll be long gone by then. *Long gone*, mister. *Truly*. Thanks heaps."

When they left Hector struggled to his feet and locked the door. Shannon said, "He's creepy."

"You said it," Hector said, looking for his Colt. "*Very* creepy, kid. C'mon, honey, let's see if we can't find you something happy on the radio to listen to. Maybe some Christmas show."

Jimmy returned an hour later. Hector said, "Your doctor friend is beyond insane. Palpably nuts. You should just shoot the sick son of a bitch and save the courts the cost."

"I've thought hard about doing just that thing," Jimmy said. "May yet come to that. Speaking of the mad bastard, I say we vacate this hovel without informing the front desk of your departure. I'd hate for this place to be occupied by some hapless traveler in the next day or two in case that bastard *does* attempt to follow-up with you three."

"Yeah, that'd louse up someone's Merry Christmas, but good." Shannon was sleeping on the bed with Meg, whom Hector thought was also asleep. But no: Meg said, "Where's Kate?"

Jimmy just looked at Hector and then at Meg.

Hector answered. "Katy didn't make it through, sorry to say."

Meg winced. She said rawly, "Oh, *God.*"

"A tragedy," Jimmy said. Hector couldn't read his friend's suddenly flat tone.

Something there? Or maybe *not.*

Meg said, "Where are we now?"

"Hotel room not far from the police headquarters," Jimmy said.

Hector said, "You and I were both shot, honey. The bullets are out and we're going to be okay, though not exactly fit for a few days. Still, we need to move our rooms and really ought to do that *now*, if you're up to it."

"I'll make it," Meg said. "Just do whatever you two think we need to. I'll cope." She hesitated, then said, "Shannon, she didn't see Katy—?"

"No," Hector said, "she didn't."

"Thank God for that at least," Meg said.

Jimmy said, "Indeed. Either of you two need pain medication? I filled your prescriptions." He held up a pair of paper envelopes.

"I'm okay I think," Meg said. "But let's make this move fast, if we can. And I need a different favor from you James, and quite soon, if you'll do it."

That neutral tone in his voice: Hector couldn't quite figure what was up with Jimmy. The Irish cop said, "Ask it of me, Miss Dalton." A beat, "And then we'll see."

Meg nodded at Shannon, asleep in her arms. "Stores will close soon. I'd like her to have some kind of a Christmas."

That softened him: Jimmy nodded and held up a big hand. "Say no more, lass, I'm surely your man."

Shannon was still asleep when Jimmy placed her on the back seat next to Meg. He'd wiped down the interior of the Chevy—not a spot of blood to be seen.

Hector said softly, "Regarding Katy's fate, Shannon doesn't know, Meg. She still expects Katy to turn up eventually."

"I'll tell her when the time is right," Meg said. "I need to be the one to tell her. I'll break the news about Katy. Don't know how yet, or when, but I'll see to it. It should be me."

Jimmy said, "I agree you should be the one. For certain, that's true."

26

Hector stood smoking outside their new motel room with Jimmy in a wet-falling snow. "We should get a move on," Jimmy said. "Stores will close soon."

Hector said, "You have any idea what to buy that kid?"

"Miss Dalton made me a list," Jimmy said, passing Hector a slip of paper. Hector looked it over.

"Something is missing," Hector said. He took a pencil from his pocket and put the list down on the window ledge of the room's single window and scrawled down a few extra items.

He passed it to Jimmy along with some money. Jimmy looked over the addendum and smiled. "You goddamn sentimentalist, you. You sure about this, Hec? I mean, your car...?"

"That's why the box and all those newspapers."

Jimmy nodded. "And you, Hec? What do you do, now?"

"My own Christmas shopping," Hector said. "Headed across the street to that lot there to buy myself a tree. Then I'm going to hit that five-and-dime yonder and get me some decorations and lights for that tree. Then I want to make a stop at that jewelry store yonder. It's Christmas for Meg, too, after all."

Jimmy said, "Seems to me, Meg's gotten her gift."

The author shrugged. "Circumstances kind of cast a pall over that present, pal, yeah?"

"Yes. One would think." Jimmy folded up the Christmas list and shoved it in his pocket. He cast down the stub of his cigarette and it sizzled in the snow. "But all that shopping is the near-term thing," he said. "I was asking you your plans in terms of the longer game. At our age, what could be a happier accident than the prospect of the instant family? Still, that child's going to need loving when she learns what's happened to Katherine, isn't she?"

Hector lightly ran his right hand over his wounded left arm. "Let's let Shannon have her Christmas, eh, Jimmy? Let's get some distance from this holiday before we tell her about Katy. Would be a shame for her to think of every Christmas as some memorial to her supposed mother."

Jimmy thought about that a while then said, "Upon that we're agreed, Hector. Sound thought coming from a man thinking through the fog of high-tone pain pills. So be it, brother."

Hector ducked back inside and shook the snow from his coat with his good arm. He found Meg limping around the room. He said, "Meg, please don't push it. You don't want to make yourself worse or tear open any stitches."

She smiled, shaking her head. "Who dragged a five-foot Christmas tree across the street with one arm, then manhandled it into our hotel room?" She coiled the lights around the tree another turn and then limped back from it a bit to survey her work. "What will the hotel manager think when he comes across this?"

"He'll smile and think it's Christmas," Hector said. "It's whimsical. We should probably plan on leaving day after tomorrow. By then I should have enough range of motion to steer the damned car. Be good to be moving in that holiday migration pack, too. You know, anonymous and in the crawling thick. Just one more in a sea of cars of families headed home to somewhere."

"We haven't even celebrated Christmas yet," Meg said. "Do we have to talk about it being over already?"

"Sorry," Hector said. He handed her the box. "Merry Christmas, Megan."

She smiled and wrinkled her brow. "I don't have anything for you."

"Sing me a song tonight and we'll call it better than even."

"Can I open it now?"

"I insist."

She did that. "It's beautiful jewlery. Put it on me."

Hector pointed at his left arm. "Can't, not with this bum wing."

"Sorry, of course. Steady me?"

Hector held her around the waist with his good arm as she leaned her cane against the foot of the bed and used both hands to fasten the antique necklace around her throat. "How's it look?"

"Perfect," he said. They kissed. He heard the bedsprings squeak. Shannon was shifting on the bed in her sleep. "We probably should wake her soon. She'll be up all night otherwise."

"Probably." Meg looked up at him with sleepy eyes. "She insisted she was going to nap to improve her odds of being up when Santa comes."

"Calculating little thing, isn't she? That trait come from your side?"

Meg suddenly looked very sad. "Thank you for all this, Hector. I mean saving us, of course, but I also mean these things, the tree and the lights. And having a friend like Jimmy who'll go shop for dresses and dolls. God only knows what he'll come back with."

"He'll find some comely young thing to help him make the right choices. Then he'll end up spending Christmas Eve with her. Old Jimmy's never drawn an uncalculated breath."

"I don't know about that," Meg said. "James doesn't strike me as a ladies' man. I think you're confusing him for yourself."

"Perhaps," I said. "He does run a little more courtly than most do these days."

Megan said, "Despite what I said about not ruining our holiday before we have it, this uncertainty is eating at me. What are we to do next? Where do we go? What becomes of Shannon… What becomes of me?"

Hector looked at the little girl asleep there, smiling at something in her dreams as she clutched harder at her doll. "What about your family back in Missouri, Meg? They still have that farm?"

"Lost to bill collectors before Daddy was even buried," Meg said. She limped back to the tree, leaning on her cane, then reached up over her head to adjust the star at the top of the tree. "This look straight?"

"Perfect," Hector lied.

"My mother still lives in the town on a smaller place my brothers help pay for."

"Think Vito would remember about your Missouri roots?"

"Given that the really important stuff is slipping through the cracks of his brain, probably not," Meg said. "But I don't want to live in Missouri. I don't want Shannon to settle there. There's no *there* there. Not in that little town."

"You remind me of Gertrude Stein with alliterative assertions like that."

"Gertrude who?"

Jesus, but Meg was such a kid in some ways. Those age digs of Jimmy's were still eating at Hector. But Jimmy was right: the cultural gap between Hector and his younger women just seemed to get deeper and wider with each passing year.

He wrapped his good arm around Meg's shoulders, appraising the tree. "I'm not thinking of condemning you to a life in the sticks, darlin'. Just thought it would be a safe place to take stock for a few days. Maybe be a good place to plot better, longer-term strategies. And, frankly, you and Shannon are not going to live legally as mother and daughter in this country. Not for a long time, anyway. The system is stacked against you on that front. I think we're talking about you two settling in Canada or maybe even down my way. We could set you up in Juarez. You'd still just be a short drive away from me there."

She said, "Not ready to move to Mexico to live with us?" Hector checked her expression: it was matter-of-fact. He sensed she meant it. He wasn't at all sure about any long-term prospects with this one.

"I might be persuaded to cross the river now and then," he said. He kissed the soft down on the back of her neck.

"Changed my mind again," Meg said. "Don't think I can think about it anymore tonight."

"Me either. It's Christmas Eve. Wish we had some spiked eggnog. A fireplace, too."

Meg looked sad again. "Maybe next year, when our lives aren't so... well, so bizarre? Not so bloody."

"Looks like we're ready to hang the bulbs," Hector said. "Time to wake this little girl up, don't you think? Let her help decorate?"

Jimmy and Hector were in front of the hotel again, their asses parked on the trunk of the car this time, burning through cigarettes and casing angles.

"Radio reports are breathless, Hector," Jimmy said. "Seems some things were leaked to the press, probably by Gibson or one of his minions. They've cast poor luckless Katy as some sort of corn-fed Joan of Arc. And Shannon? She's become some kind of latter-day Lindbergh baby, thanks to the goddamn reporters. The whole world will be keeping an eye peeled for her. I don't envy those two, or you, the road ahead."

Jimmy blew a couple of smoke rings and shook his head. "And all that press attention puts bloody Vito in the unlikely position of simultaneously trying to portray Kate as misguided or insane while putting himself across as a doting husband and father. He's hired a bounty hunter, Hector. One from down your way. Some lad out of Arizona who is one-half Pima Indian. Redskin paints himself as an über old-school tracker. Part Sam Spade and part Tonto, maybe. Vito's also hired some offshoot of the Pinkertons to find Meg and Shannon. I mean, now that the assumption is they're out of Ohio."

Hector shook his head. The Buckeye State, bless it, had presciently banned the Pinkertons years ago, rightly reasoning they constituted a threat to democracy. A forward-looking state, Ohio… in some respects, anyway.

"Well, that's all wonderful news," Hector said. "Let's inventory our enemies: we've got corrupt federal agents and honest ones, bent cops, honest cops, potentially every mobster in North America, a bounty hunter, cocksucker private investigators and now every mouth-breathing yokel with a radio, one of those televisions or just some coins for a damned newspaper. Did I miss anyone, buddy?"

"That homicidal doctor in the Dayton Veterans Administration Center," Jimmy said.

"Another reason to get ourselves out of this city," Hector said. "We're up against it for certain."

Jimmy hesitated, then said, "This 'we' thing...? I'm with you, Hector, all the way to hell and back again, you *know* that. But you and me, Hec, we're going to have to put some space between us for a time, I think. I've used up my vacation and have some casework I need to do before year's end. I can hook up with you in a few days when the calendar year turns and my allowable time-off freshens. But in the interim, we need to keep distance, I'm afraid. I'm clearly being followed and all my phones are tapped now. Maybe tapped several times over. I shook tonight's tails, but it's only a matter of time, no matter how careful I am. Too many resources are being fielded to find you three, and I'll simply not see that aim achieved through me. For now, I truly think you're safer without than with me."

"I hear you, Jimmy. And there's a real advantage in you still being in circulation out this way, still in touch with various of these parties."

"And for the moment I *am* being courted on all sides," Jimmy said. "It's not just Vito and his guinea hoodlums who want that woman in there and whatever papers of Katy's she might have access to. It's fecking Kefauver's stooge, too. That little Alamo on the police station steps upped the ante many times over for Gibson. He has to get something from all this now."

"So this is what it takes to make that attorney care?" Hector looked up at the sky. "Jesus Christ."

Jimmy said, "To that end, have you run across whatever it was Katy had of her husband's ledger?"

"No, but I haven't exactly looked all that hard." Hector felt around his pockets and found his car keys. He passed them to Jimmy. "Kate's stuff is still in the trunk. Let's do that now."

Jimmy the cop handled the search—patting down jackets and skirts and frilly, silky underthings. He got out a penknife and cut out the linings of Katy's luggage even though he had helped Kate pick out the suitcases just a short time before she was killed—that timing almost certainly precluding them containing anything hidden in that way.

Nothing.

They sorted through Shannon's smaller suitcase, as well.

Fruitless.

"Well, damn it anyway," Jimmy said when they were clearly finished. "What a sorry quandary we're in."

"What's Eliot's take on all this, Jimmy? Or do you know?"

Jimmy closed Shannon's suitcase and slammed shut the car's trunk. "I suspect Eliot saw all this as a ticket back to a badge of some kind. In some respects, suddenly, there's some tension there between Eliot and me. He's pissed I let you run from the scene of the shooting."

"I'm sorry."

"It's not important," Jimmy said. "That said, I don't rule out Eliot putting some kind of tail on me. Maybe Sagalyn or one of his other Cleveland stalwarts. And that's another reason you and I should stay apart for a time. Maybe I can plant some false trails for you. At least draw fire."

"I could call your tapped lines and let some things slip," Hector said. "We'll send those Feds and mobsters and pseudo-Pinkertons on wild goose chases to Frostproof, Florida, or Missoula, Montana."

"I like it," Jimmy said. "It's a salutary notion. Before we part ways, Hec, I'll write a schedule for you. These will be favored watering holes and the nights and times I'll be in those joints. We'll save those conversations for the *real* information exchanges."

"Brilliant," Hector said.

"Do you have some endgame in mind, Hec?"

"*Nada.* Meg's pressing for the same kinds of answers. You know we've been winging it up to now and I'm flush out of inspirations."

"Not even a notion?"

"Not beyond hitting the road and keeping those two girls far from inquiring eyes. I'll grope along the county two-lanes and avoid all the toll roads. Wait for some bolt from the blue, maybe. Short-term, I'm headed to Missouri. Meg has family there who may put us up a few days while I cogitate some more."

"Won't Vito know about the family homestead?"

"Meg thinks not. Says he's too foggy. More I hear, more I wonder how that bastard's holding on to power. He sounds pretty far gone between the ears."

"I'd like to take his measure in person," Jimmy said. "Just wish I had some pretense to roust him."

"I've been thinking about calling him up myself," Hector said. "Have us a talk, man-to-man. But not tonight. It's Christmas Eve, buddy. Merry Christmas, Jimmy."

"Happy Christmas to you, Hector. Are we opening presents tonight, or in the morning?"

"Tonight. Shannon napped so long, Meg couldn't wait and put your purchases under the tree. Meg convinced Shannon that Santa came early."

"Good," Jimmy said. "I won't miss anything then."

"You have my other gift?"

"In my room," Jimmy said. "I'm holding off, just as you asked."

"*Your* room?"

"I checked in, two doors down. I told you, it's too risky to be followed back here again. So I'm with you through morning. And, I have a little surprise of my own for the wee one."

"Good. Only risk I see to us then is our cars being spotted in the lot here."

"Give me your car keys," Jimmy said. "I'll unload the luggage and move your car to where I have my Chevy parked."

Hector looked around the lot. "Where are you parked?"

"Rental's only someplace patently brilliant," Jimmy said. "They're closed for the holidays, so there's no risk of being towed."

"Towed from where?"

"The Chevrolet dealership around the corner." Jimmy smiled. "I'm the kind of cop, I'm *always* trying to find ways to screw my own. It's often useful to think like your potential quarry. So let's see those maybe dirty, but certainly less-inspired-than-me badge-carrying officers find our Chevys *there*."

Hector thought then he might have hugged Jimmy if he had two working arms.

27

Shannon made short work of the packages. Wrapping paper and discarded boxes littered their hotel room. When she was done opening all of her presents, and looking a little glum, Meg said, "What the matter, honey?"

Hector waited for her to say, "I miss Mommy." Or something like that. The moment came in a wrenching blur.

Fortunately, it was a bad call on his part, which made some part of Hector feel sorry for Kate. By now the woman was cold and naked on some pitched tray, likely. Probably being pumped full of formaldehyde and powdered over.

Shannon said, "I didn't get a puppy."

Meg said, "Oh, *honey*... maybe Santa's waiting until we're settled in our new home. Maybe when we're not in cars or hotels all the time."

Hector started to say something, then Jimmy said to Shannon, "Easy there, colleen. Father Christmas—er, *Santa*—came early. Maybe he'll come yet again." Shannon shook her head sadly as Jimmy slipped out the door.

Twenty minutes later there was a knock at the door. Hector was reaching for his Colt when he heard the tenor-inflected,

"*Ho-ho-ho.*" Then, "Open the door for an old elf, won't you, Hector?"

Jimmy had rented himself an honest-to-God Santa suit, plush crimson velvet and a big white beard. Hector said softly to him, "Now who's sentimental?"

Jimmy ignored him and bee-lined for wide-eyed Shannon. Jimmy pulled the little white puppy from behind his back and handed the dog to Shannon.

Megan's eyes were glistening.

It was easy enough for Hector to read her lips:

Thank you so *much.*

About three in the morning, a tiny hand tugged on Hector's wrist. It was Shannon.

Hector said, "What's the matter, honey? What's wrong? Doggie keeping you up?"

"She's asleep," Shannon said. "It's my dolly. She's crunchy. She keeps waking me up."

Oh, for God's sake. "Crunchy?" *What the hell?*

"Yes," Shannon said. "She's making strange noises when I hug her. She's been doing it for a few days. I can't sleep with her doing it now."

"Do you have to sleep with her?"

"Yes."

"Then I guess I'll take a look," Hector said.

He took the doll from Shannon and padded into the bathroom. He closed the door, turned on the light and prodded at the doll. It *was* making strange noises—sounded like crumpled paper. He went back out to the nightstand and shook Megan awake. "Do you have sewing kit, Meg?"

"Yes. Why?"

"Come in the bathroom with me for a moment. I think I'm onto something."

Sitting on the closed toilet lid, Hector undressed the doll, then slit the seam up its back. He thrust his good hand inside the doll.

He said, "Son of a bitch."

The doll's torso was filled with ledger sheets: blood money notes scrawled in closely cramped hand. Pay offs, accounts receivable—all of Vito Scartelli's nefarious doings laid bare.

Hector said, "I'm going to put on some pants and take these down to Jimmy. You best take that tissue box and stuff Shannon's doll and sew her back up. Maybe these slips of paper can yet buy us a way out of this mess."

28

Two nights later, Meg finally broke the news to Shannon about Kate's death.

Hector stuck around a few minutes, then felt like an intruder on the little girl's muted grief. He wandered outside, lit a cigarette, then walked to a phone booth to make the latest of his calls to Jimmy's stipulated watering holes.

The news wasn't good: the attorney, Gibson, happily accepted the ledger sheets from Jimmy but insisted Meg be brought into to establish "provenance" for the damning account records. "I really don't see what good these records do me without a witness to tie them directly to Scartelli," Gibson had told Jimmy.

Hector cursed and gripped the phone harder and said, "Jimmy, at least make Gibson acknowledge publicly he now has the records. That admission alone might take heat off Meg and me."

"I already tried that," Jimmy said. Hector could hear barroom sounds on Jimmy's end—glasses tinkling and a jukebox in the background.

Hector suddenly wished he was there.

Jimmy said, "He wasn't going for it, Hector. Gibson said he doesn't want to 'raise public expectations' on himself. Cowardly politician. So some journalists have been hounding me for interviews. I'm going to roll the dice, Hector. I'll tell the newspaper boys about the papers I've turned over to Gibson. Well, the ones I gave him, anyway. As a precaution, I held out some of the most damning ledger sheets. Maybe I'll offer those to Kefauver or Hoover directly, if we can reach them. Put some heat on the attorney that way. I'll maybe get myself a reprimand, but screw that—it'll be goddamn worth it. And, like you say, it might take a wee bit of edge out of Vito's manhunt for you. But only a wee bit. Remember, you have his daughter. Publicly, Vito has to look like he's pulling out all stops to retrieve her. Failing doing that, he looks less the concerned father."

"We'll talk again tomorrow night," Hector said. "Oh, by the way, Meg broke the news to Shannon tonight."

The neutral tone returned: "And how did that go?"

"About like you'd expect. I left them in the room, sobbing together."

Jimmy waited long enough before speaking to prompt Hector to ask, "Jim, you still there?"

"Still here," Jimmy said. "It's a hard and terrible thing, Hector. What else is there to say?" Something in his tone again, something Hector would yet be a time learning. Jimmy said, "So what now for you, Hec?"

"Car's packed. Just need to go fetch the girls and hit the road. I swiped some dealers' plates from that car lot where you hid our Chevys. I'll rotate those every few days, try and buy myself some time that way. We'll drive by night the first twenty-four hours or so. Try and get ourselves over into Missouri."

"Sounds like a plan," Jimmy said. "Listen, Hec, I've done a little research on this bounty hunter that Vito's put on your trail. He's a truly scary boyo. No photos known to exist of him, so I don't even know what to tell you in terms of a description. But his success in finding folks, even smart and well-hidden folks? It sounds downright preternatural. Über spooky."

More good news. Hector said, "This fella have a handle?"

"Tomás Hawk," Jimmy said, "though he has another moniker he's hung on himself he seems to prefer. Almost funny in its way."

Hector said, "Let me guess: Tomahawk."

"On the nose."

"For Christ's sake," Hector said. "It just keeps getting better. What nullifies this bounty hunter, Jimmy? What are the rules governing extradition by bounty hunters, north and south of the borders?"

"I'll have to make some inquiries along those lines and subtly, of course," Jimmy said. "A certain percentage of the knowledgeable are going to assume if I put that kind of question to them that you're going to run north or south. Canada or Mexico."

"And they'd be right."

"Well, good luck, Hector. It's going to be a rocky road for you, I fear. I'll try and reconnect soon as possible along the bloody path. You just try and make it through to 1951, won't you?"

"That's the name of the game now, Jimmy."

Hector hung up the phone. He dithered a few moments. He stoked up some anger and edged himself over into recklessness. Then he dropped coins.

He got passed around a bit before he was put through to the man.

The novelist said, "Hey Vito. I'm that hombre you're hunting. Hector Lassiter."

There was some bluster and then Hector heard papers rustling. Vito Scartelli said, "You're that man… that… *Lassiter?*"
Hector could tell the man was reading it off some slip of paper.

"That's right, you senile son of a bitch," Hector said. "One
chance. You drop this thing and call off your jackals and I'll
let you stay in this world. Otherwise, I promise I'm going to
kill *you* in the slowest and bloodiest way I can devise. That's a
naked fact."

A torrent of profanities ensued. The tirade ended on,
"You're in *no* position to issue threats, Lasher."

"*Lassiter*. And sure I am," he said. "You keep up this chase
and I swear you won't see Valentine's Day from the right side
of the sod. I'll come back to Ohio and I'll find you. I will
see you dead. That's a solemn promise. You push on down
this road and I'm afraid you've gone and bought yourself an
authentic vendetta, Vito."

Vito said, "I'll see a bullet between your eyes before you
ever get a shot at me. You're dead, Lattimer! That cunt Megan
is fucking dead! Shannon is—" he stopped himself there.

Hector drew a deep breath, then said, "*When* I come for
you, Vito—and now I *am* coming, I'm determined on that
point now, regardless of anything else—I'm *not* going to shoot
you to death. It's going to be something infinitely worse than
that. It's going to be slow and painful beyond your worst imag-
inings, but not beyond *mine*, and I've got *a lot* of imagination,
hombre. Hell, I've got more imagination than anyone you've
ever met in your sorry excuse for a life. And I have a very *dark*
imagination, as you're going to learn at bloody length. This a
solemn promise from me to you, old pal. If you have any sense
left in your diseased brain, put a gun in your mouth tonight
and pull that trigger. You're going to hate what happens next
between us. That's a pledge that will be honored."

Hector racked the receiver. His good hand was shaking.

Brave words. Hector sorely hoped there was something backing them up.

Sometimes your muse failed you; sometimes even your *darkest* muse did that.

29

They crossed in darkness into the state of Indiana. About half the expanse of Illinois was driven in dusk, too.

The girls slept in the back of his Chevy, curled up in one another's arms under blankets. Meg kept muttering in her sleep, seemingly always in the throes of some bad dream.

Hector kept himself awake with country radio and black coffee from filling stations stopped at along the way. He sipped the bitter brew, tapping time on the steering wheel to Gene Autry's "Rudolph the Red-Nosed Reindeer." Gene gave way to Hank Snow's, "I'm Movin' On":

"It's all over now…"

A few miles short of the Missouri border Hector knew he'd pushed himself too far. He found a motor court and signed in with a sleepy-eyed young clerk who had a bad case of acne.

He would have liked to carry Shannon in rather than wake her up, but his left arm wasn't there yet. So he walked the groggy little girl into the room and led her to a bed. He helped Shannon off with her shoes and pulled the covers over her, too tired even to help her put on a nightgown.

Meg leaned hard on him as they made their way into the room; her limp was pronounced. She looked at the two beds, then said, "Which one should I fall into?" Meg smiled tiredly. "Or would we sleep right away?"

"Your choice of beds," Hector said. "As to the other, 'tween my left arm and your right leg, it's going to be a trial for a while. And even if we *could* get frisky, we can't do it with that kid just feet away."

"Then I'll sleep with Shannon tonight," she said. "She's woken up the past two nights with bad dreams. Crying for Katy. Did you know?"

"Must have slept through it," Hector said. "It's a terrible thing to be a young child and lose a parent like that. Just thank God there was nothing either of us could do to change that sorry outcome."

Meg bit her lip and said carefully, "You almost sound like you speak from experience. About losing a parent, I mean."

Hector shrugged, struggling to get his coats off. "Had me a time too, about that same age."

"Here," Meg said softly, limping over to him. "Let me help." She draped his sports coat over the back of a chair, then folded his overcoat and placed it over the back of the same chair. "Where are we, by the way?"

"Just a few miles from the Missouri border," he said.

"Which side?"

"Still in Illinois."

"Then I'll try and savor this night," she said. Solemn eyes. "I do *so* loathe Missouri."

If Hector had known then what he would come to know later about the bounty hunter Tomás Hawk, he might have guzzled black coffee and popped amphetamines—spurring himself south and over the border into a non-stop drive for southern Mexico.

But he didn't know any of that yet, so they tarried there along that other border.

Shannon sat playing on the floor with her female puppy that she still insisted upon calling Hector.

From time to time, the little girl would put questions to the writer about death and what happens after. Hector told her all the things others believed and seemed to draw comfort from. He painted heaven as some big floating party-cum-reunion. Though he thought he knew better then, some part of Hector hoped it somehow true. Hell, there were plenty he'd dearly love to see again.

When Shannon finally fell asleep, the puppy curled in its box on the floor by her side, Hector coached Meg for the phone call she was to place to her mother.

"Keep it short," Hector said. "Don't say anything that'll give away our location. If pressed, make it sound like we're in the Dakotas or the like. Or maybe as though we're making a run for Canada. See if your mother sounds natural, or if she maybe doesn't sound coerced. See if she sounds friendly and warm and therefore maybe receptive to putting us up for a few days when we surprise her."

Hector's arm was improving and Meg was getting around better on her cane. He decided to risk spending one more night at the motor court to catch up on sleep and give their wounds that extra day to heal. He ordered in some pizza and soda pops for dinner. After their meal, while Meg gave Shannon a bath, he called Jimmy at the next of his favored bars.

"I suppose he tells me all this to scare me," Jimmy said, jumping right in.

Hector said, "He *who*? And *he* tells you what to scare you?"

"I mean Gibson, Hec. I suppose he hopes to scare me into scaring you into turning yourself and the woman in."

"What's Gibson saying to terrify us, Jimmy?"

"The good attorney claims J. Edgar has shared transcripts of phone conversations taped of Great Lakes region mob-types regarding you and Meg. The boyos seem to think see-ing Meg and the tyke dead is the most expedient of their options."

Hector snorted. "*Options*? They have *options*? What's the alternative to killing the girls?"

"That would be the prospect of killing Vito themselves," Jimmy said. "But Gibson discounts that as a serious consider-ation. He swears we'll never see it exercised."

"Why not?"

"Gibson's assessment is the boyos don't grasp the extent of Vito's mental degeneration. At least as it's claimed to be wors-ening by Meg and by poor Kate. Seems these lads also have arcane rules, folkways and tropes within their bloody little boys club. They carried all these quaint customs over from the Old Country that Gibson says precludes them ever seriously attempting some kind of *coup d'état*."

"All of that's interesting to a mob aficionado maybe," Hec-tor said, "but frankly there's not much new in there to terrify me. No bracing revelations buddy."

"Perhaps not, viewed in a certain light," Jimmy said. "But before it was just Vito throwing resources at getting you. Now the *other* boys, if this taped chatter is to be believed, have thrown in after you, too."

"Grand, as you would say," Hector said. Looking for the silver lining, he said, "Tell me, Jimbo, the mob have much presence out here in the sticks? I mean, I always thought of them as more of an east coast and west coast, urban phenomenon."

"I don't think they're as organized out there in the heartland, no," Jimmy said. "That's why they have these Pinkerton cast-offs, I suppose. Those losers know no boundaries, near as I can tell. Maybe they're actually worse than the real Pinkertons, if you can conceive of that. I mean that in every sense, Hector. These are feckin' thugs of the first water."

"Don't need to warn me—those thugs' reputation is too well-known to me. Too bad there's not some labor strike they could focus on instead of us, the bloody sons of bitches."

Jimmy said, "That's one good thing if you'd have been able to make a stand here in the Buckeye State. Ohio passed a law years ago banning the Pickertons from operation here. Seems some long-dead Ohio politicians feared the Pinkertons could conceivably become their own standing army. They are a near legion, after all."

"I had heard that, and you're still not helping my morale," Hector said.

"And then there's the bounty hunter," Jimmy persisted.

"You have any more on him that might be useful?"

"Afraid not, Hec. Man's a cipher. Part of his mystique is being a blank, I suppose. It's something he cultivates. He plays it very mysterious."

Hector grunted, said, "Any *good* news?"

"It's the twenty-eighth of December," Jimmy said. "A Thursday. I don't work weekends. Get yourself through tomorrow night and I can see about getting back with you around New Year's Eve—Sunday night. I've already put in for vacation starting Tuesday the second."

"Really sure you want to buy a ticket back into this mess?"

"Of course," Jimmy said. "And it's an investment in my quality of life back here. Hell, must be some reward for toppling the Buckeye don in terms of a cleaner Cleveland for us cops."

"Maybe," Hector said. "But I suspect the Mafia, like nature, abhors a vacuum."

"Perhaps. But God willing, maybe the next boyo will have both oars in the water."

"Well, I'd surely love to have you back here at my side, Jimmy."

"We'll talk again tomorrow night. Stay alive, Hec."

"I always seem to manage at least that," Hector said. "That's me—a survivor, often despite myself."

"So don't going changing your ways this late in life."

Jimmy broke the connection. Hector was about to hang up when he heard a second click on the line.

He cursed and racked the receiver.

30

Megan's mother lived in a careworn farmhouse far from any main roads.

Fact was, they had to follow such a stubborn tangle of unnamed, twisting, branching dirt and gravel paths Hector doubted he could find his way back to a main road with a compass and a full tank of gas.

He was consequently heartened any would-be pursuers would be at least equally flummoxed if they came looking for them.

Meg said, "Sadly, this is almost nicer than the house I grew up in. Cows... sheep and some crops. That's what makes mother's living." Meg said it with some disdain.

Shannon, whom Hector sensed had never been outside the city, sat stroking her puppy, looking around with eager eyes. She smiled and said, "Hector is going to love this place."

A lone tallish woman stepped out onto the porch, pulling a hand-knitted shawl closer around her shoulders as they rolled to a stop in front of the old weather-washed white clapboard house.

Meg rolled down the window and called out to the woman. Meg's mother stepped down from the porch and leaned into the window, one hand on the door of Hector's Chevy. The woman kept her nails very short. Hers were strong, working hands.

She leaned in and kissed Meg on the cheek. The woman said to her pretty daughter, "Just look at you—dressed all sophisticated and the like. Like a cinema star, aren't you?"

"I don't know about that," Meg said, clearly uncomfortable.

"I thought you might be coming," Meg's mother said. "We don't have the television of course, but we've got the radio now." She pointed to an aluminum antenna that towered over the house. "And we have *that* radio, too—a ham rig your brother put in. You can talk across three states some nights with that monstrosity if the wind is running right."

The woman looked enough like Meg that Hector could have picked her out as such in a crowd. Still pretty. Her hair was white-blond like Meg's but shot through with a few stray strands of silver. Her nose and cheeks were freckled from the sun. She had laugh lines Hector liked. And she carried her Missouri accent unselfconsciously.

Where her daughter was dewy and lissome, the mother was attractive in an earthy, charismatic way. Some real presence there. Maybe that was all born of self-reliance and a kind of realist's bravado. Something else, too, something that burned brightly inside.

Either way, Meg's mother was surely attractive. And she wasn't at all what Hector expected.

Meg's mother said to him, "You can unload the car here, mister. There's a barn out back. You best hide your ride in there. There are a few other old cars already stashed inside. Park amongst those and pull a tarp off one of the junkers. Do please cover up that hi-tone car of yours. Neighbors will have seen you drive in and will surely have taken notice of such a car. Afraid some of them might even talk to those who may come looking for you."

Hector closed up the doors to the barn, struggling with his bum arm against a stiff wind that tore at the rickety door. He got a splinter in his good hand for his trouble.

Snow flurries were beginning to kick up. The sky was dark gray and the cloud ceiling pressing low to the ground, increasingly ominous looking. Hector wandered across the wind-combed field, that wind whipping at his graying brown hair and making his eyes tear up. He stepped up onto the porch and stomped snow from his boots then let myself in. He secured the screen door with a catch-and-eye hook and locked the storm door. He had to force the latter closed against the gusting press of that wicked wind. It was some nasty front shearing down from Canada across the Plains.

"Storm's coming hard, wouldn't you say," Meg's mother said behind him.

Hector smiled. "Which radio said that?"

"I said it," the elder woman said.

"I just felt it," he said. Holding out his working hand, he said, "I'm Hector Lassiter."

The woman shook his hand once in a downward jerk. She had a good grip, but her hands were rough and callused. "Hallie Dalton. Thank you for all you've done to protect my daughter and grandchild. They're cleaning up, by the way." He winced as she pressed at the splinter in his hand.

Hallie frowned at the blood on her palm and turned his hand over to inspect it. She said, "Let me see to that." She shook her head. "Gee, that's in pretty deep. Must smart like crazy."

His still gripped by her hand, Hector said, "How much do you know about what's been going on?"

"I expect I know all of it, now," Hallie said. "Including the fact you haven't known Meg for long at all. Not long enough to be a party to the mess she's made of her life. That makes you more the hero in my eyes."

Hallie took his good arm and led him over to a nook in the wall above an upright piano. On the shelves were a few knick-knacks, some pieces of antique glass and a few well-read books. He saw two paperbacks with his name on the creased spines. "I don't have much use for the motion pictures, and there aren't many opportunities around these parts if they did interest me, but I do like to read," Hallie said. "You write very good books. You write about people with real urges and feet of clay. People I can care about, who frustrate me, yet who I believe in."

Just like that, Hector wished she could be one of his critics. She said, "Have you written more books than those two?"

"A few," he said, lowballing. "I'll see a box of them is sent you when all this is done."

"No, I couldn't pay for them."

"My gift to you, for putting me up."

"You're here with Megan. No payment needed."

"Call the books a belated Christmas present, then. A simple gesture."

"I surely hope some of your good rubs off on my daughter," Hallie said, smiling. He liked her smile. "Now let's see to that hand before it infects or festers," she said.

He bit his lip through the burn as Hallie spread some Merthiolate over the place where the surprisingly long, thick splinter had resided, then secured a bandage over the wound. She patted the back of his hand and said, "All set."

"Thanks a million." The sound of water splashing in the bath.

Studying his face, she said, "As you've no doubt gathered by now, Megan could use more sand. And solid grounding." It was pretty clear from her expression Hallie Dalton was sizing Hector up, calculating how much of either quality he might provide her daughter by example.

Hector just shook his head and said, "I may not be the best candidate for all that. I mean, you've read some of my books. I'd like to say my imagination was that big, but…"

Hallie waved a hand. "Please. You're capable and intrepid. A headstrong rambler. I can tell that already. A maverick and a rover, like you write about in your books. Yet you're the kind that doesn't just let the gale of the world push him around. You go where you want. Am I right?"

Refute that? How could he dare? He smiled and said, "Right. That's me all over."

Meg and Shannon were bedding down in a guestroom together. Hallie had hauled out some old footlocker full of Megan's childhood books and dolls for her granddaughter's amusement. Meg was presently reading fairytales to Shannon.

Hallie and Hector sat at the kitchen table sipping coffee and playing 500-rum.

"Megan was going to be a singer," Hallie said. "Even as the littlest thing, at four or five, she insisted that was what she was going to do with her life. And Meg has the voice and the looks, obviously. Reason why we have the piano in the other room, there. Saved and saved and got it from the Penny's catalogue.

When she left a few years ago, her plan was to go to New York and sing in cabarets. Make some connections in the Big Apple and get a recordin' contract. So how did she end up in Ohio, with child by that gangster?"

"I honestly don't know," Hector said. "Our lives goes sideways, sometimes. You know that."

"That I surely do. At our age, we *both* do, yes? You want some bourbon, Hector?"

"That would be real nice," he said.

Hallie rose and opened a big old mahogany cabinet. She stood on tiptoe, reaching up to the top shelf. Hector watched her. Hallie's cotton dress was simple but seemed almost tailored. She was slender yet still had enticing curves. Hector tamped down some urges, shaking his head. After all, he was sleeping with her daughter. *Jesus, but I have me some sorry drives*, he thought.

Hallie smiled and smacked down a couple of cut crystal glasses and a matching decanter. "Dave, Megan's father, enjoyed a drink every night, and I did, too, but I'm not going to become one of those solitary drinkers," Hallie said. "Don't want to be some gin-soaked widow."

"Well, you've got yourself a world-class drinking partner tonight," Hector said. "And you've got some time to make up for, Hallie. So let's splash that main brace."

Hector poured them both a couple of fingers of bourbon and they tapped glasses.

Smooth yet fiery stuff.

Feeling the liquor spread out to warm his belly, he said, "How long has Dave been gone?" Remembering things Megan had said here and there he was guessing about five years.

"Too long," Hallie said. "He'd have been fifty-one in two weeks."

Ouch. Hector was just a shade younger than Megan's old man. All his women seemed to get younger, just as Jimmy had pointed out, but this time Hector was actually starting to feel a tad uncomfortable about all that. And it suddenly occurred to Hector that Hallie and he were near peers. He figured her for her late forties.

"She's sure made a mess of it all for herself this time," Hallie said. "I've tried to teach her how one decision can change the whole of a life. Tried to impress upon her actions have consequences. Not sure those lessons ever took. Pretty sure in fact that they didn't."

"Some never learn those simple things," Hector said. Hell, he figured he was probably a contender in those same sorry stakes, at least in the eyes of some. Too often heedless of likely outcomes—that had sometimes been Hector.

Hallie said, "You think you can really get them through this?"

"I mean to try to see them to safety. And I've got some help, some more-than-capable friends here and there who may prove useful. One of them may hook up with us again in a few days. We could make it." He could tell from her expression he didn't sound confident enough.

Hallie said, "Mexico? That's where Megan said she thought you meant to take them."

"That's right," he said. "She can't conceivably try and go through American courts to claim custody of Shannon, not even if Vito Scartelli and all his legions disappeared an hour from yesterday. Down there, south of the border, they can better reinvent themselves. They can maybe get lost out there in places most gringos don't even know exist. Out where there are no courts to cope with. And, hell, who knows—ten, fifteen years on, maybe they can come back. There's a bounty hunter after us, too, a nasty piece of work by all accounts. But he can't pull anyone out of Mexico. They'd hand him his head if he tried. That would leave only these former Pinkertons to chase us, and south of the border, those low bastards will tend to stand out. They'd draw themselves other flavors of grief that should soon convince 'em the job just ain't worth it."

"Why are you really doing this, Hector?"

He traced the rim of his glass with a finger. "Did Megan describe how we met?"

"She did. Told me nearly everything, I expect."

"Well, it's been like that, over and over," he said, blushing. That was something pretty unfamiliar. "Always one more crisis and one more thing to see them through, over and over. I haven't had the time to take a breath and have a think in order to sensibly opt out of this mess. Which any son of a bitch with any *sand* at all would have done at least two gunfights ago."

Hallie smiled sadly. Something in it reached him. "The way you put things?" She sighed and said, "With Meg, well, frankly, there may always be one more thing, Hec. She has a talent for findin' trouble. Or maybe for helping trouble find her. Either way, it ends the same. It's not just bad luck. I hope you understand that. Our three boys have never been much of a problem. Not Meg's older sister, Colleen, either. Megan's always been my wild one. Always running from responsibility, running from reality. The running kind, period."

Hector sipped more bourbon, but still managed to hold his tongue.

Hallie said, "Her brother, Rayburn, is coming by at seven in the morning. He's going to take Meg back to his place and her siblings will meet her there. They haven't seen her in years, and it sounds like the one chance Shannon will have to meet her kin. Think it'll be safe enough?"

"Don't see why not," Hector said. "Roads back here are surely a maze, even to an old horse soldier like myself. And I was extra careful not to be followed."

"They're not as confusing as you think," Hallie said. "If you stayed here a week or two, I expect you'd get around just fine." Hallie poured them both more bourbon. Her cheeks were red from the liquor; this glint in her eyes that put more unworthy thoughts in his head. "Well, at least Megan finally seems to have found herself a real man in her time of greatest need."

There was no graceful thing to say to that, so Hector sipped more bourbon. Hallie said, "You figure on settling down with Megan if you can see her through this? Figure maybe on raising Shannon as your own?"

"I don't figure on anything," he said. "I hardly know Meg, really. Shannon's wonderful. I like the kid a lot. But there hasn't been time for thinkin' or woolgathering. I'm no likely family man at this point in my life. Nearly certainly more days behind than ahead now. And anyway it's been run, duck and dodge from the get-go. And diggin' out bullets." He pointed at his arm.

"She told me about that. You're really something, caring for the two of you under those circumstances. I can't conceive of that. You seem more than a capable man."

He smiled "Something tells me you'd manage just fine." Hector said, "I can see you in Shannon's face." He amended that. "Well, I see some of her in your face."

"She does remind me of pictures I've seen of myself as a child," Hallie said. "Reminds me a little of Meg when she was a tiny one, too."

"And Meg now?"

"That's a little like looking in a long-gone mirror, too," she said.

"*Not* long-gone at all," Hector said. "Not by a longshot."

She smiled. "So nice of you to say. You are a silver-tongued devil, sir."

He stroked his chin. He badly needed a shave. "You maintain this place all on your own?"

"Mostly," she said. "Boys come by once in a while, but mostly it's just me."

"I'm amazed," he said.

"It's plenty manageable," Hallie said. "Pretty tiny compared to what Dave and I tended when we still had our place. And plenty others do it, and every day. This is not a remarkable life, you know." She looked around with sad eyes. "And yet this place has never quite become home. I expect it never will. You know… no shared memories here."

"I live alone too," Hector said. "I live in too big of a house for one person."

But he never spent any time at his place, not really. Not like Hallie seemed to spend on her lonely farm. He thought then that the solitude must be crushing for such a vital woman. Hallie said, "I'll make you breakfast in the morning. An honest, home-cooked breakfast."

"You don't have to do that, Hallie." But Hector thought it sounded wonderful.

"I *want* to. It'll be a treat, even—I mean as it's just for the two of us and I don't have much reason to make the effort these days. It's no trouble at all. What do you like?"

"Whatever you want to fix would be wonderful," he said. "It's been a lot of diner food and the like, lately. Grease-laden, but speedy service."

"Sounds gosh-awful," Hallie said. "Eggs, bacon, sausage and toast come the morning?"

"Sounds delicious."

"Maybe a few other things too."

"I can swear I'll be lookin' forward to it."

She looked up at the clock on the wall. "You must be exhausted after that drive. I've made my bed up. You'll sleep there tonight."

"No way," he said, "the couch will do me fine."

"Really—with that arm, you need the room to sprawl. Don't argue with me, Hector. You can't win."

The look she gave him, and the timbre of her husky voice, convinced Hector he was indeed wasting time pushing back.

And she was right—he could use a good night's sleep in a comfortable bed where he could stretch out his wounded wing. He'd be useless, otherwise.

Particularly as it might prove out to be the last peaceful night he'd sleep for some time.

31

Hector awakened early, as he always did, awakened despite the comfort of Hallie's big feather bed. The fresh sheets still somehow smelled of her. He reached over to the nightstand and turned on a light and picked up his Timex, squinting at its face in the dark. Four a.m.

He'd set out his notepad and some pencils on the nightstand the night before. He propped the down-filled pillows up behind himself and rested the notepad against his knee and wrote until the sun was visible through the cracks around the drapes.

At six, he put on some pants and a shirt and wandered out into the kitchen. Hallie was fixing breakfast for Meg and Shannon. She said, "If you want a hot bath, Hector, you're next in line."

"Sounds good," he said. He stroked Shannon's hair and said, "You need me to watch that dog for you while you're visiting?"

Shannon shook her head firmly. "She's coming with me."

Meg smiled at Hector and he said, "Okay, honey. That's fine." He gestured to Megan and beckoned with his finger for her to follow him back to her mother's bedroom. He pulled a forty-five from his suitcase and held it out to her. "Just in case, Meg."

Meg looked at the gun and shook her head, this strange look on her face. "I don't think I can touch it again. It'll be okay, probably. And if it isn't, my brothers are all hunters. They carry shotguns or rifles in their cars and trucks and have them around their houses. They'll see to us."

Hector searched her face. "You're certain?"

Meg glanced again at the gun; she looked a little queasy. "I'm certain, Hector."

She kissed him on the cheek then.

On the cheek. He half registered that.

She said, "We aren't going to stay here long, are we?"

"I reckon not," he said, weighing her tone.

"My mother's quite impressed with you. She kind of confiscated all my books of yours that you bought me."

"I'll replace 'em."

"It's okay," she said. "The more I learn about you, and the more I read your books, well, the more I find I it hard—"

Hector pressed his index finger to her lips, shushing Megan. "Just stop. I think I know where you're going with that and you're not the first to say it. Not even close."

She said in a funny, awkward voice, "Anyway, mother is clearly fascinated by you."

Hector rinsed the shampoo out of his hair and cut off the water. He groped around for a towel then dragged it over his head and dried off. He stepped out onto the bath mat, tying the towel around his waist. As he reached for his razor, he heard a male voice:

"Don't you lie to me, woman. If you do, you'll so surely suffer for it. You'll suffer far out of proportion to any cause you might conjure. Pain is how I ensure future cooperation from those yet to come."

Hallie responded, firm voiced. "I haven't seen that sorry girl in five years. You've heard of a family's black sheep? Of course you have. I figure you probably are the one in *your* clan. Well, that girl's ours. The blackest of black sheep. Though not a monster like you are."

The voice: "When one's in trouble, young ones in particular, when they rabbit, they tend to run down familiar holes, woman. They dash back to mammy and daddy and the like. Out here, so far from the cities, Meg might think she could get herself lost. From most, that would surely be true. But I ain't most. I am far from most. I'm the best at what I do."

The voice was low and menacing. Very masculine. Hector leapt to the obvious conclusion: it was the bounty hunter, Tomás Hawk.

"We forbid her to ever come back," Hallie said, sounding haughty. "We didn't want her corruptin' her brothers and sister." Next Hallie let her voice go hard and flat: "That girl made herself a whore with that Italian gangster. We didn't want her shameful example for our grandchildren." A long pause. "I can't believe her, sleeping with that Italian slime." Hallie was cool as ice. Cunningly calculating. If Hector didn't know better, he figured he'd have believed her.

The voice sounded impressed, too: "You say that with conviction. You may even feel it in some part of yourself, *ma'am*. But the maternal instinct is a strange and powerful thing. Has a mind all its own. Has its reasons that reason can't know. It's a mystical thing that can thwart all intention. I wager, even if you feel as you say you do, if Miss Megan came back here looking for help, you'd not deny her. No true mother would. I can look around this place, at the photographs on your fireplace mantel. At the artwork from your grandchildren I can see taped on the icebox back there in the kitchen. I look at that little sweater on the chair there you're knitting for some child, and I can see you're a true mother. A woman of deep feeling and commitment to kin. A woman surely lying to protect her own child." A pause, then a new edge in that voice. "And look there on that pretty old piano—a picture of Megan, the whore."

Hector heard the sound of breaking glass. He reached for the doorknob, then hesitated. He was nearly naked—unarmed but for a straight razor he doubted he'd get a chance to use. His Colt was in Hallie's room, under her soft pillow. But getting there to his gun meant walking down the hallway visible from where he guessed "Tomahawk" was standing.

The voice said: "Look—now Meg's ugly. That pretty face so like your own all disfigured and the like. Would you wish the real article to look like this? Or maybe your own face to look this way?"

"You get the hell out of my house," Hallie said, her voice hard and firm. "You have no right to be in here."

"Who's that in the shower?" Hector could hear the smile in the bounty hunter's voice. "Must be some kind of coward or Megan, because whoever it is, they ain't rushing out to your aid, ma'am."

"That's my husband," Hallie said. "He had a stroke a couple of months back. He's blind in one eye and deaf in both ears. I need to help him before he hurts himself. Get out of my house now, mister. You have no rights at all here."

"That's right," the voice said. "I have no rights, so I therefore have *every* right. I'm not police, so I don't have to fret over nonsense such as due process, search warrants, subpoenas and such. I go where I want, take what I need. Live as I choose."

Hector heard something; tried to place the noise. When the man started talking again, Hector realized what he'd heard—the whisper of a knife being drawn from a leather sheath. Hector realized he was bathed in sweat now; his heart was racing. He picked up the straight razor. It wasn't going to be pretty… an ugly way for Hector to die in service to a lost cause, taking a dainty straight razor to a buck knife fight.

And then lovely, brave Hallie? She'd *still* be alone with that monster.

The man said, "I haven't bought a meal or paid for a dinner in two years. I live like olden days, catchin', cleanin' and cookin' my own. Rabbit, squirrel and deer. Snake and woodchuck, if need be. I could strip that pretty arm of yours down to clean white bone in less than the time it would take for you to get out your second scream, ma'am. In my world there are no rules and therefore no consequences. Me and conscience parted ways a time back. My job is to take your daughter back to Mr. Scartelli. I have to take the child back to him too. Mr. Scartelli don't much care if I bring Megan back alive, or dead, or in pieces. He's frankly not much more particular about how that child comes back."

"Get out of my house," Hallie said again, her voice still steady. Did she really think Hector could make a difference like this?

No—he figured she was just steel. He started to recalculate in terms of strategy. He could make a dash for Hallie's room, try to get his Colt. But by then, Tomahawk would have his Bowie knife to Hallie's throat.

The bounty hunter said, "Megan doesn't have friends back in Ohio. Not the kind that would risk helping her under these circumstances. She was in Cleveland, we know that. I know she was last seen in Dayton. That means she's headed west. Headed out this way. Headed home. I do believe that. You've got other kin around these parts. Those pretty kids there in those pictures. I'll go talk to them, next. Even if I find her at one of those houses, I want you to know, I'll come back anyway and I'll skin that left arm of yours down to bone for lying to me. It's an investment in my own future, you see. For a man like me, reputation matters. Still counts for something in this lukewarm, piss water world." Parting words: "I hope you believe me about my coming back if I find you lied. I do mean it. You best know I'm speaking fact."

Hallie said soft but firm, "I surely do."

Hector heard heavy steps—the bounty hunter sounded like a big enough man. Then the screen door slammed. He heard Hallie running down the hallway toward the bathroom. Hector flung open the door to meet her. He was opening his arms, but she pushed him aside, running to a closet. He shrugged and moved quickly to the bedroom to get his Colt. Maybe he could shoot the son of a bitch in the back on his way to his car.

Hallie handed Hector an old Winchester. He looked at the rifle, then said, "Call your son! Warn him that son of a bitch might be on his way over there."

"They don't have the phone out to his place," Hallie said, looking annoyed at Hector. "That little reunion was handled through my daughter. He's got the ham radio but that only works if he's got it turned on, and I doubt he will at this hour. And you're wasting time! You know what you have to do."

Hector heard loud noises outside, some kind of music he didn't recognize. There were lots of drums and blasting guitars.

He searched Hallie's eyes, "You realize what you're saying?"

Hallie squeezed his bare arm. "Yes, I do! That man needs killing. If you can't do it, then give the rifle back to me and I'll try!"

Hector nodded and ran to the sitting room. Through the front window he saw the car—a forty-eight Woody—rolling away. He'd never get a shot at the bounty hunter once Hector struggled through the front door locks with his lame arm.

"Damn!" he said. Then, "At least he has to go looking for that next stop, too. Maybe I can overtake him on the way. My Chevy's fast."

"No traffic back this way," Hallie said urgently. "And all he has to do is follow Rayburn's tire tracks in the snow—all the way back to his place."

Fuck on a bicycle… darlin' Hallie was so right.

Hallie was running toward the kitchen now. She fumbled with the locks. "Road curves around the back, Hec. If you run straight across the back field, you can maybe just head him off along the rear boundary of the farm. There's a tree line to the west, so he won't see you moving across the field. But you'll have to be fast—he strikes me as a lead-foot."

Hector just nodded. "How many shots in this thing?"

Hallie winced. "I don't know, at least one… maybe as many as three."

Hector kept hold of his Colt: the Peacemaker wouldn't be much use except at close range, but it sounded like it could come to that if there was only one shot in the old Winchester.

He dashed out the back door nearly bare-assed into the wicked snow to kill an Indian.

32

It was cold and the wind still shearing down from Canada made it seem even colder. Heavy flurries were coming down, the kind that accumulate fast and deep.

Hector was already shaking. His bare feet burned from the snow and his teeth chattered uncontrollably. Hector chided himself: this middle-aged guy with two guns, running next-to-naked across two-hundred yards of ankle-deep snow to try and kill a hardcase young buck at least half his age.

He figured it'd be a miracle if he didn't have a stroke or heart attack before he reached the northern boundary of Hallie's holding. Hector feared that if he lived, he'd still be parting with some toes.

Somewhere about halfway across the field, Hector lost his wet towel. Now he *was* naked, lashed by the frigid wind, huffing steam from his nose and mouth, his feet on fire and his fingers getting numb. There was a copper taste in his mouth and he was having a much harder time getting air.

Yet Hector kept running through the wind and snow, determined to make it in time to kill the bounty hunter.

Hector hit the back boundary and leaned hard against a big old oak. He was doubled-over and seeing spots. He had stitches in his side. He began shifting weight from one burning, numb foot to the other in the nearly knee deep drifts, over and over, his teeth chattering wildly.

In the distance he could hear the hum of an engine—heard snow crunching under tires. Then he heard the radio, still turned up loud—that obnoxious, guitar-driven stuff the young kids were increasingly drawn to.

Squinting through the heavier snow, Hector got the rifle up against his shoulder, his left arm screaming at the exertion, and peered through the curtain of snow, awaiting a glimpse of the Woody.

When he was sure he could make the shot, Hector put a bullet through the front driver's-side tire and watched the Woody start steering wonkily. He hoped the bastard's blasting radio would obscure the sound of his shot. The heavy-falling snow might even help with that, Hector thought. With luck, the bastard would think it was just a blowout.

Hector heard "Tomahawk" cursing as he swung open the door of his Woody to haul himself out to check his car. Through the flurries Hector couldn't get much of a sense of the guy—just big and strong-looking, long black hair tied up behind his ears. Hector couldn't really make out his features.

Trying to steady his shaking self, Hector took a breath, then took his shot. He saw a pink spray.

Hector jacked the lever on the Winchester and fired a third time. "The Gun that Won the West" still had at least one more shot left in it: Hector emptied that one in the bastard's face, too.

A noise behind him: Hector swiveled and pointed his Colt. It was Hallie. He moved to cover his groin with his big old Peacemaker. Was the barrel long enough? Well, it was very cold, after all.

She smiled and said, "After a husband and three sons, you think I don't know what you've got, Mister? You're freezing, poor thing." She had his clothes, boots and coat in a loose bundle. "Put these on," she said. "Won't be much help getting dressed out here, cold as you already are, but better 'n' being bare-assed." With shaking hands, Hector took the pile of clothes from her and began to dress.

Hallie pushed down the rickety wire fence bounding her property, moving to step over it.

"I wouldn't," he said. "Put two in his head."

Hallie shook her head. "You surely killed him dead enough. Even I could tell that from a distance."

"So it's going to be a sorry sight. I'll clean up the mess."

Hallie held up an old blanket. "*We* need to clean this up. And we need to do it fast in case others happen by. Can't exactly report this, can we? And I've seen plenty of blood in my time, Hector. Get dressed fast and please come help me."

When he finished dressing, he stepped over the fence and made his way down a slight embankment to the road. Hallie had already wrapped the blanket around what ever remained of Tomás Hawk's head and tied it off with twine.

She was scooping up snow and tossing it over the patches of pink, red and gray brain matter dappling the snow mantle. Hector looked at the body again. A big kid. Hector never saw his face, of course, and now Hector—nor anybody else—ever would.

Hallie said, "Too bad you shot out his tire. We'll have to drag the body out of here."

Hector was still shaking, his teeth banging against one another. He shoved his Peacemaker down his waistband and slung the Winchester into the back seat of the Woody. He popped open the rear hatch. The back seat was already down. "We'll put him in here and drive him back. It's not so far it should wreck the rim." Hector saw then how lucky he'd gotten with his first shot.

To the good, the bounty hunter had installed snow chains on all four wheels—somehow the bullet had missed all that metal.

Hector got him up into the back of his own car. Hallie—so strong, thank God—did most of the work because of his still weak left arm. He started the engine and that damned radio started blasting again. Hector turned down the sound and cranked the dial to a country station, "Riders in the Sky." He said, "Going to be next-to-impossible to break any ground for a grave in this weather, you know. I fear we're stuck with a corpse we can't bury."

"There's a dry well behind the barn, a pretty deep one," Hallie said, rubbing her arms and turning the car heater up. "We'll drop him down there. I have some quicklime in the barn. We'll empty a few bags of that atop him. Come the spring, I'll have my boys help me throw some dirt over whatever's left. Maybe even say some words, though he hardly seemed to merit the effort."

They drove to that dry well on a flat tire. They manhandled the corpse from the dead man's own car. Hector winced when he heard Tomahawk's body finally hit bottom: seemed a lonely place to spend eternity.

Hallie crossed herself; kissed her bloodstained fingers. A lapsed Catholic, Hector tried to copy the move, his hand shaking and his teeth still chattering. His feet still burned in his boots.

She took his arm and said, "You look like hell, honey. Need to get you in a hot bath, now before you start losing parts of yourself."

As Hallie drew the bath Hector sat shivering by the fire. Through the window he saw that the snowfall was still heavier now: hardly any visibility at all. The man on the radio was predicting at least six new inches of snow. Hallie said, "It may make getting out of here in a hurry real trouble. I hope that bounty hunter didn't tell anyone else where he was headed."

Yes, Hector hoped Hawk didn't tell anyone like ex-Pinkertons or mobsters. Not crooked Feds, nor cops.

After a time, Hallie came and took his right arm and hauled him up to her. His teeth still chattered and his toes throbbed. He saw she had washed the blood from her hands and bare arms. Her arms were strong and muscled from all the work she handled all alone around the farm.

"C'mon, fella, don't be foolish." she said. "You're still freezing. Don't want you getting pneumonia or losing your toes."

In the bathroom, she began to fumble with his buttons. "I can undress myself," he said.

"Not with your hands shaking like that, you can't," she said. "Besides, I've already seen it all, remember?"

Not really. Hallie hadn't gotten a good look at all of his body. As she stepped behind him to take off his shirt he heard this sharp intake of breath. She said, "My Lord, what happened to your back?"

"Cat-o-nine tails," Hector said. "Happened in Paris, well really *under* the City of Lights, in February, 1924."

This tone in her voice: "We weren't at war *then*."

"There are wars and there are wars," he said. "I was in the latter kind that year. Paris in the old days was a crazy time. It's a story you don't want to hear now." Hell, if she'd read enough of his books, if she'd read *One True Sentence*, she might already know that story.

This knowing smile on Hallie's face as he watched her in the mirror. She asked, "What was her name? Which one was she?"

"Which one? Which one, what?"

Hallie gave him a look. "Which one of your women in the books. Brinke? Molly? That other, Duff?" Another smile. "Never mind." Then, "It looks like your arm is healing okay." Then, "What happened here?" She was pointing at his lower left leg.

"Just more old trouble. Some of the oldest, actually."

"God, what you've done to your body." He was naked now and she held his right hand as he slowly lowered himself into the tub. His skin—particularly his toes—flared in pain at contact with the warm water.

"Believe it or not, it's lukewarm for now," she said, splashing water on him and rubbing at his arms and back and legs.

Lukewarm? It felt like fire.

She said, "We'll make it warmer as we go, draw that cold out of your bones."

He sat there and let her work on him; feeling embarrassed and a little like some overgrown child being cared for. Mostly though, Hector watched Hallie—watched the muscles in her arms and capable hands. He watched the way she stopped now and then and used her forearms to brush back stray strands of hair that fell in her face as she scoured at him. The bath was very hot now and he thought he might want to spend what remained of the day in the tub.

Hallie said suddenly, "That man out there, he's obviously not your first kill. Between the wars—the ones they give names to and your private campaigns—" Hector had to smile at that, but a rueful smile, "—how many would you guess you've… let's call it *handled?*"

"I couldn't put a number to it," he said. "Hell, I wouldn't. Not the kind of thing to count. I don't cut notches in the butt of my Colt. I'm not that breed of jerk. Listen Hallie, I want you to know, if he really had tried to use that knife on you in the sitting room—"

"You'd have come charging out to help me and we'd both be dead now," Hallie said. She winked. "I'm glad you had the sand and good sense to await your moment. I was really trying to buy you that time, Hector." She looked at his body and smiled and said, "Looking your poor body over, I'd have you use that good sense more, but at least when the chips are truly down, you're better than effective. You're a survivor. You exude grace under pressure."

That last phrase dug into him more than a bit, rightly or wrongly—it was too associated with an estranged friend.

Hector noticed Hallie's hand was moving slower now. Her left arm was in water up to her elbow and she'd been rubbing at the calf and thigh of his left leg. Her hand moved higher. Her teeth nervously worked at her full bottom lip. They looked into one another's eyes a time, and her hand strayed there.

She'd started it; Hector more than meant to finish.

He leaned forward, cupping the side of her face with his good right hand, and kissed her. It was slow and soft and warm. Then their kiss grew hungry. He could taste his blood on his tongue from her teeth. She stopped suddenly, panting, her forehead pressed to his so he couldn't see her eyes. "This is more than *wrong*," she said hoarsely. "You've been with her. You're my daughter's man."

Hector wasn't so sure about that, not at all.

And he didn't really care at the moment. He also didn't care what that said about him.

He forced his mouth back against Hallie's. He massaged her full, firm breasts and she pressed his hands harder to her chest.

He then reached behind her and down. He tugged her sweater over her head. His hands stayed to her back, felt the muscles carved there by years of hard work in the fields and barns. Her hand was there again, stroking him. He tore her skirt trying to get it off her. He pulled her into the tub atop him, as naked now as he was.

It was variously slow and hard; hungry and frenzied.

They lay together in the bath after and she said, "This was terribly wrong. A calamitous mistake."

As she said it, Hector realized that for the first time in decades he'd made love to a woman close to his own age.

In his youth Hector had been drawn to worldly older women like the one Megan had asked about from his novel *The Last Key*. Brinke had been about five years older than Hector. Sometime in his mid-thirties, the pendulum had swung the other way. All the women after that seemed always to be in their early twenties. And the gulf just got wider over the years, just as Jimmy had pointed out.

Hector kissed Hallie's flushed throat, his hand gliding down her flat belly. He closed his hand between her legs and said softly, "Actually, this might be one of the few right things I've ever done."

Hallie turned around to see his eyes. "You're serious," she said.

"I'll be fifty-one in a few days," he said. "High-time I gave up chasing after girls."

Hell, everyone told Hector that was so, they'd been doing that for years.

She smiled sadly and brushed the hair back from above his right eyebrow. "Hec, your kind never truly grows up or settles down. Lovely as this was—and it was passing heaven—this can't happen again. It just never can, Hector."

"I'm not sure yet I'm prepared to accept that." Hector said. "I mean it. This is something new for me."

"Like I said." Her hand there. "You're just a big kid. There's way too much boy in you, still. Too much of the handsome rover."

33

Despite what Hallie said, of course it did happen again. And later, yet again, on a carpet in the sitting room in front of her crackling fire.

At four, Hallie's son Rayburn made contact via ham radio to say the cut back onto his property was hopelessly drifted closed.

With a foot more of snow on the way, and more severe drifting expected, even with a tractor he'd fitted with a plow blade, he couldn't get Meg and Shannon back before morning and maybe not for a couple of days after that if the drifting kept up.

As she heard that assessment, Hallie gave Hector a look he couldn't quite read.

So Hector just smiled at her. After a time Hallie smiled back, a sad half-smile.

They stood in the stable, staring at the big, fidgety stallion.

"My husband bought him a year before he died," Hallie said. "Dave had notions of breaking him. Someday, maybe of even breeding him. Dave was ex-cavalry. One of the last I guess. He chased Pancho Villa."

"Hell, me too," Hector said, surprised. Suddenly a little uncomfortable, he said, "Maybe I knew Dave."

Probably *not*: when Pancho Villa attacked Columbus, New Mexico and killed all those Americans—prompting Woodrow Wilson to send Black Jack Pershing into the desert to try and catch the Mexican revolutionary "dead or alive"—there were thousands of men who crossed the Mexican border to hunt Villa.

Chances were, Dave and Hector never came within hollering distance of one another.

Hector flinched as that unbroken stallion kicked a back wall with a wicked hoof. The barn's slats just held.

The stallion was all muscle and spirit and defiant in its prime. It stood there fire-eyed, white and snorting steam as it pawed the hard frozen stable dirt with its right front hoof. There was something almost elemental about the horse.

"He's far more trouble than he's worth," Hallie said. "Unbroken, untamed. More than half-dangerous. Won't be ridden, and if he ever got lose, I think he'd run until he dropped with a burst heart. Another of the running kind, you know? Wouldn't know home if he found it."

"I surely do know what you mean."

It had been a time since Hector had been around horses like this one. He was tempted to try and have a hand at breaking him. He said, "What's his name?"

"Traveller, after Robert E. Lee's horse."

Hector shook his head. "Does that mean that your husband was a secessionist?"

"Just a history buff," Hallie said. "Can't bring myself to get rid of the beast because Dave loved him so. I love him, too, after a fashion. Though he's expensive and, like this, unbroken but fenced in, he's pretty much useless."

Hector smiled. "I've got me some habits and hobbies the same could be said of."

Traveller suddenly pushed his head Hector's way. "He is a majestic thing." The horse tolerated Hector's stroking of his neck.

"Like Dave, you must have been pretty young when you signed up for the army," Hallie said, watching Hector and the horse.

"Under age, but tall, and the recruiters weren't too choosy under the circumstances," Hector said. "I reckoned it would be romantic to ride horses and hunt Mexican bandits. And I wasn't too happy at home about then."

Hallie brushed that comma of hair back from Hector's forehead. "Was it? Romantic?"

"Hardly at all. Pretty nearly everything but."

"Guess you and Dave are more alike than I might have thought. Cowboys born out of their time. Too old for breaking, yet too young to tame."

Hector thought that might surely be said of Traveller. But of himself?

"Not me," he said. "I like central heating and air conditioning too much now."

Hector pulled Hallie close. He kissed her as Traveller snorted and bumped Hector's shoulder with his nose, seeking more attention. Hector broke his embrace with Hallie. He stroked the stallion's long nose and said, "I like comfortable feather beds with down covers and phonographs and radios. I love my Chevy. And I don't have to follow that sucker around with a shovel."

"What about the television," Hallie said. "You have one of those gizmos in your big house?"

"Hell, no," Hector said. "I'm a working writer. Who has the time for *that* horseshit?"

Hallie was making dinner. He'd offered to help, but she'd said, "Thanks, Hector, but I suspect you'd just be in the way. Sit by the fire, do some writing or reading."

More the morning writer, Hector turned on the radio and twisted around until he found some concert originating from a New York City ballroom.

He went to that little shelf over the piano and took down a copy of *The Last Key* and started reading it where he'd left off in Ohio. He sat there crouched close to the crackling fire and hanging on his own words. He was finally starting to feel really warm again. Maybe it was all that Key West imagery, he thought. Maybe it was something else.

As he read his own novel, he found myself drawn back to that time, his first days in the sultry Keys. He was half his present age then and so still full of illusions.

And he had been moving toward his first marriage. He was planning to wed a fellow writer: that black-haired, black-eyed beauty five years his senior. Brinke Devlin. How he'd loved that sleek, perplexing woman.

That too-short span in Key West they'd shared had arguably comprised Hector's one legitimate shot at a Square-John life.

He knew how that sorry story ended, so Hector closed his own book on some paragraph that still held promise of a bright future.

He sat there alone with this memories, listening to the wicked wind and the comforting kitchen noises, finally having some time alone with his thoughts to do some serious reflecting.

For most of his nearly fifty-one years, Hector had lived his life at a sprint. He'd lived on the run like some goddamn fugitive, even when he sometimes wasn't.

Always the running kind.

Hector and Traveller—the writer let himself think they maybe were sorry kindred.

He looked around Hallie's little farmhouse and imagined how it would look in spring and summer and autumn.

Sitting there, Hector thought about how the home would look with a fresh coat of white paint. They'd have them some big and black, flop-eared dog Hector could pet with his left hand by the fire as he wrote with his right. He'd live in quiet peace here. Just drive down into town now and again to shop and to collect mail or to fire off a manuscript or two. He'd maybe be some kind of latter-day crime fiction version of Louis Bromfield, writing while living amidst some agrarian idyll in the Show-Me State.

Mostly Hector's thoughts centered around pretty, strong, lonely and sensuous Hallie Dalton.

Much woman as they put it, down borderlands' way.

The strength in her pretty body nearly matched his, Hector figured. And Hallie's passionate, carnally charged nature perhaps actually eclipsed his own.

After so many years of solitude, she was, of course, love-starved. That quality had appeals all its own. But it wasn't just pent-up sexual hunger that so drew Hector to the woman.

Hallie was fiercely passionate by nature and came back at him with ferocity and carnal candor that left him shaking and in awe.

It seemed to Hector that Hallie was his first *woman* since Brinke and he burned at her touch.

This impulse seized him: he'd sell that crazy and rambling *casa* down along the Rio Grande.

He'd cast off all the sentimental detritus of his picaresque, oft-times deplorable life. Just bring his books and clothes back to this perfect place smack dab in beautiful nowhere and kick back. Hector would grow old with Hallie.

Oh, he'd bring his Colt, of course—Ambrose Bierce's old gun. He'd bring that iron just because around the farm there'd always be something needed putting down.

And it was a venerable old gun from a truer, surer time. Or so Hector kidded myself.

But that's all the use it would evermore see.

No more trouble.

No more blood and thunder nonsense.

Hector would live the settled life with this woman he was falling so hard and deep for.

Theirs would be a good and quiet—an honest—life.

That was the unexpected place Hector's thoughts had taken him to when Hallie called him for dinner.

34

Maybe Hallie had some kind of sixth sense.

Over more bourbon, she said, "I feel like the worst sort of heel, Hec."

The name "Meg" hung unuttered between them.

"Hallie, I'm the one to blame in this. You haven't done anything."

She was emphatic. "I have these crazy notions, Hector. Wrongful yearnings."

He took her hand. She squeezed back hard. He said, "What kinds of crazy notions?"

"About keeping you here, at gunpoint, if necessary," she said. "Notions about you living here with me as a writer and my man. No more car chases, no more killing. No more knife cuts, bullet holes or whip wounds to add to your crazy collection of scars. But then I think of Meg and how wrong it is for me to wish you from her."

Hector took Hallie's hand and squeezed hard. "My mind's been going to the same sorts of places, darlin'. I can't believe how strongly my mind's turning to it, but that's all I've been thinking about these past hours. We need to talk more about this and seriously so." He checked the clock on the kitchen wall. It was that time. "But I need a few minutes, first," he said. "I need to call a friend."

"The Irish policeman?"

"Jim Hanrahan," he said. "I hope one day you two will meet. But I do have to call now. It's a pre-arranged thing. There's just a narrow window when we can talk. Marks to hit."

"Then you'd better make your call, Hec." Hallie squeezed Hector's hand a last time and then let go to begin collecting dishes.

"Thank Christ, Hector," Jimmy said. "Can't tell you how relieved I am to hear your voice. Word filtered back this way that Tom Hawk had figured where you likely are."

The writer in Hector relished saying it. "No worries there, Jimmy—that hatchet's buried."

"Well, fuckin' *hooray* for our side! You're well, then, Hector?"

"Snowbound, but aces over kings."

"Snowbound?"

"A foot-and-a-half of the white stuff on the ground and plenty more to come. Then there are the drifts. You could hide a double-decker bus under some of those bastards out this way."

"Oh, Christ, but that's unfortunate. Really bad news, actually."

"Just say it Jimmy. What's coming?"

"I had this romantic notion Hawk would be a lone wolf, flying fully solo," Jimmy said. "But Gibson's wire taps indicate otherwise. Hawk tipped those ersatz Pinkertons. Gibson says they're coming in after you, and I mean in force. May take them longer to reach you because of all that snow, but they're coming, and with you all but snowbound, sounds as if you running isn't an option, either."

"It's not," Hector said. "Not by car, anyhow. I'm cut off from Meg and Shannon, right now. Maybe cut off for a few days because of the snow."

"Calamitous luck, that."

"Those Pinks will likely have to come back in here on foot," Hector said. "Or snowshoes," he added, trying to lighten the mood a bit. "You don't suppose they can get themselves access to sleds and some huskies, do you?"

Jimmy wasn't playing along. "Honestly? I put nothing beyond the reach of that bunch. Remember how they were in bad old days? They knew no boundaries."

Hector knew his history well enough. He knew what you could lay at the feet of the Pinkertons, proper. These cast-offs by all accounts went darker still.

A hard swallow. "How long do you think I've got, Jim?"

"If you have the whole of another day, it would pleasantly surprise me," Jimmy said.

"I best get a move on, then. God willing, we'll talk again tomorrow night. We can set our rendezvous then. And by tomorrow night, maybe I can tell you the brilliant thing I haven't even thought of yet to get the girls and me out of this mess."

Hector hung up. Hallie frowned. She said, "It's bad?"

"Very bad. See if you can raise your son on that radio gizmo, won't you?"

Hector could hear the strain in Megan's voice. "So what are we going to do now?"

"I'm still trying to think of that thing," he said.

Megan, who sounded a little drunk, said, "No more Jimmy Hanrahan-like friends in Missouri? You don't have any fellow, thrill-seeking, crime writer friends around these parts?"

Hallie was watching him. Hector shrugged and said, "If I did, they have no advantages in this weather that we don't have."

He bit his lip. Maybe that wasn't quite true.

He clicked the mic button and said, "You all stay close to the radio, Megan. A friend may be contacting you on that thing shortly. Fella name of Les Dent. You can trust him, all the way up."

Hector handed the microphone to Hallie and headed for his luggage to dig out his little black book.

35

His old pulp writer pal Lester said, "Didn't know you were a ham radio buff, Hec. If you're radioing all the way from La Mesilla, you've got to tell me what kind of unit you're using. I need me that one, too."

That was good old Les—always the technophile and gadget guy. It was Les' penchant for gizmos that landed him his bread-and-butter job as chief writer for a long-running, recently-canceled pulp series focused on globe-trotting doctor-adventurer Clark Savage, Jr. and his intrepid crew of lesser supermen. It was the only pulp magazine Hector had kept reading as the years ground on, mostly out of love for Les.

"I'm on a friend's rig," Hector said. "I'm just a few miles due south of you." Les and his wife, Norma, lived on a family dairy farm in La Plata. Hector said, "Do you still have that aerial photography business?"

"Have a near fleet of planes now," Les said. "Have to have some income since that damned woman cancelled Doc. You know she skipped publication of one of the last ones I wrote? Great thing tied to the Russians having the bomb. Probably the best of the Docs I ever wrote. Called in *In Hell, Madonna*.

Maybe the title was too brainy for her. You think that was it? Hell, it's Billy Shakespeare, don't you know?"

"Likely it was too brainy for her," Hector said. "That bitch always did have sorry literary tastes." She'd spiked a story or two of Hector's, too. He hesitated, then got to it. "Snow has stopped down my way, at least for a time. Is it possible to fly in this weather?"

"Sure... possible," Les said. "Advisable is a far different beast."

"And what about landing? Say in a field? Could you do it?"

"If it was flat enough and had enough room to roll. We've got some crafts equipped to do that."

"Then I need a big favor, Les. It's a hell of a tale, buddy."

Hector told Lester Dent his story.

Les agreed to call Rayburn via ham radio and tell him what he'd need Rayburn to set up by way of a marked landing strip. All of that was now between Les and Rayburn.

Hector was out in the barn changing the tire on Hawk's 1948 Woody. He'd just put on the spare and tightened the lug nuts. His left arm ached from hauling the old tire off and mounting the spare, but he was getting by. Hector was setting about putting the chains on the front tire when Hallie slid into the barn and pressed the door closed behind her, shutting out the blowing snow. She rubbed her hands over her arms and said, "So what's the plan?"

"My friend Les Dent will land his plane on your son's farm," Hector said. "Rayburn will set some fires or smudges to mark the strip so Les can find it from up there." Hector jerked his head upward to indicate the sky. "Then Les will fly

Meg and Shannon on to Kansas City. There's another friend of mine there who'll hook up with 'em. A rough customer who owes me a favor. He'll see the girls safely to me, somewhere around Wichita. Once they're back in my hands, I'll make that final run for Mexico. I'll try and hook up with Jimmy somewhere along the border. We'll get the girls safely into Mexico and see 'em established, but well lost from searchers."

Hallie nodded. "And then what?" This quaver in her voice. She waited for it.

A cautious smile. "Then I'm going to go to Cleveland and find some way of shutting down Vito's business for all day and more," Hector said. "I mean to put that monster down for keeps if I have to. Cut off the problem at the source, in other words."

She searched his face. Bless her, she wasn't one to toe around the central issue or the big questions. She just put it out there, naked and frank. "Will you find your way back here after you've done all those impossible labors, Hec?"

He smiled and stroked her jaw. "I surely will. Have to come back here for my Chevy, for one thing."

Hallie wasn't in a joking mood. He wiped the smile from his face and said, "I mean to get back here, Hallie. I truly do mean to do that. And if you'll have me, I won't be leavin' next time I come here. Not leavin' alone the next time, anyway."

Hallie smiled and said simply, "I believe you." She kissed him hard. "I want you, back here, safe and whole. I think you need me as much as I need you."

That was all she said.

It was enough—hell, everything.

She helped Hector with the tire chain. "Why are you leaving your car here?"

"Because of all those ex-Pinkertons working their way back here," he said. "Hawk's fearsome reputation was such partly because he kept his identity deliberately murky. No photos of him or the like are in circulation. You're probably one of the few people to have ever seen that bastard's face."

"I didn't see it either," Hallie said. "He was wearing his hood up. Had on sunglasses and a scarf covering his mouth and nose when he came here and confronted me."

"That's even better news," Hector said. "He must have been truly paranoid about his appearance getting out. So I'll wear Hawk's scarf. It's still there on the front seat. See, I'm going to see if I can find those ex-Pinkertons on my way out. I'll pass myself off as Hawk and tell 'em I have word Meg and Shannon and me have doubled back east. Do my best to lead them away from here so you and your family won't be bothered anymore by their bloody likes."

"That sounds well beyond risky," Hallie said.

"But well worth that risk," Hector said. "I really think it can work. Critical thing now is that Les Dent get that plane of his down and then back up safely." As Hector said it, he thought he could hear the distant buzz of an engine overhead somewhere.

God bless, Les—he was always the best of the *Black Mask* boys, and the only one Hector had stayed close to because Dent was so very solid.

As though she had again sensed what he was thinking, Hallie said, "You have good friends to do crazy, brave things like this for you at just a request. Mr. Dent's a real man's man flying in this weather. That kind of loyalty speaks well of *you* as a man."

Hector waved that away and moved to rear driver's side door of the Woody. "Les wrote almost all of the Doc Savage pulps. Doc's kind of the ultimate American hero. The distance between old Doc and Les isn't as wide as the gap between most writers and their characters."

"Then in that this Lester sounds more than a little like you," Hallie said.

"Maybe." Then he mumbled, "But the Les in his works reads nicer than I do in my books."

On that note, Hector dug around in a container Hawk had resting on the floorboards behind the front seat. He whistled low. It was full of guns and rifles and knives. A nasty looking double-barreled sawed-off, some WWII-issue hand grenades and even a longbow and some arrows.

Hector fetched the box of confiscated guns from his Chevy and added them to Hawk's arsenal, just in case.

Hallie asked, "When will you leave?"

His fingers combed through her hair. "I'd hoped to spend the night."

Hallie pulled him close. "Let's go inside then. Let's not waste anymore time."

He lay in Hallie's bed, stroking her strong, bare back.

Rayburn had contacted them earlier to confirm that Les had safely taken off with the girls.

Still later, Norma Dent had contacted Hector to confirm they'd safely reached Kansas City and were in the hands of his other friend there.

Everything seemed to be going perfectly to plan, a condition that always stirred the cynic in Hector.

Then the phone rang.

Hallie slid from under the warm covers, her slender bare body silhouetted in the moonlight through the window.

She shrugged on a warn, warm robe and padded into the kitchen to answer the phone. Hector reached for his Timex and switched on the bedside lamp: he was sorry to see it was already tomorrow.

He could hear fresh sleet lashing the window glass. Then he heard floorboards squeak. Hallie was headed back. She kissed him, hard and urgent again, their tongues tangling. Then she said, "You'd best dress. And be damn quick about it, Hec."

He threw off the covers and reached for his pants. "What's happened?"

"That was Lootie Wohill. Her place is five miles east of here. At the edge of that tangle of roads, as you put it. Fifteen, perhaps twenty men were just at her place asking about Meg. Asking about me. They were combing her farm when Lootie risked calling. Seems those Pinkertons or whatever they are are working their way back over our way. They're acting like some occupation force, Lootie said. She said they have a bus and a dump truck with a snowplow mounted on the front. Sounds like the weather won't be much of an obstacle for them."

"Sounds that way," Hector said.

Damn it all to infernal hell.

"I already packed Megan and Shannon's things, all the evidence they were here," Hallie said. "While you load the car, I'll make you some sandwiches for the road."

He slung his portable typewriter into the back of the Woody and slid behind the wheel and started her up. As he did that, Hector realized he'd never thought to check the thing's tank. He got lucky—more than three-quarters full.

He twisted the keys to his Chevy off the ring and put them on the front seat of his car and then pulled the tarp back down over the Chevy's door. Then he pulled the Woody out of the barn and locked the barn door behind himself. Somewhere in the night, he heard Traveller bray and pound the frozen ground.

Hector smiled ruefully thinking of the distance they might cover together if only that big unbroken horse would accept a saddle.

He found Hallie in the kitchen, finishing up his provisions.

He felt sick for what might be coming her way. "I'm so sorry for all this," he said. "If I hadn't brought the girls here?"

"Those men would have presumed Meg might have come here anyway," Hallie said. "Hawk certainly did that. This isn't your doing, heart-of-my-heart. Not any of it. You know that. To my eyes, you're nothing less than an angel doing all this, Hector."

Angel? Not of any stripe he'd ever heard tell of.

"I'll do all I can to keep those men from coming back here to harass you and yours."

Hallie smiled sadly. "I know you will do all that and more. And that scares me a little. Scares me for you, I mean."

"Keys to my Chevy are on the front seat in case you need to move or hide it," Hector said. "Pink slip's in the glove compartment in case I don't—"

Her fingertips were quickly there, pressed against his lips. "Hush, now. You're coming back for that goddamn car. And when you do, you just try and leave again. This is your home now, Hector Lassiter. But for now, for this night and maybe the next few nights, you need to use all your past talents for running," she said. "Use that sorry skill. Do it for all it's worth."

Hector almost said, *It's what I've always done best,* but he held his tongue for once.

He kissed Hallie hard and held her close. "You be careful with those Pinkertons," she said. "Don't try anything crazy, thinking that you're maybe protecting me." Hallie shook loose from his hug and handed him a piece of paper. "I drew you a map to get you back to civilization." Then she handed him a paper sack filled with food and a long silver thermos full of black coffee.

They kissed again, then he stepped out onto the porch into the chilly, wet wind. The sleet was coming down harder, and he knew it was going to be a white-knuckle drive along those twisting and confusing, moonlit back roads. He wished the weather and light was better so he could take another look at his future home to better commit it to memory.

Sighing, he slipped behind the wheel of the Woody and dialed around the radio until he found a country station. He pulled on some gloves, tied Hawk's discarded scarf around his face and got his stolen wheels in gear.

Hallie waved to him from the porch, a dim figure in his rearview mirror. He honked the horn twice and headed off down that icy, washboard road, swearing to himself all the while he would find his way back to the farm and Hallie.

36

Hector had to keep turning on a flashlight to check unnamed roads against Hallie's hastily scrawled map.

About three miles or thereabouts from Hallie's house, he saw big headlights boring through the sleet and snow. As he came closer, Hector saw the vehicles seemed to be stopped. Three men were silhouetted in the blinding beams of the lead vehicle, waving rifles above their heads and signaling Hector to stop.

He slowed his stolen car, pulling his Colt from under his coat, cocking it and then laying it on his lap under Hallie's map.

As one of the men approached, Hector pulled the scarf closer around his face, covering a little more of his nose. He turned down the radio and cranked the window down a couple of inches to talk through it. His left arm burned at the exertion required of rolling down the window just a crack. As one man approached the driver's side door, another man stepped into Hector's headlights, squinting and checking his license plate against something on a clipboard.

One of the ex-Pinkertons said, "It's Hawk, right?"

Hector recalled the bounty hunter's voice from his confrontation with Hallie. The difference between a southern Texas accent and one from southern Arizona was negligible to all but locals, Hector figured, gambling he could get by:

"That's right," he said. "Get those vehicles over so I can get by. I'm trying to make up some ground, goddamn it."

The rogue Pinks didn't seem to care about his objectives: "We're heading in to comb these shithole farms," the man said. "Hell, *you* got us all dragged out here in the first place, from what I hear. You telling me that now you're tearing off?"

"That's right," Hector said, surly. "They lit out of here too long ago. But I mean to overtake them."

Hawk had left his knife in its sheath on the passenger sheet. Hector held it up where the bastard could see. "Had me a little talk with some of this Dalton whore's kin folk. She's rabbited again. Her and the crime writer have doubled back. They came back this way to try and lay a false trail, to make us think they're running north with the notion of heading up into Vancouver. Make us think they're going to lose themselves somewhere in Northern Canada."

"You saying they *ain't* back here?" Some smart boy Hector had drawn in this one.

"Got out just ahead of the freshest snow," Hector said. "They're really running back *east* figuring we'd never figure them to do that. I'm going to try and catch 'em before they reach the coast. I know where they're stopping along the way. Now make fucking room for me to get by."

"Ease up, Geronimo," the Pinkerton said. "We got guys fucking everywhere. We can head 'em off and save you a shitload of driving. Just tell me where these safe harbors are and—"

"I have my own arrangement with Mr. Scartelli, asshole," Hector said. "Do you want me to tell Mr. Scartelli how you queered my shot at catching this skirt before she could get to the Feds back east?"

The man held up his hands and backed away. Bastard folded far faster than Hector had expected him to.

Hector told himself he deserved that break.

The ex-Pinkerton climbed up on the step to duck his head in the driver's side window of the big dump truck with the front-mounted snow shovel. The driver steered over closer to the side of the road and the bus behind followed. Hector drove slowly past them and picked up Hallie's map, using their headlights to check his next crossroads. He didn't want to foul up and have to double back and maybe run into the would-be Pinks again.

Hector watched the rearview mirror, then sighed in relief.

Thank God—the sons of bitches were turning their vehicles around to follow him out. Looked like Hallie and her children would be spared after all. Hector gave the Woody some more gas then. He figured he'd try and get some distance on the bastards before they could really try to follow him in earnest.

When he finally hit a main, marked and properly paved road, Hector dropped the hammer. He drove for ten miles as fast as he dared go on the slick pavement. He pulled over just long enough to get at Hallie's coffee to steel himself for the longer drive ahead.

Hector's country music station had faded somewhere coming down out of the sticks. He turned the radio up on some crime drama, sipping his coffee and burning down the road.

37

The radio was Hector's sole companion across the state of Missouri—more crime dramas, country music when he could find it, and disquieting news out of Korea when he couldn't.

Seemed to be lots of night attacks being mounted by the Chinese and North Koreans. *Harry S. Truman*: seemed to Hector every Democrat administration in his lifetime brought with it a bloody and arguably avoidable war.

The Korean news gave Hector a sour stomach. He'd had several newspaper syndicates and magazines approach him the past months with stringing offers to cover that "conflict," the so-called "police action." Whatever they were calling this one to keep from properly calling it a war. But this time, Hector wasn't biting.

He'd had his fill of those sorts of wars. Europe and the last big show had ground out whatever capacity Hector had for that scale of carnage. Or so he told myself.

In a truck stop outside Wichita, he waited under a canopy, smoking a cigarette and watching the flurries fall. He watched those eighteen-wheelers come and go.

Hector had figured Meg, Shannon and their escort would beat him to their rendezvous site. Their lateness worried him.

But then after loving Hallie, the prospect of reuniting with Meg unsettled Hector, too.

Because of that unease, the awkward mess he'd made for himself falling for Hallie, he'd given Jimmy an aggressive schedule to reunite with him at Hector's hacienda in La Mesilla.

In effect, Meg and Hector would have to drive twelve hours straight through, switching off driving duties and stopping only for food-to-go and to fill up the Woody's tank.

Hector was on his third Pall Mall when he saw the old '41 Touring Sedan lumber into the truck stop. He waved and the headlights flashed once. Hector cast down his cigarette and walked out to meet them.

Jake Carmony, rodeo-clown-turned-stuntman, turned-grizzled and wall-eyed character-actor, thrust out a big hand and pumped Hector's good arm. "By Christ, Lass, I'm relieved to see ya after the ear fillin' I've been getting. You're really playing it edgy takin' on these Dago types."

Hector smiled and twisted a toe atop a cigarette stub. "You try to choose the fights you can win," he said. "That said, sometimes the fights choose you. Thanks for takin' this job on, and on short notice at that. And thanks for doin' it in this lousy damn weather."

Hector could see Shannon's luminous eyes in the backseat so he was curbing his language. The usually salty tongued Jake seemed to be doing the same. Hector said, "I wish to God there was time to catch up, buddy, but we've got to fly."

"Understood, and no sweat, Hec. You give 'em hell, pal." Hector fished the roll of bills he owed Jake from his pants pocket and passed it to him in the guise of a last handshake.

Hector was positively hemorrhaging cash, this bloody escapade.

Jake said, "Next time you make sometime when you come this way, hear? I'll stand you to some world-class barbecue."

Hector walked around the Packard and took Meg's hand, drawing her up to him. Seemed she was getting around better—Meg was foregoing a cane.

But her breath smelled of gin. She helped Shannon out and Hector ended up carrying the box with Shannon's dog—little "Hector" the bitch—sleeping inside.

Hector popped the rear hatch on the Woody and slid the box inside. He'd picked up an air mattress during a stop for gas in a small berg halfway between Moberly and Wichita: he just couldn't bear the thought of the girls sacking out on the same surface that luckless Tomás Hawk rested upon during his final, brief ride to that dry well's frigid bottom.

Shannon squealed when she saw the cushions and cozy pillows and blankets in back. She crawled in, kicking off her shoes and snuggling up with her puppy. Meg leaned in for a hug and gave Hector her cheek.

Given circumstances of which she surely wasn't aware—namely Hector's torn carnal allegiances—that was okay by him.

He said to her, "We're driving straight through, I'm afraid. We'll switch off driving duties if you think your leg is up to it. If not, I think I can push on. Just twelve hours more, give or take. A little over seven hundred miles. We'll likely risk bunking one night at my place to freshen up and reconnect with Jimmy, then we'll make the final border run."

Meg slid into the front seat of the Woody and Hector closed the door after her.

When he slid behind the wheel, he saw she'd already started the engine and turned up the heater. They started rolling and Hector could feel the road bumping up against those tire chains through the thinner veneer of snow out that way. He figured in another fifty or so miles due south they'd have to stop somewhere and have those snow chains pulled off.

Meg said, "Where'd you ever find that guy Jake? He's unbelievable. I felt like I spent the last several hours trapped inside a B-movie. Is he for real? I mean, *really*? I think he thinks he's George Raft."

"Jake's real enough," he said. "You had to at least like Les."

"Lester was wonderful," Meg said. "I love him. And he was terrific with Shannon. She's never flown, and the flight was pretty terrifying at points because of the weather. Lester is a very brave man. And Lester made up this elaborate story for Shannon as he flew us. A wonderful, weird, funny story that he kept going for hours. I wish I had had a notebook and pen to take dictation for him. I think it was easily publishable."

"Les is the best of men," Hector said. "And a damned fine writer."

"Yeah..." A long pause, then, "Driving straight through is a sign that things are getting even worse, I guess," Meg said. "And you've switched cars. I hope you didn't find yourself forced to sell your Chevy in exchange for this heap."

"My car's still at your mother's," Hector said. "I'll get back there in a few days to pick it up. Once you two are safe, I mean."

"Then what's the story on this jalopy?"

Hector told her in as much detail as he could with Shannon maybe eavesdropping behind the seat.

When he finished Meg said, "My God, how horrible."

"Your mother is fine, by the way, despite all that happened to us after you left."

Meg nodded. "Thank God for that." Her gaze drifted to the silver thermos resting on the seat between them. In this strange voice she said, "That was my father's."

It sounded like an epiphany.

"Your mother loaned it to me for the road trip," he said. "I'll get it back to her when I pick up the car."

"Sure." That tone... Just like that, Hector sensed something between them changed.

Something ended.

To his possible discredit, Hector figured, he felt immense relief sweeping over him. Hector thought, *Okay, then. So be it.*

In a town called Liberal, hard along the Oklahoma border, Hector finally had to stop at a service station to scrap those snow chains.

The grease monkey kept giving Meg the eye, not in that lustful way, but more in recognition. Hector had the sense the mechanic would be dropping a dime on them as soon as they pulled out. That meant their car would be made.

Watching the man watching Meg, Hector stepped inside the garage's office to pour himself a cup of coffee. There on the desk next to the cash register was a copy of the *Kansas City Star* with a picture of Megan on the cover. The paper was covered with greasy fingerprints obscuring some of the type. Still, Hector tried to scan the story to get its gist. Damn fool reporters had misspelled his last name. Sloppy amateurs.

But either way, that wire-service article had torn it.

Hector pulled out his penknife and cut the station's phone chord.

The car handled better with those damn chains off and he gave her some gas as they cut across the northwest corner of

Texas, jumping jurisdictions lickety-split in case that grease monkey had found some other close-by phone and alerted any Kansas cops.

Hector at last allowed himself a deep breath when they at last crossed over into New Mexico.

Driving through Tucumari, Hector said, "We're in my country now. We'll stop for some more grub in Vaughn. Should make it to my house before sunset."

Meg nodded, looking a little nervous... maybe even a little sad.

38

Everything was quiet around his hacienda. He asked the girls to stay in the car while he walked the grounds, checked around back.

Mostly it was quiet. Just the sound of coyotes baying and the slap of the Rio Grande as it hit the bend and flowed on down south.

Hector took a long, hard look at his house, two stories of stucco with a wrap-around second floor porch, just as he had described it to Meg. He suddenly had trouble really seeing himself letting it go.

Sensing motion, he looked down and saw a scorpion. Those critters Hector wouldn't miss.

He ground the deadly bug under his boot heel and went to fetch the girls.

Hector locked the garage door with the Woody inside, parked alongside the forty-one Chevrolet Cabriolet he'd never quite brought himself to unload. He finally had some plan for that car now.

Hector lugged in the suitcases and locked up the front door behind them.

Meg had turned on some lights in the front of the house. Hector promptly doused those lights and made the place look derelict again.

Dropping the luggage in the foyer, he wandered the hallways of his big, lonely house, looking for the girls. He found them in his book-lined study. Shannon was rolling pool balls across the billiard table.

Meg smiled sadly, "It's everything I imagined, and yet so different. It's a wonderful place. I don't know how you ever leave such a place."

Hector couldn't think of anything to say to that, so he just smiled and shrugged.

Shannon quit playing with the billiard balls and picked up her puppy. She pointed at a large oil painting behind the bar. It was a nude woman standing in full view, pretty, but her body was disrupted by little half-open doors and compartments. It was a piece of surrealist art he'd picked up in Paris several years before. Shannon said, "That's creepy."

"It is," Hector agreed.

Meg arched an eyebrow. "Friend of yours?"

"The model and the artist," Hector said. "Surrealist painter of my acquaintance. Friend doesn't quite fit, though."

"Sounds like another novel," Meg said. "That one at least have a happy ending?"

"Jury's still out," Hector said. "You two take my bedroom. It's the biggest bed in the house, and it's on the second floor and therefore defensible. I'll shack out down here. With luck, Jimmy might yet make it here tonight. Help me stand guard."

"You look exhausted. You need sleep, Hector."

"I'm going to stay up and make some calls," Hector said. "I'm owed a few favors it's time to call in. Maybe I can rustle up some sentries if I work the phones aggressively."

While Meg and Shannon settled in, Hector poured a single malt and sat at his writing desk with the phone and his drink, staring up at his surrealist painter friend's sexy, unsettling self-portrait and thinking.

Rachel... Like Meg, Rache was a bird with at least one wing down.

The kind of woman who too often made Hector a goner despite his knowing better.

That was another old, bad habit he surely meant to change.

Hallie wasn't damaged like that. Hector smiled, thinking about her.

Then he scooped up the phone receiver and started calling around to local bars and whorehouses, either side of the border.

Hector was fresh from a scalding shower, just hitching a towel around his waist when Meg barged in. "I saw a man outside, Hector! He had a rifle."

Scooping up his Colt Hector said, "Easy now, it may not be what you think."

He ran downstairs and parted a curtain and searched the night. A man outside the window raised his pistol and waved. Hector waved back and turned to find Meg limping down the stairs after him.

"That fella is Raoul Reyes, a local boy who answered the call," Hector said. "There should be at least four more just like him out there now. Tough customers, sure, but they're our thugs."

Meg sighed and shook her head. "Do all your friends live the same way? I mean toting guns? Running toward trouble instead of away from it?"

"Suppose if they didn't do all that they simply wouldn't be my friends," Hector said.

Meg seemed committed to testing things about then. She stepped up close and put a hand familiarly on his hip. Despite himself, Hector stirred under the towel. She said, "Shannon's asleep..."

She was pushing up against Hector when the doorbell rang. That tenor voice called out, stopping Meg just as she was leaning in for a kiss. "Hector, open up! The cavalry has arrived!"

Pulling away, Meg said, "Jimmy. His damned timing..."

Yeah. Good old Jimmy.

About that timing: Hector thought it perfect.

The three of them sat in Hector's book-lined den, James and Meg on a leather couch and Hector in his leather armchair. He'd dressed and dragged a comb through his hair. His left arm was finally feeling like it was regaining something like full range of motion, and not a moment too soon, he reckoned.

Jimmy said, "Who are those thugs outside? Jesus, I thought I was a dead man."

Hector said, "Locals. Passing acquaintances. Amazing what the offer of booze and twenty bucks for a night's work will buy a man here in the borderlands."

"Let's just hope they're loyal then," Jimmy said. "Hate to see the allegiances of that bargain-basement militia shift from us to our foes for a mere few dollars more. Still, they look, ya know, capable."

"They look capable of anything, more like," Meg said. "Ferocious."

Hector said, "And therefore perfect for our needs. Anything new on your front Jimmy?"

"Not a jig." Jimmy sipped his whisky and rolled his head, stretching his neck out. "I've been cut out. Gibson's pretty much closed down on me. Seems pissed I never produced the two of you. So I figure I was followed by all sorts coming down this way. But I tried my best to be careful and to confuse things. Flew to Texas and came across the New Mexico border from there. Switched cars and drove down roads nobody could follow without making it clear they were following. I think I'm clean."

"Gas station attendant recognized Megan a ways north of here," Hector said. He hadn't told Megan about that, and she looked at him, suddenly flustered. "Your picture was all over the newspaper in his office," Hector said to her. "Anyway, I figure the opposition—be they mob, or be they ex-Pinkertons—know we're running for Mexico. So we're just going to have to reach the other side and keep going. Thank your stars for a broad national border. If they do follow us across, we'll do what we can to thin the herd."

"Then let's talk strategy toward that very bloody end," Jimmy said.

Meg struggled up to her feet. "I'm sorry, but I just can't listen to this. I'm already a wreck. Going to go upstairs, try and sleep." She kissed Jimmy on the cheek; kissed Hector fleetingly on the mouth. She said, "You'll be staying up late?"

Hector said, "Better figure I will be. We're down to the important last hours. Strategy counts most of all now, especially against the inelegance of such thugs."

"Of course," she said. She picked up her glass. Then she picked up the bottle of gin and limped out of the study.

Jimmy said softly, "That limp of hers looks like something that might last. Poor beauty." He paused and said softly, "But her elbow seems more limber than memory recalls."

Jimmy and Hector talked for about an hour: they mulled thrusts and counter-thrusts. Contingency plans and distractions. After a bit, he said, "Hec, you look like hell. You really need to sleep. And she's waiting up there, I think."

That was when Hector confided to Jim about Hallie. He told Jimmy all of it.

"It is getting to be that time of life, been getting to be that time," Jimmy said, clearly pleased but trying to hide it. "Neither of us is kids anymore, Hec. It's past time to settle down. Sounds like you've found yourself a good *woman*... at last."

The Irishman looked up at the ceiling and said, "That one up there, well, Meg's still got a lot of vixen in her, and Lord knows you've have had enough of that in your life."

Jimmy hesitated, then said, "Besides, she... well..." Jimmy broke off and waved a hand. "Never mind."

"Say it, Jim."

"Hardly seems to matter anymore," Jimmy said. "Some other time, maybe. Go to bed, Hector—in whichever bed you intend to bunk down in tonight. I'll not judge you for that, not this night. I'll go talk to those nasty boyos prowling your property. I'll make sure they're still on our side and endeavor to keep them there."

PART III

— CIUDAD JUAREZ, MEXICO —

"The longest road out is the shortest road home."
— Irish proverb

39

Before dawn, Hector was freshly showered, dressed and at work in his garage, transferring all those guns they'd been collecting since Youngstown and all those weapons Hawk had—moving them from the Woody to the old Cabriolet. Hector checked the glove compartment of his older Chevy to make sure the pink slip was still in there.

After, he talked to his ragtag brigade of soldiers. They said they'd seen lights in the surrounding hills. They'd heard voices northwest of Hector's place; overheard many car doors slamming.

Later, they'd spotted campfires.

One of Hector's boys crept out and saw a massing army—two-dozen, maybe as many as three-dozen men silhouetted against the wine-red mountains.

Sounded to Hector like their time was growing terribly short. He fetched Jimmy and gave him the fill. He then set Jim to finishing packing Meg and Shannon's stuff in Hector's old Chevy.

While Jimmy did that, Hector paid off their overnight guard, then handed them the keys to the Woody.

He said, "Car's yours boys. Just drive fast that-a-way," He pointed a bit west of where the ex-Pinkertons and their ilk were camped. He said, "And don't you boys dare stop for *any-thing.*"

It was a little like a suicide mission, but Hector's recruits looked game for it.

And as Jimmy said, they were capable enough. Hell, they might even make it.

And they'd maybe buy the rest of them time, send that crew of brigands running west while Hector and company ran south across the border to lose the girls in the desert's wastelands.

A short time later, Hector's boys set off in the Woody.

He listened to their engine roar; heard others start up.

Hector saw this big dust cloud rise out there on the horizon. Heard gunshots… heard screams.

Meg was squeezed between Hector and Jimmy. Little Shannon and her puppy were stretched out atop their hidden weapons' cache. Hector figured that tactic might dissuade border sentries from a too-aggressive search of their car.

They caught a break at the border—they drew a couple of guards Hector was well enough acquainted with, a fringe benefit of his frequent crossings in and around Juarez.

The guards and Hector chatted briefly and they waved them through. In the rearview mirror, Hector saw some other cars coming up fast on the checkpoint, some Pinks who hadn't been fooled, he figured.

There was also a too-familiar bus.

Jimmy saw them too. He said, "Two cars at least. Four men to a car. Maybe five."

"And the bus, too, of course," Hector said. "Figure as many as fifty in there, maybe."

Meg looked sick. Hector floored the old Chevy. Jimmy said, sour-faced, "You got yourself a notion here, Hec? 'Cause I'm frankly dry." Jimmy, too, looked nauseous.

Hector couldn't say he felt so wonderful himself. He said, "Other side of the city, there's an old road. It's narrow and runs between hills. There's an old one-lane bridge there across a dried up arroyo. Only one car can pass there at a time. Call it a natural chokepoint. You and I will make our stand there, Jimmy," Hector said. "The girls will go on without us."

Jimmy's blue eyes searched Hector's, long and hard.

A grim smile. The Irish cop finally said, "Hokey-doke, then. Looks as though that's the way it'll be, Hec."

They drove through a jumble of Juarez streets, just losing themselves for a short time there. Then Hector headed for that old and narrow desert road to make their last stand.

There was a solitary cantina not far from the bridge, the kind of joint that never *truly* closes. Hector pulled into the parking lot and climbed out. He lifted sleeping Shannon up and moved her to the front seat where Jimmy had been sitting.

Hector got out the box of weapons and handed it to Jimmy who said, "Jesus, Hec, what's in here?"

"An arsenal. So be careful—some explosives, too."

Jimmy's eyes went wide.

Hector pulled Meg from the back seat. "You have to go on alone now, I'm afraid, darlin'. You have to do that fast, Meg.

I wanted to help you set up your new life with the little one, I truly did. I wanted to help with all those logistics. But we don't have that *luxury*, now. We need to hold these bastards off to buy you escape time."

Meg searched Hector's face with scared eyes.

She looked a bit hung-over. Her chin was trembling.

He said, "Thing you do now is put me and Jimmy from your mind and start driving south. There's money in the glove compartment, enough to get you started and see you through a year or two, here. Cost of living's *much* cheaper down here. You can stretch those dollars a good ways if you're real resourceful. And the car is yours, too. If things get tough, sell the wheels and buy something cheaper. You should get a few hundred for it, even this side of the border. Pink slip is in the glove box. Along with your forty-five."

Meg looked panicked. "I don't even speak Spanish, Hector."

"In a month you will," he said, "enough to get by, anyway. That little girl of yours will pick it up even sooner, I'll wager. Tykes are sponges that way. Little natural linguists. And there's no other choice and damned little time left us now. You run, Meg. Both of you go hide so good that even *I* can't find you. You best figure if *I* can't find you, or if Jimmy can't, then nobody else can either."

Meg clearly wanted to talk more, to stall somehow, but there wasn't time.

Hector urged her through the dust to the driver's side of his old Cabriolet. "You hustle now, darlin'. And don't you ever look back."

Meg's eyes pleaded, "Shannon, she'll want to say good-bye to you two."

"Let her sleep, Meg. You need to make time and distance, and I mean *now*. Burn down that road, dainty foot to the fire-wall. Really go. Do that now."

"But you two…? You're *goners* if you stay back here."

Jimmy pushed her into the car and slammed the door. "We're survivors, this magnificent heathen and me," Jimmy said. "There is no reason to fear for the likes of us. Now go, lass."

Hector leaned down and kissed her hand. "You said you're the running kind, Meg. Prove it to me."

She said, "Will I ever see you again, Hector?"

With a sad smile Hector said, "Don't take this the wrong way, darlin', but I surely hope to God not. Now *go!*" He slapped the roof and Meg flinched, reflexively giving the Chevy the gas.

A cloud of dust.

Jimmy and Hector stood in the cantina's sweltering parking lot with a box of weapons at their feet and an army headed their way.

The dust kicked up by his departing car sifted slowly back down, settling on their shoes.

Jimmy said, "So what next, Custer?"

40

Hector winced as he lifted one end of the box of weapons. Some rebelling ache flared high up in his left arm. "Help me stash this alongside those trashcans there," he said to Jimmy.

They carried the box into the shade alongside the cantina and he opened it up. Jimmy whistled. "Jesus! We could actually win this war with this stuff if we only had a dozen more like us."

"One miracle at a time," Hector said. He pulled out five or six grenades and held them curled in his arms. There was some discarded twine and rope curling around the trashcans. "Grab that, too," he said, setting off toward that rickety old bridge.

"What do you have in mind?" Jimmy asked, fast-walking to catch up.

"We're gonna blow up that bridge," Hector said.

The dead arroyo's dusty bottom was about ten feet below the road grade—with the bridge gone, no cars would be passing over that way. The ex-Pinkertons—or whoever was chasing them—would have to drive another thirty miles east or west to find another crossing if they meant to maintain their wheels, Hector figured. That equated to more critical get-away time for Meg and Shannon. It was all down to that now, Hector told himself—all about buying those two get-away and get-lost time.

Hector lashed some grenades to the rusting struts at the end of the bridge on their side of the dry creek bottom.

There was a jumble of boulders on their side of the dusty arroyo Hector figured to use for their cover. He strung the rope through the grenade pins and played the rope out toward the big rocks. He caught a break in that the rope indeed reached the boulders with two or three feet to spare.

Jimmy looked at the rocks and said, "I'll go get that box now."

As Jimmy was huffing along behind the rocks to set down their weapons cache, Hector saw a cloud of dust and heard rumbling motors.

Didn't sound like cars, though.

Across the morning heat shimmer he finally made out what was coming their way: a motorcycle gang. It was a passel of young toughs with a few hard-looking women clinging to their backs. Hector counted fifteen. They looked like much worse than simple rough trade.

Jimmy shot him this look and rolled his eyes: "Oh Christ, you're not thinkin' of…?"

Hector stepped out from behind the rocks and waved at the bikers to stop. The leader rolled to a stop a few feet from Jimmy and Hector and planted his feet in the dust. He pulled up his goggles and said, "What gives?"

Americans… better and better, Hector thought. He smiled and said, "I have a proposition, brother. Buddy and I need a little earnest back-up, *pronto*, on a situation about to transpire with some ugly types. Could use the appearance of some serious muscle to dissuade those coming from pushing back."

The head biker snorted and shook his head. "We look like Samaritans to you?"

"Not at all, and that's precisely your appeal," Hector said, smiling again. "And I'll pay you in hardware. You each get a gun or rifle. After these others clear out, the weapons are yours to keep. And after *that*, I'm buying drinks at the watering hole over there yonder for you and yours. *Lots* of goddamn drinks. Ya'll can drink on me until you're just short of blind."

The head biker snorted. "Guns we don't want if the price is some son-of-a bitchin' strangers' blood. We don't need *that kind* of trouble."

"Won't be *that kind* of trouble," Hector lied. "I'm not asking you to shoot anyone. Just point the guns at some folks if need be. Look menacing. No shock in me saying that won't be a reach for you fellas. The women can wait in the bar. They can start that tab running while we close-out cases."

Hell, the women could stay and fight as far as Hector was concerned. Some looked meaner than most men.

The chief biker frowned. "Who are these guys you're looking to stand down?"

Hector looked the bikers over; took a gamble based on things he'd increasingly heard about drug trafficking and the biker gangs down Mexico way.

"Narcotics agents, working undercover," Hector said. "Of course they have no jurisdiction this side—they're crooked, too. Probably have a good supply of contraband with them. And hell, any drugs you can have, too."

The leader of motorcycle gang nodded, sucking on a lonely front tooth and thinking about that. He looked at his comrades, who shrugged, almost as one. He turned back to Hector and said, "Exactly what kind of guns ya got?"

Jimmy did a rough count: there were still ten handguns left; a few stray grenades and that longbow and some arrows. He said, "Gonna make a run over to the cantina, Hector. See if I can't scrape up a few more recruits."

The bikers followed Jimmy over there to park their motor-cycles in the lot—to keep 'em safe from stray bullets and on the right side of the bridge if things went crosswise.

Ten minutes later Jimmy returned with a dozen young Mexicans: scrawny bucks ranging in age from maybe fifteen to twenty-five.

The handguns ran out and the youngest of the boys, grinning with gold-capped front teeth, picked up the longbow and fitted an arrow. He whooped like an Indian. His burly friend scooped up the last of the grenades.

There was another big dust plume out there on the horizon. This time it sounded like a bus engine. Hector's stomach kicked. Jim gave him this wild-eyed wink: the Irishman's adrenaline was kicking in—Hector knew the look. Jimmy wasn't alone in that way—Hector was feeling it, too.

Hector looked at their crew. "Motley" didn't do this bunch justice.

But they'd have to do.

Hell, Hector figured they'd prove out just fine; they seemed awesomely feral. It had been a while since Hector had his my own guerilla outfit, not since Paris and the liberation.

Jimmy cocked a rifle and gave Hector this last fond look, smiling and shaking his head. "*Jaysus*, Hec. Here we stand, likely about to go down like Jim Bowie and Davy Crockett, and I've rarely seen you look so happy."

Hector shrugged. He truly didn't expected to die this day. He had something—someone—to get back to, after all. And the tide, it seemed, had turned in their favor.

"We're gonna have us a time, Jimmy," he said. He jacked shells into a double-barreled, then checked his Peacemaker. Hector smiled and said, "Let's call it a last blast."

41

Hector had a very particular vision: he'd stand up on top of the pile of boulders and call across the bridge—give that busload of hard cases a chance to turn around and skedaddle back across the border without ever engaging them.

And he'd promised the bikers no risk of real trouble, though he really had in mind forcing the fight on them, much like he had with those Feds back in Cleveland.

Diplomacy at the point of a gun—that was Hector's first impulse. Call it a rough wooing.

And, when the time came, it started that way well enough—diplomatic, like.

Hector scaled atop the sprawl of rocks, holding out his hands to get the bus stopped while it was still on the far side of the bridge.

The bus and a couple of touring cars trailing behind it stopped in an engulfing cloud of drifting alkali. Air brakes wheezed. One of the former Pinkertons stepped down into the dust, and Hector started stating terms.

Then one of Hector's conscripts, his blood up, whooped like an Apache.

It was the young boy with the gold front teeth—'Carlos' was his name, Hector would later learn. The kid pulled back that gut string on his bow and let fly with a deep thwang.

The Pinkerton looked down at the arrow in his heart, this funny, quizzical look on his face. Then he fell dead in the dirt.

Bullets started flying; more arrows.

A slaughter ensued.

As ambushes so often go, it was a decidedly one-sided affair. Hector's side didn't lose any—not even a flesh wound suffered among his rag-tag crew.

The remaining occupants in the cantina stood out in the parking lot, watching that private little war, quaking even as they quaffed. El Paso residents, Hector remembered reading, long ago sat on their rooftops, watching Villa's attack on Juarez, back in the day. *Call it history on repeat cycle*, he thought.

Hector looked over at Jimmy, the Irishman had a look of disgust on his dusty, sweat-streaked face. The slaughter was all too much, even for Hector, truth be told.

Jimmy said, "At least we spared the bridge. Why don't you unwire that feckin' bomb before somebody trips on the detonator cord? I'm going to go talk to that tavern keep before he decides to call in the local law. See if I can't buy him off. What do you say we offer him those two cars for his silence?"

Jimmy pointed at the sedans behind the bus.

"Sure," Hector said. "Get the drinks flowing, too. I'll see to the mop up." Hector figured it was the least he could do.

He held back the Mexican kid with the gold teeth and his young friend. They'd both been looting the bodies—boy surely didn't seem to mind getting their hands dirty, or even bloody.

Jesus, even the bikers, disappointed to find no drugs, hadn't had the stomach to pat down the tattered and bullet-riddled corpses for wallets or the like.

With the two wildest boys' help, Hector hauled them up and inside and piled the bodies in the back of the bus.

The duo followed Hector in one of the sedans as he drove the bus deep into the dust flats to abandon it.

Far from any road, Hector took the grenade rig he'd pulled from the bridge and wrapped the bundle around the bus's axle near the gas tanks.

Hiding behind the sedan, Hector pulled the cord.

He figured the resulting fireball must be visible all the way back to the cantina.

The ensuing mushroom cloud looked a little like newsreel footage Hector had seen of atomic bomb tests conducted in his home state of New Mexico.

Given the terrible evidence whose destruction the swelling cloud portended, it seemed to the novelist a sublime and lovely thing in its terrible way.

The boys did the driving back to that watering hole where Jimmy waited; Hector sat in the backseat, watching desert scenery whip by.

The boys turned up the radio extra loud on some barely-there mariachi station. Hector ordered them to keep dialing. They at last settled on a somber cover version of "Prairie in the Sky."

Hector stretched his arms out and tipped his head back against the seat, eyes closed, smelling the desert air and savoring the music, thinking of the quiet farm and that woman awaiting him in rural Missouri.

42

Eventually, a couple of shell-shocked bikers agreed to give Jimmy and Hector a lift back to Juarez. The two men brushed dust off their clothes and crossed the border bridge back to the States. They took a taxi back to Hector's hacienda.

There, they showered and slept maybe just a little like all the new dead across the border.

The next afternoon, the two drifted back across the border, purportedly to belatedly celebrate Hector's fifty-first birthday and the New Year now that there was time for that frivolous kind of thing.

The Irish cop and Hector were in the Kentucky Bar, slumming and slamming them back, pointedly avoiding the subject of the bloody slaughter back there on the outskirts of Juarez.

Jimmy toasted Hector's birthday again. "We drink to your coffin, Hector. May it be built from the wood of a hundred year old oak tree that I shall plant tomorrow."

Hector laughed and said, "Sure, to that."

Slurring a little, Jimmy told Hector again how pleased he was Hector had found Hallie.

Jimmy suddenly squinted into the mirror behind the bar, then turned around for a better look. "Holy Christ, look what the cat dragged in, Hec. It's Francis himself!"

Distractedly, Hector said, "What? Who?"

"Francis—Frank. You know—feckin' Sinatra."

Hector looked up from his tequila. It *was* Sinatra. Frank and Hector were half-assed acquaintances. Rumor had it Sinatra had been getting down Juarez way more often in recent times.

Frank had Ava Gardner on his arm, a dark-haired, dark-eyed, walking wet dream—the kind of woman to draw out every last inch of the fool in a man.

Hector swiveled back around and lowered his head, in no mood for mock civility and the "star scene" that would ensue if Frank spotted him.

Jimmy turned back around and shook his head. "Question is, what exactly did we accomplish back there, Hec? We wiped out *that* lot, sure. Meg and Shannon are safely lost in all that big empty out this way, at least for the moment."

Jimmy started into his glass. "But Vito can just hire more brigands. Maybe even find himself some *Mexican* bounty hunter who won't be so easily lost or put off as all these Italian torpedoes and ex-Pinkerton thugs he's been sending our way. I feel like we just bought those two gals some short measure of additional time, and that's about all we did back there."

Too true… maybe. Jimmy's dark thoughts echoed Hector's in some ways, sure they did. He said, "I hear you, Jimmy. I wish I could tell you I'm thinking otherwise."

This loud slap on Hector's back that stung.

That voice, all Jersey bravado: "Jesus, Heckso, I thought it was you! Ava, looky here, it is Hector!" He said Hector's name so it sounded like *Heck-tuh*.

Sinatra: he'd shed the sports coat and tie he'd been wearing when he'd come in a few minutes before. Frank's collar was open now and his sleeves rolled up. He'd left on his porkpie hat though—this unseasonable bid to hide his spreading monk's bald spot.

The Chairman of the Board took up a stool by Hector's side. He patted the empty stool next to himself and said to Ava, "Take a load off, Kitten. Park that luscious caboose right here. Me and Heckso have some serious catching up to do."

Frank slapped the writer's back again. "When was it last? Jamaica, I'm thinkin'. You and that limey hump in the hotel bar? The playwright, fuckin' Coward? No offense, and maybe he ain't even your friend, but what a flaming, light-in-the-loafers queen that one is. I made a promise to myself to personally castrate that limey hump Noel with a pair of safety scissors if he crosses paths with me again. Jesus, but he's touchy-feely."

Hector leaned back so Frank could get a look at Jimmy. He introduced them. Frank said to Jimmy, "Fuckin' Irish, clearly—but good fighters, ain'tcha?"

Jimmy shrugged and gave Old Blues Eyes a crooked smile. "So they say. Hector can serve as a reference."

Frank winked and said, "And now, thinkin' of the goddamn Irish, just like that, I'm cool to the fucking mescal I came here thinkin' I was craving." Frank slapped his hand on the bar and said, "Fuckin' keep—I want a bottle of Jameson and another of Bailey's right here." Frank pointed at the bar in front of him with a finger. "Right here." He said to Ava, "IRA Cocktails—you'll fuckin' love 'em, dollface."

Frank pulled out a cigarette case and Hector fired him up with his old Zippo. Frank said, "Heckso, we don't see you so much around the old good places in the Big Apple no more. What's with that?"

Hector lit his own cigarette and flipped closed his Zippo. "Hell, Frank, I'm just kind of tired of the same old scenes. Everything around New York City just keeps repeating itself for me, these years. Nothing good there for me."

"Well, I hear that," Frank said. "Guess that's why we're down here now. Just did the Berle show and after I wanted nothing more than to get out of that town and away from the weather and fucking Uncle Miltie. I know what you're saying, Heckso. I do. All the suck-ups and sycophants back East? *Chee-rist.*"

"Fuck 'em all," Hector growled back, playing to Frank. "Francis, you're the only one I can countenance."

Frank smiled. "Jesus, sounds like a fucking Harry Ruby lyric." The singer bit his lip, then patted Hector's cheek. "But I dig the sentiment, baby. It's getting' late in life and that is no season for suck-ups. I'm simpatico, Heckso. I'm up to *here* with both coasts, myself. Hell, I'm for real Quitsville with that bunter East Coast scene. *Again.* I think you've got the right notion, Heckso. I mean all this *clean* desert living. But why are you lookin' so hangdog? You want I should secure you and your Irish pal a couple of broads? I can get some señoritas sent over with Charleys out to here."

Hector watched Ava roll her dark eyes and got the sense Frank's act was playing out for her. Frank was oblivious, however.

The crooner said to Jimmy and Hector, "No jokin', boyos, just give the word if it suits your Clydes. If you're not up to the full course, I can guard the john door while the ladies play tonsil hockey with your birds. How's about? Jaw-jobs sound good to you boyos?"

Hector shook his head. "Maybe later, Frank. I've been having myself a time with some folks. Just tryin' to get even from that."

Frank's smile went away. He didn't make eye contact directly, just looked at Hector in the mirror behind the bar. The singer's eyes seemed to go a little dead. "Ah, yes. The Dalton twist. Well that is *the* talk in certain circles. All that, and your role in it, kid."

Ava excused herself then, wandered over to the jukebox, all luscious hips and languor. A few dozen sets of eyes wandered there with her.

But not Hector's. The novelist was still looking at Frank in the mirror behind the bar.

And then Hector realized what was happening. "You being here, finding me like this," Hector said. "It's no accident, is it, Frank?"

"Wish it were otherwise," Sinatra said. "But word is you're down this way, and I was down this way. So a friend asked me to talk to you. We should get us a booth now, Hec."

"Let's do just that," Hector said carefully. "Jimmy hears this too, though. He and I are in this together."

Frank gave Jimmy another look and said, "That's your call, Heckso."

The booths were all taken, but Frank gave some gringo tourists the eye and they cleared out for their vacated seats at the bar.

Frank slid into the booth beside Hector and wrapped an arm around the writer's shoulders. "Let's just cut to the chase, yeah? Momo is *not* pleased, my friend. Things are unsettled like they've never been, and with that fucking woodchuck Kefauver in the mix? Well, trust when I say there is much unhappiness due north. Momo is looking for a way to calm the waters. He thought maybe you'd want to help with that."

Momo—that would be Sam "Momo" Giancana.

"I'm going to assume you know even more than you're letting on," Hector said to Frank.

Sinatra smiled. "Always a safe fuckin' assumption, Lassiter. Go on..."

Hector wet his lips and said, "Has Mr. Giancana heard that Vito Scartelli is going, you know, *nuts*?"

"There've been rumors," Frank said, checking his manicure. "There are always humps who like to work their mouths. But I think—strictly my opinion—that Momo thinks such talk about his Ohio friend is just low gossip."

"It isn't," Jimmy said. "Scartelli's certainly losing it. And Vito knows it, too. His memory is going away like a night train with the hammer down. That's why he *writes everything down*, Francis."

Hector sensed he and Jimmy were thinking along same lines about then.

"Writes down," Frank said, brows knitted. "Everything... Like, a *written record*?"

"Every damned thing," Hector said. "All of it put to paper. Show him, Jimmy."

Jimmy pulled out some last folded ledger sheets from his wallet, the more damaging ones he'd held onto for a hole card when Gibson had so disappointed them. Jimmy spread the papers out on the table in front of Frank.

"Pretty damning stuff," Hector said, taking one of the sheets. He looked it over and had to bite back a smile. His luck was running good. "And look right here, Frank. Here's some notes regarding some transaction between Vito and a certain 'Sammy G.' And down here, a 'Momo' notation. Small world, ain't it? Unusual nicknames? They're vanity's tiger traps, if you ask me."

Frank's voice was low. "This is from the fuckin' ledger that dead broad Kate stole from her old man?"

"That's right," Hector said.

Frank's blue eyes bored into Hector's. "Where's the rest? There are only four or five pages here."

"Feds got the rest," Jimmy said. "Back in our early naïve days, when we thought cops would care for material such as this, we gave them the rest."

Frank looked like he was ready to rip out Jimmy's throat. The Chairman of the Board said, "And fucking Momo was written up in those pages you gave to Kefauver's stooge?"

"Jimmy purged the book before we turned it over," Hector said quickly. "Jimmy thought we should hold the best or most damaging stuff back. Keep some options open for ourselves."

Frank grunted. "One forward lookin' Mick, that's what you are, Harleyhand."

"Hanrahan, and thanks, boyo," Jimmy said. Something in Jimmy's voice: now Hector was starting to fear a little for Frank.

"So these pages…?" Frank's voice trailed off.

"Those are all that's left," Hector said. "They're yours to give to Momo. Say it was our gift to him. We just want two things in return."

"I can figure one," Frank said. "The girls walk. Yes?"

"As much as can be expected, that's right," Hector said. "I just want a vow from Sam he'll see the chase is stopped. Let those two fillies disappear and live on in obscure safety, here to forever. They're no threat anymore. Meg just wants to raise her little girl, and Vito doesn't give two squirts for that kid's fate." Hector knew how that last would go down with a proud Italian. Hector said, "Old Vito, he's just not a family man like you or me."

"I'll convey," Frank said coolly. "And the second favor?"

Hector said, "It's my understanding that the prospect of Sam—or even some of Vito's stooges—taking Vito out, despite his growing senility, is verboten."

"It's complication-laden, yeah," Frank said.

"So have Momo clear the road for me," Hector said. "I ask safe passage back to Ohio and Vito."

Jimmy saw where Hector was going and clearly hated it. He said, "*Hector...*"

"Stop, Jimmy," Hector said, holding up a hand. "In fact, you go now, Jimmy. I insist."

Jimmy looked like he was about to come across the table at Hector. "It's not like you think," Hector said. "Please, Jimmy. Just allow me two minutes alone with Frank."

Eyes smoldering, Jimmy slid out of the booth. Possibly just to needle Frank, Hector suspected, Jimmy wandered over and chatted up Ava at the jukebox.

Frank said, "Now cut to the chase, Lassiter. Are you saying if Momo pulls off Vito's guards *you'll* do the job? You'll personally kill the son of a bitch?"

"Same as. Close enough. By that, I mean old Vito will be dead for certain. Promise."

"And what would you want for a *favor* like that? What's your reward?"

"Knowing the girls are safe, like I said, here to forever."

"That was favor number one, Heckso. That's granted. I'm asking, what do you want in return for removing Scartelli from the chessboard? Because seems to me that's a different fucking favor."

"Nothing, honestly. Vito's given me plenty of grief these past few days to justify my wanting to hand some back with lethally compounded interest."

Frank smiled thinly. "That I can feature. Everything is always personal with our kind, am I right? I'm gonna to go make a call. You and your Mick friend have another round on me and watch over my gal. Don't let anyone get fresh with her while I'm on the horn back east. When I get back, let's forget this whole conversation, right? Forget these sides of one another we just shared, yeah? Let's not let this become a *thing* between us." An edge in Frank's voice. The Italian street-punk and Mafia suck-up showing through the crooner's suave veneer. "Ya better be with me, Lassiter."

Hector said, "Sure, Frank, I'm with you, and I mean the distance. Sure."

Frank patted his cheek again. "That's my pal. Lass, you are one suave son of a bitch and a class act. Next life, I'm comin' back a Texan."

When Frank returned, it was just like he said.

He shot Hector a thumbs-up, then launched into a long ramble about the current shambles of his career. "But I'm chartin' my course back, brothers," Frank vowed, raising his glass. "Gonna find me the short path back to Comebacksville. Going to be on top again and soon. Swear to Christ, Fifty-one will not pass without some triumphs for me."

Ava just watched Frank with bored eyes. She looked at Hector occasionally, inquiringly. Or so he flattered myself.

Hector shifted in his seat and tried not to make eye contact with her. At some point Jimmy started teaching Frank the lyrics to "Carrikfergus." That exercise seemed to shift Ava's interest from Hector to Hanrahan. Frank then sang a version of "Danny Boy" that reduced several gringo tourists to tears. Jimmy wasn't far behind them.

Hector managed to hold it in. He was thinking of his future.

When Hector and Jimmy finally left Frank and Ava in the bar to head back to Hector's hacienda on the other side of the border, Jimmy said, "What deal exactly did you cut with that Dago devil?"

"*I'm* not going to murder Vito," Hector said. "It's not what you think, Jimmy, truly."

It was true enough. Personally killing Vito really wasn't Hector's plan. That much he was being honest about.

His Irish friend said, "There are worse things than killing a man, Hector."

Indeed, Hector thought. Good old Jimmy—now he was getting warm.

43

Hector made a slow ramble up to Ohio; Jimmy had flown back home to Cleveland well ahead of the writer.

Of course, Hector made a point of passing through Missouri on the way. He tarried for a few days in Hallie's bed and her claw-footed tub.

He helped her with some chores around the farm, just trying it out, he told himself. The novelist assured himself he merely wanted to see if this envisioned new life truly agreed with him. It did—so much so it actually scared Hector a little. He decided he could indeed live out his days this way. Working around the farm would put all those muscles back into his arms and legs he'd had in the Keys when he had his own boat, The Devil May Care, and near daily engaged in strenuous sports fishing with Gulf Stream leviathans.

Hallie and Hector made love several times a day. They gradually murdered a few bottles of fine wine he'd brought along. They danced to the radio: swayed to "Raglan Road" and "The Lily of the West."

Nights, warm and tangled up together in her feather bed, they read books deep into the night before turning out the lights. Hallie read Hector; Hector read the books of peers, rivals and contenders.

They stood in the chilly morning air, sipping coffee and watching Traveller trot and test fences. Hector was growing to love that presumed-to-be-untamable beast.

He figured the biggest danger in his beautiful new life that he was plotting was going to be the ungovernable urge to one day mount that silver stallion. He reckoned it was going to be impossible not to try and ride Traveller up into the high country.

Yes, that was the way it would be. He'd break that horse— just enough to accept one man's saddle—and they'd go for long treks up into the surrounding hills in the sun and snow, a couple of headstrong mavericks bound together by wanderlust and sheer cussedness.

Eventually, though, Hector couldn't stall much longer. He had to get down to this last, bloody job.

Hallie, tangled naked and damp around Hector in front of the fire, said, "You'll really come back to me? *Really?*"

"Forever," he said. "Just need to do this one last thing to keep your kin safe," he said.

"Isn't there a line in one of your books—forever's just pretend?"

Hector held up a hand. "I say this only to you, my love. My art imitates my life, never the other way around."

Solemn, Hallie told Hector she loved him. Hector told Hallie he loved her too. She pulled him closer. They kissed.

Hector thought leaving her soon, even for a short time, was perhaps the hardest thing he'd ever do.

Using Hallie's more carefully drawn map, Hector drove back to civilization a few days later in his Chevy.

He left the farm clear-headed, clear-eyed and intent upon closing out cases with Vito.

He regarded it as his last campaign.

After he done that, it was Hector's plan to spend a last week or two saying good-bye to the borderlands before heading back to Hallie's farm.

Call it a kind of bachelor's *La Frontera* farewell.

44

Sam Giancana succeeded in exceeding Hector's expectations.

It really was like Momo had arranged to open all doors to the writer.

When Scartelli's guards saw Hector approach the grounds of the sprawling northern Ohio mansion, they lowered their guns and opened the iron gates to Vito's estate.

Then they vanished.

Hector got the same treatment at the front door, imposing thugs simply stepping aside with strange smiles, easing away. They pointed toward stairs and bedrooms before "being gone."

It was starting to make Hector a little uneasy in terms of how easily it was all going.

Things turned a bit when he reached Vito Scartelli's bedroom.

It was nearly eleven p.m., and Meg had told Hector that Vito was a go-to-bed-at-seven sort, particularly since the disease had really dug in. It was worse, Meg said, at night.

But this night Vito was burning the midnight oil. And he wasn't alone.

Scartelli was up playing cards with some stooge who evidently didn't get Momo's orders.

The young buck drew down on Hector with bloody intent.

But Hector already had his gun out.

As his finger spasmed a last time, the mortally wounded young thug accidently put a round in his senile boss's leg.

Hector dragged Vito bleeding and screaming through his grand house, down the steps and out the door to the Chevy.

Once Hector got the mob boss in the backseat of the Chevrolet, Hector pressed a rag drenched in chloroform over Vito's mouth and nose and put him to sleep. Hector then wrapped a tourniquet around Vito's thigh. It was not the careful job he'd done tending to Meg, but Hector really didn't care whether or not this gunshot victim lost a leg.

In fact, Hector rather anticipated just that sort of thing ensuing for luckless Vito.

The writer cuffed the mobster's hands behind his back, then strung a seatbelt between the chains, securing Vito to the backseat.

The mobster was whimpering, pleading for a doctor.

Hector said, "Enjoy the ride. It is indeed going to be your last, you sorry damned fiend."

Then Hector started driving southwest.

The crazy old mobster awakened somewhere around Springfield, Ohio.

Seeing those corporation limit signs once more again put Hector in mind of Brinke Devlin—it was her hometown. He'd dreamed of her the night before: Brinke coming to Hector in his sleep to tell him we was doing the right thing loving Hallie.

Vito snarled, "Do you know how fucking dead you are, even now?"

"Please," Hector said. "You don't even know who I am. And have you forgotten you were shot? Are you really that far gone upstairs now?"

Hector surely hoped not. There'd be no satisfaction in what he had planned if Vito wasn't sufficiently sane to realize what was happening to him and why.

And by whose design.

There was a long pause, then Vito screamed, "Oh my God! I am shot. You did this to me?"

"No, your own bodyguard did that to you," Hector said. "Your own guys gave you up. It went that way from the top down. By the by, Momo sends his regards. And by the way, my name is Hector Lassiter."

"Who? Hector what?" The mob kingpin stammered, "Who the hell are you?"

So much for savoring *that* moment.

But then events so rarely lived up to Hector's imagination.

Vito said again, "I need a doctor!"

"Happy accident then," Hector said. "We're heading to Dayton. I know a guy there who's eager to see you. He's a doctor. I mean, sort of. He's a sawbones after a fashion."

Hector checked the map again as they drove on.

After a while, Vito snarled, "Lassiter! That's your name! I know you now. You're that hump that's been protecting that whore Megan!"

Now it was perfect.

Hector figured the smile on his face would be a terrible thing to see. So he avoided the rearview mirror and instead checked his watch. Hector calculated that by now the man he was taking Vito Scartelli to see would already have signed himself out of the Dayton Veteran's Administration Center.

Hector shrugged off a sudden chill and turned the car heater up a little higher.

Looking to distract himself from his own dark thoughts, Hector inadvertently found an appropriate tune on the radio. Pasty Cline softly sang, "I fall to pieces…"

45

Hector spent a week in Mexico, trying to get a line on Shannon and Meg.

He couldn't find even the thinnest clue to their whereabouts, goddamn it. He couldn't fine a clue to their whereabouts, *thank God.* Hector concluded that despite all her worries, Meg had done well covering their tracks. Seemed logical to assume that if Hector couldn't find them with all his good reasons for doing so, nobody with ill intentions could ferret them out, either.

That search was a last gesture to Meg and Shannon, and a promise kept to Hallie to ensure her daughter and granddaughter's tracks were indeed well-covered.

Content the Dalton girls had truly lost themselves somewhere down in the relative safety of the Mexican desert or beaches, Hector headed back to the border to begin dismantling his hollow old solo lobo life in order to build a new and better one with Hallie Dalton.

Jimmy was due at Hector's place in La Mesilla, soon. The cop was coming down to help Hector burn down that empty old existence, to help Hector spend a last few days carousing through Juarez.

They'd mentioned trying to reunite their old crew from that desert war they'd fought to buy Meg and Shannon their time to escape.

That sounded a daft and therefore perfect endeavor to Hector's ears when Jimmy ventured the prospect over the phone.

It sounded like a hell of a time, a fitting end for Hector's hell-raising days.

46

Man proposes; God disposes: talk about your plans, and He will laugh.

This particular trouble started in a bar, as too often was the case, one of those places where there are never any happy endings to be found.

Bad news? No, the *worst* news. A nightmarish revelation; one bad decision equating to years of ensuing grief.

It all started with a different kind of nasty truth: the first in a series, that day, as it happened.

Jimmy, a little drunk, hesitated and said, "Something I never told you, Hec, because, well, what purpose would it serve back then? Guess now it's academic so far as Megan goes. And maybe knowing will help you see how you're making the right choice. The right choice in settling down with darling Hallie, I mean."

Hector put his glass down and leaned back in his chair, studying his friend's face. "What the hell are you talking about, Jimmy?"

The Irishman wet his lips, then took the plunge. He said, raw voiced, "That day in Dayton, when the bullets started flying so fierce and wild and with such terrible results? Well, hard as it may be to believe, Hec, I mean with so much iron being deployed…"

"I'm not following you on this one, Jim," Hector said. "Not at all. Give me more. Say it straight. One true sentence."

Jimmy frowned and shifted his butt on the stool. "Well, Hector, amidst all those guns being fired wildly on that city street, even for all that, there were only three pieces firing forty-five caliber shells."

Jimmy paused and stared into his glass. "So far as the forty-fives go, there was your old Colt, my usual gat, and that gun you gave to Megan Dalton."

Jimmy paused again, then said, his voice as raw as Hector had ever heard it, "I know where my bullets went, Hector."

"Okay." Hector swallowed hard, resisting his intuition. He said, "Where are you going with this, Jim?"

Jimmy said, "When they dug the slugs out of Katy's face they learned she was killed by three shots—all of them forty-five caliber slugs."

Hector wet his lips. Jimmy said, "I don't like it, Hec, but for an instant there, I thought maybe you shot that sorry bitch Kate. God forgive me, the thought did occur to me, but just for an instant."

Hector felt the muscles in his jaw tighten. He said, "So what changed your mind on all that wrong thinkin', buddy?"

Jimmy sighed. "I found the slugs you dug out of Meg and yourself in your shirt pocket while the *doctor* was treating you. One of them was from a forty-five. *Doc* figured from the relative sizes of your wounds that that was the one from Meg's leg."

"He guessed right," Hector said. "And…?"

"And while the 'doctor' was treating Meg—you were unconscious by then—he pointed to Meg's dress and showed me the powder burns on the fabric there. The crazy bastard giggled and told me how it was obviously a self-inflicted wound. He said it took him back to the Great War and all the self-inflicted leg and foot wounds he saw there as a medic." Jimmy hesitated and made a sour face. "Cocksucker laughed the whole time he was telling me Meg shot herself in the leg. You know, for cover."

Hector went cold all over, saw spots. *So it was like that. Hell's belles.* Meg had had the ice to do the job on Katy herself and then to put one in her own leg to cover her tracks. Some tough young thing, darling young Megan. More mettle there than Hector ever sensed.

Hector supposed on the spot he had to chalk it up to maternal instinct. He kidded himself that made it if not okay, at least a bit more understandable. Katy didn't love that pretty little child, after all.

Hell, even that bounty hunter had commented on the strength and durability of a mother and her child's sacred bond. Hector had seen how deep such ties ran when Hallie was prepared to die to protect Meg and Shannon.

Sure: motherly love—that's what it had been about.

Love gone sideways and bloody, sure. But love in the end.

Jimmy said, "I'm sorry, Hector. It was selfish to share that, but I just couldn't carry it alone anymore."

The writer took a deep breath, let it out and said, "Jimmy, we need to drink a sea of booze this round, old friend."

Sighing, Jimmy said, "Aye, Hector. That we surely do." He freshened their glasses from the bottle they'd ordered. "And that we surely will."

The two of them did that for a time. Drank hard and in near silence.

But yonder came Hector's ultimate undoing, breezed right through those swinging doors with a flashing smile, raven hair and perfumed skin.

Craig McDonald

Like Hallie said, the course of a life can too often turn on a single bad decision. The reason Hector resisted notions of God and master plans. Take one wrong turn and your life can go down a dark, damned path. Hector knew that as well as anyone… maybe even better than most.

A group of young Latina women drifted into the cantina, pretty, spirited and all of them slightly drunk: dewy, vivacious and ripe low-hanging fruit.

Their "crew" from the battle outside Juarez started pairing off with some of the young women, one or two at a time.

Jimmy and Hector stayed at their table the longest, but then Jimmy, too, got led off by a pretty young husky Latina named Inez.

That left one beauty at the bar, all alone.

She was the prettiest of the lot by far, black eyes and long black hair that nearly reached her fetching tailbone. The young woman had a pretty smile and her skin was the color of whisky. She had the kind of matinee looks that intimidated, kept all the others at bay. She'd been making eyes at Hector for a time.

There was far more than possibility perched there on that yonder barstool, Hector figured.

Sorry tomcat urges: even sincere love for another woman can't quite tamp those down in a man.

A sorry admission, sure, but there it was: men simply aren't strong in *that* way.

So for safety's sake, Hector wandered to a quieter part of the cantina. He found himself a phone.

It took a while and a few operators to get himself connected to Hallie's phone.

Hector savored the moment, waiting to hear his true love's voice. He wanted to share some loving talk with Hallie to firm his resolve to walk out of that damned cantina alone.

A man answered the phone. He was pretty shaken up.

Soon enough, he wasn't alone in that state.

It was the stallion that was to blame—Traveller.

Evidently Hallie was doing something in the stable when the horse lashed out with a too-powerful hoof.

The blow caught a kneeling Hallie in the temple.

It was impossible to tell how long she'd been there on the floor of the stall with that big pale horse standing over her, Hallie's son, Rayburn, said.

She was alive when her son arrived to check on her after too much radio silence.

Hallie had survived the bumpy, long ride along that twisted maze of country roads and across twenty miles of frozen-over freeway to the hospital, he said.

Rayburn said Hallie had lingered in a coma for two days.

Hallie had passed away in her dreams, they reckoned. She just never came to.

There were surely worse ways to go. Hector had imagined or inflicted upon others most all of those other ways. He'd done that on the page and, sometimes, even in person.

The family was presently massed at Hallie's place for the expected post-funeral gathering.

Hector was too late even for that wrenching ritual.

They talked a bit more—an awkward, choked-voice exchange filled with pregnant pauses.

Hector at last hung up, shaking, standing at the edge of a void that called all too seductively. He'd stared down that hole once before almost exactly twenty-five years ago—stared it down in every sense. But he'd been a younger man, then. Literally half his present age.

Swallowing hard, Hector wandered back to the cantina. He found his stool and ordered another drink.

That Mexican beauty was staring at him again. Now her flirtatious glances seemed mixed with flickers of concern.

Hector needed to get away from himself, fast. He desperately needed to run from the barking, harrying black dogs of his own mind before they maybe brought him down for all day.

There are distractions and there are distractions: that black-eyed Latina beauty looked like the latter.

She was everything Hector wanted in a woman just then and not a thing he needed.

But, after all, it was just for a night, *sí?* Just long enough to get him through these first few, hard hours of adjusting to a darker, still-meaner world with no Hallie Dalton living in it.

Time to adjust to the loss of this beautiful new settled life Hector had almost had within his grasp.

Hector took a deep drink of tequila; savored the familiar burn. A line from "Carrickfergus" ambushed him:

> *But the sea is wide and I can't swim over*
> *And neither have I the wings to fly…*

Raw-voiced, Hector called out to that pretty young Mexican woman. He called over, "Darlin', why don't you join me? I'll buy you dinner if you're simpatico."

The stranger smiled and looked Hector over a long moment. She smiled and said, "That might just be wonderful."

They moved to a table, drinks still in hand. The young woman sat down across from Hector and he ordered them some fresh tequila and fish tacos.

The girl was even lovelier up close. She had a sultry mouth and a husky voice.

And something positively *wild* there in her eyes—something Hector might be a long time coming to understand.

But he wasn't thinking about any of that just then. He had no such eye to the future.

Hell, he wasn't thinking much beyond the next minute.

He said, "My name is Hector Lassiter. How do they call you, beauty?"

In a smoky voice, the woman smiled and said, "*Me llamo* Maria."

PART IV

— SAN ANTONIO, TEXAS —

July, 1966

"If we knew the road's end, would
we ever set off down that sorry path?"
— Bud Fiske
(Excerpt from the liner notes for a rare, 1969 Irish
pressing of Frank Sinatra's *My Way*)

47

The line of book-buyers was finally dwindling down. The author's signing was nearly finished, just some straggler book-buyers, Hector and the author's lately FBI shadow, one callow young agent named Andrew Langley.

Hector signed hardcovers for three more elderly fans, then looked up and saw a ghost.

A pretty young woman who looked just like Megan Dalton said, "Hello, Hector. Gosh, but it's been a long time."

He did some quick math: Meg should be about forty. This woman didn't look much older than her early twenties. She smiled and said, "It's me!" She held her hand about waist-high and said, "Shannon! Don't you remember?"

"I've never forgotten," Hector said thickly. It was true—he was a man positively cursed with memory. He stood up on shaky legs and hugged her tightly to him. "God, hardly a day's gone by I haven't wondered about you and your mother," Hector said. "She doin' okay?"

A too-enthusiastic smile. "*Yeah...* Sure she is."

Well, that didn't sound too awful convincing. But Shannon hurried on: "We ended up in Veracruz. She talks about you all the time. Mother buys all your books as soon as they appear. She sees every movie your name is attached to."

Hector caught Shannon looking at his left hand and the new wedding band there. Her demeanor shifted a bit. "And you? You're still well?"

"Still north of the dirt, anyways," Hector said. "Vertical and published—every author's dream. God, look at you. You've gone and gotten beautiful, kiddo."

Now he checked Shannon's left hand. There was an engagement ring there. She saw Hector looking at her ring and said, "That's why I'm here. I saw you're touring around Texas in support of your new novel. So I decided to come up here and pop the question, so to speak. I'm to be married myself next month. I wanted to ask if you'd consider giving me away. It would mean the world to me."

Hector surprised himself with his own near-loss of self-composure.

"It'd mean the world to me, too," Hector said with a cracking voice. He dug a knuckle at his eye.

They went to dinner that night, just the two of them.

Later Hector couldn't remember much of what was said. He just spent most of the time staring at Shannon, struck by how much she resembled her mother. Dazed by how similar their mannerisms and voices were.

Even more though, Shannon reminded Hector of Hallie, and that hurt. That similarity fired a pain Hector savored in some strange way, maybe just because it made Hallie seem somehow close by again.

Hector got the sense Meg was still unattached. He sat there, twisting his wedding band, listening as Shannon talked of their lives in the years since Hector and Jimmy had watched them drive away down that dusty Mexican road sixteen or so years ago.

Hector listened to tales of sixteen years he might have shared with them if he'd chosen to go that way.

They parted after Hector promised he'd escort Shannon down the middle aisle of some pretty, crumbling old candle-lit mission in balmy coastal Mexico.

That night Hector called Jimmy long-distance and told him whom he'd seen.

They talked about old times, lost loves and lingering mysteries.

Between them, Shannon and Jimmy stirred old ghosts who dogged Hector's dreams that night. Half-forgotten faces and long unthought of names, dead enemies and lost loves:

So many specters.

Estes Kefauver, grandstanding, buck-toothed politician: in the end, that cocksucker's mob inquiries probably sold several hundreds of thousands of television sets, Hector figured. People sat in bars or in living rooms, eyes glued to that flickering cyclops as mobsters straight from central casting played to or fell apart in front of the unblinking cameras.

Some crazy show, but that's about all it really proved to be in the end. The mob soldiered on when it was all over. Just pushed on unfazed and largely untouched. Always the grandstander, Kefauver later shifted his sights to the comic book industry, and then later still, to the men's magazines whose short story markets still sometimes buttered Hector's bread.

That pissed the author off, plenty.

Then toothsome Estes made the mistake of going after a fleeting, panting acquaintance of Hector's—Bettie Page, she of the black bangs, buttery curves and casual nudity.

One December night a few years later, while hanging out with a country musician friend in Gatlinburg, Tennessee, Hector caught sight of Senator Kefauver leaving a restaurant.

Buddy Loy Burke and Hector trailed the senator to a parking lot. Hector kicked Estes in the back of the knees and then slammed Kefauver's face into the trunk of his own car. Twice. *Shame on me,* Hector thought, standing over the unconscious politician as the snow sifted down around them.

True Crime magazines got a lot of mileage out of Vito Scartelli's mysterious disappearance in January of 1951. Wild stories still abounded about lieutenants so nonplussed by their skipper's burgeoning senility they allegedly drove him down to the Everglades and fed him to the gators.

Other canards placed Vito's corpse in the cornerstones of various buildings around the Buckeye State.

Of course, the wildest of the conspiracy buffs never came close to the true circumstances regarding Vito's Houdini-like disappearance at Hector's hands.

Eliot Ness died a virtual pauper on May 16, 1957 after a string of failed business enterprises.

Ness stopped to buy himself a bottle of scotch, walked into his kitchen and keeled over, dead of a massive heart attack. He'd recently finished working on a book about his life with a hack writer named Oscar Fraley. The book came out after Eliot's death and made Ness and his "Untouchables" legends when the wildly exaggerated accounts of their Chicago exploits made the leap to television. But Desi Arnez and Lucille Ball made plenty more on that TV series than Eliot's struggling survivors ever did.

Christ, but Eliot had the rottenest sort of luck.

Eliot's prime suspect for the Kingsbury run murders long survived him, was indeed still rotting in some Buckeye mad house, so far as Hector knew.

Jimmy Hanrahan had finally retired and went private. He still endeavored to put the Cleveland Butcher away, for *keeps*. Eerie thing was, about every six months or so, some torso or headless corpse still turned up here or there around Ohio, often times around Dayton or neighboring Yellow Springs and that particular crumbling veteran's center.

Rod Serling carved quite a name for himself as a screenwriter. He made his fame with some killer teleplays, to Hector's mind—*Requiem for a Heavyweight* and the like. Hector would catch Rod's anthology show on the television now and again. The kid did okay for himself, Hector figured. "Shadows and substance," indeed.

Rod had offered Hector a chance to script an episode of his *Twilight Zone* follow-up, a Western called *The Loner*. Hector was still toying with trying.

Francis Sinatra found his way back to the top, and plenty fine. The Chairman of the Board successfully mounted his campaign to "Comebacksville."

Yet rumors of mob ties still dogged the crooner.

Frank and Ava split, and by all accounts Sinatra always carried a wicked torch for her.

For her part, Ava bedded bullfighters down in Old *Mehhico*. She swam nude in Hem's Cuban pool. Hector and Ava, eventually—a time or two—became better acquainted, horizontally.

The critics claimed Frank's grief at Ava's loss pushed him to some of his best work. Seemed the silver-tonsiled magnificent bastard did what all the real artists were supposed to do: Francis "used the pain."

Hector managed to shake his latest, much-younger Scottish wife for a few days and made that trip down to Vercruz *solo lobo* to give away Shannon on her wedding day.

Meg didn't look so good. Too much liquor over too long a time had put some serious weight on her. The Mexican sun had done no favors to her skin. A few minutes into their reunion, Meg asked, "Is James still alive?"

Hanrahan, she meant. Hector nodded. "Not in the best of health, but, yeah, Jimmy's still around, thank Christ."

Meg smiled sadly. Sometimes I remember that song he sang a time or two to put Shannon to sleep. Do you remember it, Hector?"

He rolled his neck, some part of himself wishing he was far away, too. "Yes. 'Carrickfergus,' sure. Always had myself a soft spot for that tune."

Meg cleared her throat a little and sang a bit:

> *My childhood days bring back sad reflections*
> *Of happy time there spent so long ago*
> *My boyhood friends and my own relations*
> *Have all passed on now like the melting snow*
> *So I'll spend my days in this endless roving.*

Much later, as Hector was preparing to hit the trail north, Meg, slightly drunk, confessed what she'd done to Katy.

Studying his face, she said carefully, "You don't look at all surprised, Hector. Why is that?"

"Jimmy pieced it together years ago," he said, raw-voiced. "Jimmy suspected the night we were both shot there in Dayton."

Meg had this pained expression. "And James told you?"

"Eventually."

She said, "And you did nothing, either of you?" Her eyes searched his. "Why not?"

"Hell, was a time I maybe flirted with just standing back and letting Kate fend for herself if the chips were down and those bullets started flying," Hector said. "Jimmy even confessed to me that he feared I'd do just that. But my conscience got the best of me. I saved Kate in that shootout outside that Cleveland brownstone, even though I thought I had all kinds of wrong-headed good reasons not to do that right thing."

Meg smiled sadly. "For my sake, I have to say I wish you'd hadn't done the right thing."

Hector looked at her, at this wreck of the woman he once had feelings for.

Meg was younger than Hallie had been when Hector had fallen in love with Meg's mother back in 1950. Yet Meg now looked much older than her mother ever had.

"Maybe I wish I had too," Hector lied. Hindsight: what a wicked old whore.

Meg said, "I read all that about what happened to you. The stories about your wife—you know, Maria. The rumors about you maybe having, well, *you know…*

In his head, Hector supplied the words Meg couldn't give voice: *The rumors about you maybe having killed Maria. You killed your own wife, Hector. That's what they claim.*

"I'm sorry for all that," Meg said. "So sorry for you losing your daughter like that."

Goddamn Maria…

Maria—the *one* subject Hector never discussed, not even ten years on.

At that moment, Hector just wanted far away from Megan Dalton and all the lashing memories she brought raining down on him.

The keys to Hector's fifty-seven Bel Air and his hacienda weighed heavily in his hand. They also seemed to carry the weight of so many regrets, losses and sins.

Meg smiled sadly and said, "So it's back on the road then, Hec?"

"Have to get back north," Hector said.

"Me, too, maybe. With Shannon married now, I've been thinking about crossing the border, seeing some old favorite places. To see how the country's changed."

"I can tell you here and now it's not changed for the better," Hector said, sour-voiced. "This war? This incompetent accidental president? Cocksucker shames me to be a Texan." His voice softened a shade. "But sure, go see the States, Megan. You should do that if it's what you really want."

"Yeah, just get a car and ramble," Meg said. "Maybe I will do that."

"Rambling can be good," Hector said. "You can be new everywhere you go."

Meg looked at their feet. She said, "Your present wife, is she like you? Is she like us?"

"You mean Hannah?" Hector frowned. "Is she like us? How?"

A funny smile played on Meg's mouth. "You know—is Hannah our kind?"

What? What exactly was our kind, to Meg's mind?

Did she mean a maverick—some flavor of rootless runner? Or did Meg mean a killer?

Hector decided to decide that Meg surely meant the first.

He decided to choose for both of them, one more time.

"No, Hannah's not like us," Hector said. "She not like you, or me, not at all."

He smiled a sad smile and said, "She's just not the running kind."

THE END

THE RUNNING KIND

Reader Discussion Questions

1. *The Running Kind* shares a key plot similarity with the prior Lassiter novel *Roll the Credits*: namely, the attempted delivery of a child into safe hands against overwhelming odds. If you've read *Credits*, how do the two novels compare and contrast, to your mind?

2. Legendary FBI director J. Edgar Hoover looms over much of Hector Lassiter's life, just as he did that of many writers of the early- to mid-20th Century. What do you make of Hoover and Lassiter's lives crossing as the series unfolds?

3. Hoover famously denied the existence of the Mafia for decades, finally forced to do so partly as a result of the televised Kefauver hearings (an event indeed credited for massively spiking TV sales, by the way). Why do you think Hoover resisted admitting the mob's existence? Had you heard of the Kefauver committee before reading this novel?

4. On the subject of television, a certain TV pioneer named Rod Serling crops up along the way. The Lassiter series has

centered books around writing, painting, radio, film and now, television. What other mediums or artistic movements do you think lie ahead as the series reaches its climax?

5. Mid-book, Hector falls in love with a woman named Hallie Dalton and begins to plan a settled life with her. If you know the other Lassiter novels, what most strikes you as different about Hallie when compared to most of the other women Hector falls for in other novels?

6. By this novel's end, what were your attitudes or perspectives on Hallie's daughter, Meg?

7. Jimmy Hanrahan has now appeared as a primary sidekick in two Lassiter novels (as well as making significant appearances in Craig McDonald's overlapping cycle of Chris Lyon novels). Bud Fiske was Hector's sidekick in *Head Games*. In other novels, Hector's primary foils have been historic personages including Ernest Hemingway and Orson Welles. Do you prefer Hector operating in tandem with real, or instead with wholly fictional characters?

8. Most of the Hector Lassiter novels tend to sprawl across continents to varying degrees. Apart from a late-novel trip across the border, *The Running Kind* hews largely to American soil. Do you have a preference in whether your Lassiter's are "foreign" or "domestic"? If you do, why?

9. This novel finds Hector at his own half-century mark and starting to look backward a good bit more. Are there certain ages or periods of his life when you prefer to read about Hector? As many series turn on seemingly ageless

heroes and heroines, are you attracted to or rather put off by a hero who actually ages across books, just as we do?

10. If you've read *Head Games* and recognize the name, what was your reaction to the introduction of Maria?

ABOUT THE AUTHOR

Craig McDonald is an award-winning author and journalist. The Hector Lassiter series has been published to international acclaim in numerous languages. McDonald's debut novel was nominated for Edgar, Anthony and Gumshoe awards in the U.S. and the 2011 Sélection du prix polar Saint-Maur en Poche in France.

The Lassiter series has been enthusiastically endorsed by a who's who of crime fiction authors including: Michael Connelly, Laura Lippmann, Daniel Woodrell, James Crumley, James Sallis, Diana Gabaldon, and Ken Bruen, among many others.

Hector Lassiter also centers short stories that appear in three crime fiction anthologies, *Dublin Noir* (Akashic Books), *The Deadly Bride & 19 of the Year's Finest Crime and Mystery Stories*, (Carroll & Graf) and *Danger City II* (Contemporary Press).

Craig McDonald is also the author of two highly praised non-fiction volumes on the subject of mystery and crime fiction writing, *Art in the Blood* and *Rogue Males*, nominated for the Macavity Award.

To learn more about Craig, visit *www.craigmcdonaldbooks.com* and *www.betimesbooks.com*

Follow Craig McDonald on Twitter @HECTORLASSITER

https://www.facebook.com/craigmcdonaldnovelist